RULE OF THE HIGH PLAINS

Rule of the High Plains

John Neely Davis

A FRANK RULE WESTERN COLLECTION

FIVE STAR
A part of Gale, a Cengage Company

The publisher bears no responsibility for the quality of information provided through author or third-party Web sites and does not have any control over, nor assume any responsibility for, information contained in these sites. Providing these sites should not be construed as an endorsement or approval by the publisher of these organizations or of the positions they may take on various issues.

CIP DATA ON FILE. CATALOGUING IN PUBLICATION FOR
THIS BOOK IS AVAILABLE FROM THE LIBRARY OF CONGRESS.

ISBN-13: 978-1-4328-7832-0 (hardcover alk. paper)
LCCN: 2021935000

First Edition. First Printing: July 2021
Find us on Facebook—https://www.facebook.com/FiveStarCengage
Visit our website—http://www.gale.cengage.com/fivestar
Contact Five Star Publishing at FiveStar@cengage.com

Printed in Mexico
Print Number: 01   Print Year: 2021

My ancestors with surnames—McCall, Neely,
McKelvy, Boswell, Woods, Breazeale, Davis—
had itchy feet and probably always wondered
"what was on the other side of the mountain."
And the ones I knew had an almost fanatical obsession to read.
I've tried to fulfill their yearnings with this book.

ACKNOWLEDGMENTS

Generally, only one person authors a work of fiction. But in reality, many people have input, some knowingly and some unknowing. Longtime friends Jerry Henderson and Don Lepp provided direct input for this book. Brentwood critique group The Scribblers and Franklin critique group The Harpeth River Writers made early corrections and suggestions.

Indirectly, the family core—Jayne, Cindy, Tim, Melissa, and Dave—contributed. The females prodded and encouraged. Dave provided the cover. Karen Davis was an indirect contributor through early encouragement.

The photograph on the back of the dust jacket is my father, John Brown Davis, and was taken seventy years ago.

To all of you, I am greatly in your debt.

TABLE OF CONTENTS

Though the mountains be shaken and the hills be removed, yet my unfailing love for you will not be shaken . . .

—Isaiah 54:10

★ ★ ★ ★ ★

THE JOURNEY

★ ★ ★ ★ ★

* * * *

The Journey

* * * *

Frank Rule and his daughter, Shirl, worked their way southwestward, their horses fresh from a night's rest. Spanish explorer Francisco Vazquez de Coronado had described this land in 1541: "Plains so vast I did not find their limit anywhere . . . there was not a stone, nor bit of rising ground, nor a tree, nor a shrub, nor anything to go by."

Not exactly true, Frank thought. On his previous trips across the Llano Estacado, he'd burned the locations of scattered stone *mojoneras* on his mind. The landmarks, used by Indians for centuries, peered infrequently over the sea of grass and marked water holes. Occasionally, Frank happened upon a *playa*— sometimes dry or so fouled by buffalo that the water was little more palatable than thin mud.

They came off the Llano Estacado at the palisaded Mescalero Escarpment, the southwest wind relentlessly blowing fine sand and small pebbles around or through the crudely fashioned bandana masks guarding their faces. Behind them to the east, the mesas rose, like the mirage of a giant ocean.

Throughout their long journey, Frank watched hawklike over Shirl's frailness. He did not question her about the past and her life with the Comancheros; she would talk when she felt moved. He did not need to know—did not want to know. Ever.

At night, he thought about Billy. His brave son savagely fought the Indians during the abduction of his mother and sister. Regardless of what he'd been told, it was beyond Frank's imagination that this courageous boy would willingly have gone with the Comanches. Frank was certain—he had to believe—that Billy was waiting for an opportunity to escape and return home.

Some days, Frank and Shirl traveled less than ten miles, breaking camp late and settling early at day's end. They forded the dun-colored Pecos and later, after the rolling plains, crossed the verdant Jicarilla Mountains. Two days after that, the unforgiving blackness of the forbidding *Malpais* glistened in the afternoon sun.

"Tomorrow," Frank said to Shirl. "Tomorrow, we'll be home."

Her eyes misted; she lowered her face into her hands and sobbed.

That night, after Shirl's deep breathing told him his daughter was asleep, Frank walked away from the flickering light of the campfire. He removed his hat and looked up into the blue-black sky. *God, help me to be a better man. Forgive me if I have not watched over my family good enough in the past. Help me to never put them in danger again. Bless them all and heal Shirl.*

Ellen looked northward for weeks, her heart racing at the sight of dust rising from the desert floor. Sometimes it would be a buggy: a family traveling southward toward the Great White Sands, and, after that, the desolate land south of the border. She would stand in the shade of her house, hoping the travelers would stop for water. And if they did, she would look enviously at their togetherness. Other times it would be a solitary rider, and she would fear it was Frank, that he had not found Shirl or, worse yet, he'd found her but she was dead. At these times, Ellen's heart felt as if it were rising in her throat and choking the life from her.

It was a wash day, and Ellen built a fire under the black, cast-iron kettle. At the edge of the yard, Joseph played in the sand, creating low mounds and decorating them with twigs. Mr. Reyes had given them a dog, a large brindle cur—for company and protection, he said—and the animal became her young son's constant companion.

The dog growled, hackles and ears erect. Ellen turned toward the creek and saw Frank's black hat bobbing above the mesquite. He came through an opening in the brush, and Ellen saw the second rider . . . saw the blonde girl.

Her knees weakened and would not support her weight. She crumpled to the ground, her keening rolling out across the harshness of the countryside.

The family sat at the kitchen table enjoying Shirl's favorite dessert—a one-egg cake and milk.

Frank and Shirl had been home for almost a week. The girl spent hours with her mother in low whispered conversations, telling stories Frank would never know. Trailed by Joseph, he mended fences and tended chores neglected during his long absence.

Frank carefully waited for the right time to have a discussion with Ellen. He needed to talk about moving and their future.

"This man, this Ben Greer, up in Texas at a place called Longsought," Frank said, as he raked yellow crumbs across his plate, "he told me that there was lots of ranch land available near him. Seems like folks got the land through something called land entry from the government. They had to live on the place for five years. Had to farm it, build a house, outbuildings, stuff like that. Then the government would give them a clear deed."

Ellen thought about the years they'd worked on their small place. "Give them the land! Good gracious. Can't believe free land. Could we have done that?"

Frank was happy that the thought of *free* piqued Ellen's interest. "Well, it did cost them something—maybe fifty cents an

17

acre, maybe less. Somehow, lot of them didn't follow through with what the government wanted, so they never got title. Some of them worked through everything and then just took off. Just give up and went back east. I hear tell, now the land is pretty much available to anybody that wants it."

"Why would anybody want to claim the land and then not go through with their ranching plans?"

Frank did not look up from his plate. "That Texas feller, Greer, said it was Kiowas and Comanches. Said they had run a bunch of ranchers off several years ago. Ranches just setting there now . . . deserted . . . kinda like nobody owns the land."

Ellen smiled. "Sounds like you're trying to tell me something without saying it straight out."

Frank nodded. "I . . . I really like the men from Longsought. I'm not sure I'd have ever got Shirl outta that Comanchero camp if it hadn't been for them."

"Oh, Frank, sure you would. I've got more faith in you than that."

"No. It was bad. I've never been in nothing like that. Them Comancheros was 'bout as tough a bunch as I ever run into. But I gotta say, that Texas bunch was tougher."

"Go on, Frank. Say it. Spit it out."

"Greer said that if I was gonna keep going out to look for Billy, I was gonna need a base. Need to have folks I could trust while I was away from home. Folks that would help look after you and Shirl."

"We got this place. I'm not fearful."

Frank took Ellen's hand. "But I am. I'm afraid that the next band of Indians what comes through might make off with you. And the children. Next time, I won't be able to find you. I was lucky last time; might not be so lucky again."

"But we've got the Spencers and Mr. Reyes."

"They're too far away. Too far to be any help."

"I don't think I can leave, Frank. We got so much time here. So much hard work. Things are just startin'—"

"No, Ellen, they're not. We've been here goin' on fifteen years. Look at us. Dozen head of cattle. Few head of horses. Some chickens. Look at where we live. I'm not one to quit, but we . . . you and the children can't stay here. And you deserve better. A lot better. If I'm gonna keep looking for Billy—"

"You can't quit. You've got to keep looking."

Frank shrugged. "Then that don't leave us much choice."

"How far is it to this Longsought?"

"In miles?" Frank asked. "I don't know for sure. Calculate it to be . . . maybe six hundred."

Ellen blanched. "Six hundred miles."

Frank heard the reluctance in his wife's voice. She was the strongest woman he had ever known. She had fought Indians, survived a brutal rape, given birth to their children without the help of a doctor, struggled through the overpowering heat and bitter coldness of the desert, and now was dismayed at the distance he was asking her to travel.

"Six hundred . . ." she pulled her hand away from his and leaned back from the table.

"We can take our time. Maybe look at it this way. Say we do ten miles a day. Make the trip about three months—probably less."

Ellen stood and began clearing dishes from the table. She crossed behind Frank and touched his shoulder. "I'll start getting our things together in the morning."

She turned quickly, but not before Frank saw the wetness on her cheeks.

It took longer to prepare for the trip than expected.

Frank sorted through the cattle; ten were strong enough for the trip. Eight horses, including the two that would pull the wagon, were chosen. He kept the eighteen head in the pasture by the barn and fed them extra grain and grass hay. It would not be an easy journey. At least he could see they were strong at the start.

Mr. Reyes rode along the dry creek bed, then up the narrow trail to Frank's ranch. "You doin' something I ought to know about?" he asked, staring out over the barn lot at the livestock.

Frank smiled at his old friend. "We're pullin' up stakes. Going to Texas."

Reyes stroked the grizzled, five-day stubble on his chin and then seemed to study the thick stand of salt cedar growing along the creek, their feathery, bluish-green branches moving in the noon breeze.

"What about here?" Reyes asked. "You just giving up? Just walking away?"

"No, nothing like that. I reckon we'll be back someday. I gotta find my boy. He's somewhere up to the north. Kansas, or maybe in the Texas Panhandle. Can't live down here and look up there. Hate to just leave, but don't see any other way."

"Takin' your wife and children?" Reyes asked. Then, without waiting for an answer, he said, "Not smart, if you ask me."

"Mr. Reyes, it's no more risky than living here, waiting for the Hunter's Moon, and them damned Indians to come through here, raidin'. You know what happened last time. I'd druther have my family up in Texas where they'll be safe. Least there's neighbors."

Reyes squatted, arthritic knees popping like broken twigs, and drew meaningless lines in the sand with his finger. "You know I was raised up there in that part of the country. Come south with Pa. He was going to make a fortune down here. 'Gonna get out of them damn winters, cyclones, and blizzards,' he said. He was a dreamer. Never saw forty. Fever took him. I been here ever since."

Frank looked at the old man, gnarled hands, gray hair, stooped shoulders. "You ever considered going back? To Texas, I mean?"

Reyes looked up, battered hat brim hiding the top part of his face. "You invitin'?"

"Wouldn't turn down a topnotch hand like you. Always use an extra man. Somebody experienced. Sure be a help."

"I can damned sure carry my own weight," Reyes said. "Wouldn't be no kind of burden. If I was, you could just cut me loose. I could make it on my own—always have."

"Be proud to have you."

Reyes pulled a battered pipe from his shirt pocket, filled it, and made a big pretense of tamping the tobacco into the bowl. "I'll need a couple of days," he said. "Kinda get things buttoned up around my place."

Frank watched as the old man pulled himself up into the saddle on the second try. *That'll be me someday. Least I've got a wife and children. I'm not alone.*

Ellen carefully hung the wash out early in the day, feeling confident she would gather it before dark. That afternoon, a late spring thunderstorm came down the valley, whipped her bedsheets from the clothesline, and sent them flapping like huge white bats across the pasture. Near the edge of the dry creek, the sheets tangled in a field of cactus. Before Ellen could rescue them, the force of the wind shredded the trapped bed clothing into jagged strips.

It took almost a month of work to prepare for the journey northward.

Mr. Reyes moved his meager possessions to Frank's barn and insisted on sleeping in the hay. "I've slept in a whole lot worse places than a hayloft," he said. "And besides, I get to put my feet under Ellen's table three times a day. I've eat my own cookin' for fifty years, and I'm getting tired of it. Taters and beans one meal, beans and taters the next."

"How you gonna be traveling?" Hampton Spencer asked Frank. "Not figuring to put them children and Ellen on horseback, I hope."

"I got this wagon and with some work—"

Hampton shook his head. "Might make it and might not. I got this Studebaker out in the barn. There's better wagons, but it'll beat anything you've got."

Frank had seen the dust covered prairie wagon. "How much you want for it?"

"Me and the missus will die right here on this ranch," Hampton said. "I'm gonna give that old wagon to you. That way, we'll dang sure not move again. Can't think of nobody I'd druther have it than you. It brought us from Arkansas. It'll take you to Texas, I'm betting.

"Some of the bows need work, and the bonnet needs patching and greasing. Or, even better, mayhaps you can find new canvas. Right smart caulking and the bed ought to be tight enough to float—long as the river ain't too wide. You'll probably need to put the wheels in a creek for a week—swell 'em up good so everything is strong and tight. Put the water barrel in there, too. No telling how much the staves have shrunk. Be careful with it so it don't split apart 'til it swells."

The two men put the wagon wheels and water barrel in the mountain stream running behind Hampton's house. "Give her a week, and we'll see what she looks like," the older man said.

At the barn, Reyes sat on an upturned bucket in the shade. "Wagon looks durn funny, settin' there without any wheels," he

said. "I've hauled a bunch of freight in my day, but I never tried moving a wagon without wheels."

Frank and Hampton laughed at the old man's attempt at humor. "Swelling the wheels," Frank said.

"I ain't trying to be nosy," Reyes said, "but what do you plan on pulling that thing with?"

"I got some work horses," Hampton said. "And got four teams of mules. Guess we can make a choice 'tween them."

Reyes stood and circled the wagon, eyeing it as if it were an alien monstrosity dropped from the sky. "I've drove wagons a heap bigger than this one. Old big Conestogas. I've used a six-mule hitch and a eight-horse hitch, but if I was running this show, I'd get me a four-hitch of oxen. Won't make quite as good time, but they're easier handled and don't need as much feed. 'Sides that, Indians won't steal them. And you can always find 'em come daylight. They might wander off, but it won't be too far. Worse comes to worse, you can always run 'em down horseback."

Frank nodded in agreement. Then, knowing the answer, he asked, "And where would a man find such animals?"

Reyes hooked his thumbs behind his galluses. "In my pasture up in the edge of the mountains. Fact is, I've got six. They ain't been worked in a while, but give me three or four days, and I'll have 'em tamed down like spotted pups that was still nursin' their mammy."

Frank looked at Hampton. "Where you reckon I might find a man that would drive them? I don't know anything about handling oxen. 'Specially pulling a wagon."

Reyes straightened himself, stuck his chest out, and nodded. "You're purely lookin' at him."

After Hampton declared the wagon parts sufficiently water soaked and at their original size, he and Frank reassembled the wagon. "Right impressive piece of equipment, I'd say," Reyes declared after viewing the wagon from all angles.

"Show you something else," Hampton said to Frank. He pulled a leather scabbard, dried and cracked with age, from under the wagon canvas. "In here is a Sharps .50. It's probably killed more buffalo than all other rifles combined. I don't have any use for it; you might. It'll kill a buffalo at more than five hundred yards. There's talk that Billy Dixon killed an Indian at a quarter-mile distance with one. Sounds kinda suspect to me, but it is a hell of a gun."

Frank hefted the heavy rifle and smiled. "Got any cartridges?"

Hampton nodded. "Right here—fifty in a box. You're welcome to 'em."

Frank jacked the lever and dropped a cartridge into the chamber. He sighted down the long barrel.

Hampton said, "See that white rock down there at the edge of the pasture? See if you can bust it."

"How far away is it, you reckon?"

Hampton grinned. "I know exactly. It's right at thirteen hundred feet."

Frank pulled the heavy rifle to his shoulder, cocked the hammer, aimed, and fired. In less than a heartbeat, a cloud of dust erupted, and the rock fragmented into a hundred pieces.

"Damn," Frank said.

Crispness remained in the morning air, and the smell of sage was strong enough to linger on the taste buds. Hampton Spenser and his wife sat in their buggy alongside the trail watching Frank Rule and his family moving northward toward the western edge of the Jicarilla Mountains. Reyes walked on the left side of the oxen, prodding them gently with a long pole. Ellen sat in the wagon, Joseph in her lap. Shirl rode a pony close alongside Frank, the livestock between them and the wagon. The brindle cur trotted behind, tongue lolling in the nippiness of the morning air.

Last night, Mrs. Spenser baked bread and this morning shared it with the Rules. She had stood with her arm around Shirl's shoulders and told the young girl how much she loved her. "I'll miss you, too," she told Ellen. "I didn't see you much, but it was always comforting just to know that another woman was here in the valley. I'd looked forward to seeing the children grow up."

The two women hugged, each stroking the other's back as if caressing a child. Frank and Hampton shook hands, only nodding, not trusting their voices. Reyes peered from the side of the wagon. "We're wasting daylight," he shouted.

The travelers left. Except for Shirl, none of them looked back.

"Reckon, we'll ever see them again?" Mrs. Spenser asked, then watched her husband shake his head without answering. She dabbed at the corners of her eyes. "I think you're right."

They moved northward, keeping the Jicarillas to the right and Gallinas Peak to their left. The rolling landscape extended as far as the eye could see. The trail skirted narrow ravines and low bluffs. The grass was plentiful but not as lush as atop the verdant Llano Estacado.

Frank had chosen a route that stayed away from the Great Plains. He'd crossed them twice, but he'd been horseback and not encumbered by a wagon—and family. Besides, he didn't think Shirl could stand a second trip across the barrenness; her memories of the terrible events around the kidnapping would be too strong.

The journey settled into a pattern: coffee and a cold breakfast of last night's leftovers, moving at first light, lying up in the heat of the day while the oxen rested and grazed, traveling again in the coolness of the afternoon, and then setting up camp at dusk. Although they had no way of recording their distance, Frank estimated they covered fifteen miles on an average day and twenty miles on days when the weather was cool and the terrain level.

Reyes, true to his word, was an excellent teamster. He watched the oxen and rotated their time in the yoke so they would remain as fresh as possible. Belying his years, he continued to walk beside the oxen, speaking softly to them as he might a child. He had understated his cooking skills, and while Ellen prepared most of the meals, Reyes was proficient at roasting antelope and baking sourdough biscuits in a Dutch oven.

Frank fastened a metal bucket to the end of the coupling pole. In the coolness of the morning, Shirl and Joseph walked behind the wagon, gathering buffalo chips for the nighttime cooking fire. Occasionally, Reyes joined them, and the three sang haunting Mexican tunes that only the old man understood. Frank rode drag, eating dust and keeping the livestock grouped behind the wagon. At times, he could hear his family singing, and their joy almost made him forget Billy was missing from the group.

Eleven days into their journey, they reached Las Vegas, a village sitting at the foot of the Sangre de Cristo Mountains. None of the travelers had seen a town this size—or half—or a third—or a tenth. For years, westward adventurers passed here on the Santa Fe Trail. Now the town was expanding, mostly on the expectations the Atchison, Topeka and Santa Fe Railroad would reach here within five years. The Rule family camped along the Gallinas River and marveled at how the sky above the town glowed with a pale golden hue at night.

The next morning, Frank and Reyes saddled their horses and rode into Las Vegas. Their mission was threefold: Frank posted a letter to Ben Greer at Longsought saying they would be there before winter set in; they needed to replenish their rapidly diminishing supplies of coffee, salt, and sugar; and Reyes had a toothache—not a regular toothache, but an abscessed jaw tooth that made him look like a ground squirrel with an oversized acorn in its cheek.

Days earlier, Frank had declared, "A dentist will have to look after this."

"If'n I could get ahold of it, I'd pull it myself," Reyes had said yesterday morning. Now he and everyone else agreed—this was something far beyond "pulling it myself."

At the general store, the proprietor instructed Frank to take Reyes down the street to the only dentist office in town. "He's a right young feller," the storeowner said. "Ain't been here very long, but I ain't heard no complaints. 'Bout his dentist work, that is.

"Understand he came here from Georgia. Got a terrible cough. They tell me he's pretty handy with a pistol. And got a reputation as being fractious when he's drinkin'. But this early in the day, he ought to be sober. Can't miss his office. Got a sign with a tooth painted on it. Got his name, John Henry Holliday, painted on it."

Before noon, Frank and Reyes left Las Vegas. Both had a cloth sack of groceries tied behind their saddles, but the abscessed tooth lay in the enamel spittoon in Doc Holliday's office.

The storekeeper in Las Vegas strongly suggested Frank take the Mountain Route up through Raton Pass and not try the Cimarron Cutoff—way too many miles without water and way too many mean Indians, he'd reasoned.

Reyes disagreed. "I talked with some freighters once. They'd took the Cimarron Route. Said it was shorter and didn't have to go over Raton Pass. Said that pass has ruined a many a wagon. Ain't much water along the Cimarron, but we've had a wet season; bet it will be all right."

"And if we don't find water, then what?" Frank asked, weighing the horrors of Raton Pass against the dryness of the Cimarron Route.

"Reckon it could be pretty bad," Reyes said. "Hell, I can't make no decisions like this."

Ellen listened to the two men. As if she sensed her husband's quandary, she said, "What if we go on up to La Junta where the trail forks and then decide? I talked with a woman at the river this morning; that's what they're going to do."

The twenty-mile trip was along a heavily traveled part of the Santa Fe Trail; freighters and traders had used it for almost fifty years. That night, the travelers made camp at La Junta near the junction of the Mora and Sapelló Rivers.

Troopers from Fort Union under the command of Lt. George Coleman were bivouacked along the river and visited just after dark. As eager as Frank was to talk with the soldiers, they were even more eager to see a woman. Particularly a woman as pretty as Ellen. She made a second pot of coffee, and the horse soldiers responded as if they were tasting nectar sent directly from the gods.

"We've traveled the Cimarron Route, the Mountain Route, even made one trip along the Fort Union-Granada Road," Lt. Coleman said. "None of them are easy. They've all got their good points and bad ones. Raton Pass is hell on wagons . . . 'scuse me, Mrs. Rule . . . that just kinda slipped out. That military road running along the Arkansas River can be pretty boggy in places at times. 'Course, the Cimarron Route can be awfully dry. And bad lightning storms."

28

uns.

"If you had to take one, which one might it be?" Frank asked.

The lieutenant stood and emptied his coffee grounds in the sand. "Ain't no good way," he said. "Everything goes all right, Cimarron would be the quickest." The trooper shook his head. "Ain't no guarantees, no guarantees at all."

The troopers waded into the darkness between the two camps. Then Lt. Coleman called out, his voice seemingly coming from the murkiness of the fog rising off the river. "Mr. Rule, can you spare us a minute, sir?"

"Be right back, Ellen," Frank said. "Promised Joseph I'd tell him a story tonight. Won't be gone long."

Lt. Coleman waited in the darkness, a thin silhouette against the troopers' dying campfire. "Didn't want to tell this in front of Mrs. Rule. We've just come off an expedition up on the Arkansas River. Found what was left of a theater troupe, called themselves the Joyful Jones Jubilee. Musicians and the such. They was about a week overdue at Fort Union. Looked like it was Kiowas. Strewed costumes everywhere. Busted up the instruments. They didn't leave anybody alive. Even killed a couple of little boys. Killed a tame bear that was part of somebody's act—shot it so full of arrows, it looked like a porcupine. Poor thing still had its muzzle on and was chained to a wagon wheel. Looks like it was a small party—somewhere less than a half-dozen. Tracked them to where they come across the Canadian. Lost 'em, but we're provisioned up and are going back out. We'll get their sorry asses—may not be next week, but we'll get them."

The lieutenant rubbed his hands together, then continued. "It's really none of my business, but I believe it would be derelict of me if I didn't give you some advice, though you ain't asked for it. If I was you and had a family and all, I'd lay around here

29

and wait for another wagon going back east . . . if you can't do that, be extra careful."

The travelers moved eastward along the Cimarron Route, passing Wagon Mound, and fording the Canadian River at Rock Crossing. Ahead of them lay the rolling plains with crossings at Ute Creek and Carrizo Creek before they would reach Round Mound. They rested for six days at a creek north of Rabbit Ears Peak. Here they found a good spring, fair grass, and firewood. Frank killed two antelope and replenished their supply of meat.

Strengthened, they continued eastward, fording Corrumpa Creek and the North Fork of the Canadian.

They set up camp for the night at Fort Nichols. Years earlier, Kit Carson constructed the fort to protect civilians traveling along the Cimarron Trail. In its glory days, it was not much: half a dozen stone buildings and about that many stone-walled tents. Then, almost as quickly as it was constructed, it was abandoned. Now nothing remained except decaying walls and shallow breastworks.

"Might be a good place to lay over a couple of nights," Frank said, and Reyes agreed, saying the oxen could use some rest.

"What if we let Reyes look after the children a couple of hours?" Frank asked Ellen. "We could go down to Cedar Springs, maybe take a bath, spend a little time together—just you and me."

Ellen smiled. She had given the same smile all those years ago when they first met on the bank of the Rio Grande. Then her hair had been curly and fiery in the afternoon sun. He'd fallen in love instantly, and when he asked her to marry him within five minutes after they met, she'd thought him either ignorant or the most straightforward man she'd ever met. Three weeks later, they married. She had never been sorry.

"Maybe I will take a couple slices of yellow cake," she said.

"And, if I'm not wrong, I believe there is a jar of wine somewhere in the wagon."

They had their swim and then sat in the slanting afternoon sun on a rock shelf overlooking the spring.

"You haven't changed," he said. "You were my first girlfriend. Turned out to be my only one. I'd never seen a woman as pretty as you were. Still haven't."

She smiled at this man, this short man who wore glasses, this bald man who'd taken her heart. "Three children and fifteen years in the desert sun. No, I haven't changed. I've just turned into an old woman."

"That's not true," Frank said. "You still take my breath away. Make me feel like a little boy seein' his first Christmas present."

She pulled him close and took his hands in hers. "You are all I've ever wanted, all I ever needed," she said. "I just didn't recognize it when I first saw you."

"Ellen, I worry. I'm not sure about this move. It's more than I thought it would be. Sometimes I'm afraid I've bit off more than I can chew. We are way out here in the middle of nowhere. Not really got any idea of what's ahead of us. Sometimes, I think—"

"—think you've made the right decision. I do. We've faced things a lot worse than this. We'll make it. I've got faith in you."

It was an hour before sunset when they got back to camp. Reyes was roasting the hindquarter of an antelope, and Shirl and Joseph were playing with the brindle cur.

By morning, everyone was sick with an illness of the stomach. Nothing stayed down. Reyes made a broth of squash and corn. As evil as it tasted, it stayed in the stomach, and they gradually regained strength.

On the second night at Fort Nichols, Frank went out into the crumbling walls to relieve himself. There was a faint moon, and he picked his way carefully through the ruins. A night breeze rose and moved almost silently through the debris. But there was an additional noise, barely perceptible, little more than a low hum that seemed to rise and fall with a melodic pattern.

Muuumm. Ahmuuumm. Muuumm. Ahmuuumm.

Frank held his breath and funneled his hands around his ears.

Muuumm. Ahmuuumm. Muuumm. Ahmuuumm.

He moved until a slanting doorpost guarded his back, and then stood, shotgun across his chest, finger near the trigger.

Muuumm. Ahmuuumm. Muuumm. Ahmuuumm.

The noise grew fainter. Frank sat, eyes probing the darkness, lips puckered, the sound of his breathing no louder than the beating of a butterfly's wings. An hour passed; a false dawn tinted the eastern sky. Frank didn't move until the sun's edge emerged over the horizon.

Maybe it was the fever. Maybe he had not heard anything. He wanted to think there had been nothing out there in the darkness. Perhaps a prairie dog digging a new hole, perhaps an armadillo grubbing for food. He was uncomfortable with anything *perhaps*.

He scattered a handful of buffalo chips across the embers of the fire, then added mesquite twigs and, once the fire awoke, added larger branches. Soon, the smell of boiling coffee drifted through the camp. Reyes, ground cloth still wrapped around his shoulders, moved from under the wagon, stretched, and yawned. Ellen climbed over the tailgate and then helped Shirl and Joseph to the ground.

"I woke up, and you were gone," Ellen said to Frank when he brought her a cup of coffee. "Must have been about morning. You need to be careful wandering around in the dark. Rattlesnakes, prairie dog holes. Or at least, let me know when you're getting up." She smiled and smoothed her husband's narrow band of sleep-rumpled hair. "I got cold without you."

While Reyes yoked the oxen and Ellen prepared the wagon for the day's journey, Frank went through the ruins of the fort and out to where he thought the strange sounds came from last night. He walked an ever-widening arc through the waist-high grass, searching—he didn't know what he was looking for. Less than a hundred yards from the fort, he found a trail—bent stems and broken blades of grass—leading to a shallow arroyo. He stood at the lip of the ravine and looked down. The sandy floor had been disturbed. Perhaps the wind blew sand across antelope tracks, or maybe prairie chickens had dusted themselves. Maybe brush had been dragged through the sand, obliterating what might have been horse tracks. Whatever happened, any clues of what passed across the sandy floor of the ravine were now meaningless.

He crossed the ravine, still searching. Then he found an area the size of a metal washtub where the vegetation was pressed flat in a swirl pattern. He squatted and ran the palm of his hand over the grass and found a small mound of dirt no more than six inches across and a couple of inches high. He sifted through the dirt, letting it fall in a thin stream between his fingers. He scooped into the mound again and this time uncovered a dozen red sequins.

The oxen plodded across the prairie and around shallow ravines and scattered bushes. The livestock became accustomed to following the wagon and did not require as much attention, just an occasional touch-up with the end of a lariat. Now, Frank rode closer to his family, shotgun resting across the pommel of his saddle, aware of anything that moved or any unusual sound.

That night they made camp just south of Autograph Rock. It made Frank feel as if they were nearing civilization. Something about just knowing traders and wagon trains successfully passed this way comforted him. If others made it, surely he and his family could.

"I think I oughta sleep outside—under the wagon with Reyes," Frank told Ellen, after they had finished supper. "Just keep an eye on things better if I'm out there."

Ellen did not question her husband's reasoning. They had been married long enough she could read his body language, his eyes, his heightened alertness. "The children and I will miss you in the wagon," she said, "but I know you have your reasons."

"Daddy, I'm afraid you'll get cold at night," Shirl said. "I want you to have my blanket. Joseph and I'll sleep next to Mama, and she'll keep us warm."

Frank had watched as his daughter gradually recovered from her kidnapping by the Comancheros. She had taken over most of Joseph's care, and Frank believed this added responsibility gave her courage. But he could also see the fear in her eyes as night approached, and anything unusual caused her to stiffen. He took it as a good sign that she wanted to share her blanket, that she felt comfortable without it. He and Ellen agreed their daughter was getting better, but still he worried. While she might hide the conditions of the outlaw's camp in the corners of her mind, they were indelible in Frank's memory.

Once the wind settled, the open prairie could be quiet at night. The oxen lay nearby, placidly chewing their cuds, resting from the day's efforts and building stamina for tomorrow. Early in the trip, Frank strapped a bell to the oldest steer's neck, and the other livestock seemed content to follow that sound. Tonight the bell steer grazed around the edge of an arroyo, the sound of the bell a beacon for the rest of the livestock. The men started hobbling the horses at night, and the animals' silhouettes rose up in the pale moonlight, breaking the smoothness of the horizon. Occasionally one nickered, little more than a low, melodic sound understood only by other horses.

Reyes scraped the tobacco cake from his pipe and then reloaded. "Papa always said that was the horses talkin' to each other. It was their way of saying everything was all right. He was a good horseman, and I took anything he said about a horse as pretty much gospel."

Frank leaned back against a wagon wheel, removed his glasses, and deposited them in his shirt pocket. He pulled his hat down across his forehead. He was tired, mentally and physically. It was not within him to share his worry about the strange moaning sound, the grass swirls, the buried sequins.

The brindle cur lay beside him, occasionally twitching a leg as if pursuing a phantom rabbit through a puffy cloud of dreams. Only at night when Joseph was asleep in the wagon did the dog leave the boy's side.

"Cur dog acts just like an old brother looking after a little 'un," Reyes observed.

The stars were fading as Frank reached that stage when awareness blends with sleep. Had he dreamed, or had the haunting sounds woken him? It was faint in the thinness of his tired mind.

Reyes rolled back his tarpaulin and raised himself to his knees. "Frank. Frank, you awake? Did you hear that?"

Frank yawned, rubbed his eyes, and willed himself awake. "What? Did I hear what?"

"That humming, whatever it was. Moaning. It never come from you, and I don't think it was from the wagon. Never heard livestock make a noise like that."

Muuumm. Ahmuuumm. Muuumm. Ahmuuumm.

The cur stood, ears pricked forward, testing the night wind, sorting familiar and unfamiliar scents and sounds.

Muuumm. Ahmuuumm. Muuumm. Ahmuuumm.

"Just pull back under the wagon," Frank whispered to Reyes,

"and hold the dog. Wait to see if we hear the noise again. Tell where it's coming from."

The noise stopped. Finally, the dog lay in the sand and went back to sleep. Reyes covered himself with his tarp and resumed his snoring. Frank sat cross-legged at the rear of the wagon, shotgun across his knees. He could not recall the last good night's sleep he'd had.

Frank kicked up the fire and put the coffee on.

"Kinda think one of the horses might have got loose last night," he told Ellen as she climbed from the wagon in the first light of day. "Gonna see if I can pick up its tracks."

He walked through the scrubby brush looking for a sign, anything that might help him find where the noise came from last night. To the east, the prairie became grassland, level as a tabletop, no hiding place. The livestock had grazed south and west last night and showed no sign of disturbance. He circled north of the camp, and seventy-five yards from their sleeping place last night, he found the circle of matted grass. He dropped to his knees in the center of the swirl, raked the grass aside, and found the mound of dirt covering the sequins. Another hundred yards northward, he found where three horses had been tied to low brush, the piles of manure they'd left still fresh and damp in the morning light.

At camp, Frank helped Reyes yoke the oxen while the women packed for the day's trip. "Probably nothing to it," Frank told Reyes, "but I saw somethin' kinda strange this morning. Somebody was close to our camp last night. Don't want to scare the women, but let's you and me keep a sharp eye out."

They camped at Upper Springs that night, refilling the water barrel and resting the oxen. Point of Rocks lay ahead. When they reached them, they would be near the state of Texas.

Somewhere to the east, perhaps no more than ten days' travel, lay the town of Longsought.

"We get this next stretch out of the way, Ellen, I'll feel a lot better. Why, I wouldn't be surprised if we didn't run into some of the Longsought men. They spread out pretty wide, I've been told." Frank said this to his wife, trying to reassure her the end of the journey was in sight. But, in the pit of his stomach, there was nothing but dread; some of the toughest part of the trip might lie ahead of them.

The next day, he saw the Indians for the first time. Frank had moved ahead of the wagon, looking for a place to rest the oxen before they continued their late afternoon segment. Hampton had given him a pair of cavalry binoculars, and lately he'd used them to scan the trail ahead. He would not have seen the Indians except they sat on their horses at the edge of a small draw, their conspicuous profiles protruding above the horizon.

Frank reined his horse to a stop, dismounted, and steadied the binoculars against the cantle of his saddle. The three Indians were less than a quarter mile away, moving slowly across the prairie on a course that would intersect the trail near a copse of chinkapin oaks. They wore breechclouts; their bodies were dull with trail dust, their braided hair decorated with beads and silver coins. All three wore bone breastplates. Each carried a short bow and a quiver of arrows tied with red cords to their buffalo-hide saddle. Two of the men carried lances while the oldest of the three carried a long-barrel gun. Frank thought it strange the Indians' hair was cut short atop their right ears.

Their horses walked slowly, almost leisurely, as if the riders were in no hurry. The braves circled a low rock outcrop, and Frank could see the man with the rifle had an irregular-shaped, black case tied behind his saddle. There were red markings, perhaps letters, along the edge of the case, but the distance was so great he could not make them out distinctly. He cleaned his glasses, looked again. It didn't help.

They know we're here, know we're following the trail. They couldn't have missed the trailing wagon and livestock. They do not care. They want me to see them. They're trying to either scare me or warn me not to travel deeper into their territory. Bet they're Kiowas. Arrogant bastards.

Frank made an early camp that afternoon. He reasoned if he set up near the river with the rock escarpment at his back, at least two sides would have natural protection. He watered the livestock at the river while it was still light, then tied the bell steer to a wagon wheel in hopes the other steers and horses would remain close to the familiar sound.

Reyes gathered extra firewood. Frank wanted the campfire to last through the night.

"I've been here before," Reyes said. "It was back a long time ago. There'd been a god-awful fight the day 'fore we got here, and Jedidiah Smith got killed. Indians got him down at the river. 'Bout a dozen of his party killed, too. Three of us freighters was travelin' about ten miles behind Smith's bunch. Saw buzzards circling as thick as mosquitoes. I remember Papa cussin' when we got closer and we saw what happened. Dead folks everywhere. What livestock the Indians didn't steal, they shot up or lanced.

"Smith's men was damned tough and musta held their own a pretty good while. We found five dead Indians. They had them funny haircuts. Right side of their heads pretty much shaved. Papa said they were Kiowas. Said they were Dog Soldiers. 'Bout the meanest of all their tribe."

Frank thought of the men he saw. "Why do they cut their hair like that?"

"Papa said they done it so their hair wouldn't hinder their

aim when they pulled their bow. Musta worked pretty good. They damn sure killed a passel of white men that day."

Frank studied the old man, bent frame, white, shoulder-length hair. "I don't think it means nothin', but I saw some Indians yesterday. They're to the east of us. Three of 'em."

"The hell you say." Reyes stood and stepped back from where he was laying the night's fire, moved to the wagon, took the cloth bag containing his few possessions, and rummaged around through the clothes. He removed a gun belt, worn smooth with use and cracked with age, and buckled it around his thin waist. He reached in the bag again, withdrew a battered pistol, and settled it into the holster.

The travelers ate an early supper, and Ellen put Shirl and Joseph to bed in the wagon. The adults drank the last of the coffee. Darkness swept in from the east, and soon the evening star hung in the darkening sky like a diamond.

"I'm not 'specially worried," Frank told Ellen. "But it's better to be safe than sorry. Reyes is going to sleep under the wagon like always, but I'm going to move out a little. Once the steers bed down, I'll throw my bedroll somewhere in the middle of them. That way I'll be able to watch toward the east better. Can't never know too much about what's going on around you at night."

Frank kissed Ellen goodnight and helped her up into the wagon. "We'll get an early start in the morning. Make up for takin' out early today."

Ellen untied the canvas at the rear of the wagon and, before securing the opening for the night, reached out into the darkness, fingers wiggling. Frank pressed her fingers between his work-roughened hands.

"I love you," he said.

She held his hand briefly. "I love you and be careful."

Frank lay in the darkness, covered by his bedroll, head resting on his saddle. A coyote howled in the distance, and one prowling along the river answered. Crickets set up a chirping chorus; katydids sang an irregular song from the oak trees. Five yards away, a steer belched his cud and resumed chewing.

To the north, the Point of Rocks bluff rose from the flatness of the plains like a series of low, irregular-shaped buildings.

Muuumm. Ahmuuumm. Muuumm. Ahmuuumm.

The noise was so muted that initially Frank thought he was dreaming. Then he heard it again, this time louder.

Muuumm. Ahmuuumm. Muuumm. Ahmuuumm.

The sound was directionless.

Muuumm. Ahmuuumm. Muuumm. Ahmuuumm.

Frank closed his eyes, turned his head slowly, body tense, willing himself to discover the source of the noise.

Five days ago, the Kiowas came upon Frank Rule's trail. They dismounted and studied the signs: a wagon pulled by four oxen, a dozen head of cattle, a half-dozen horses, two horsemen, and a dog. They paid special attention to the dog tracks.

The father, Apiatan, translated as Wooden Lance in English, was a Dog Soldier, a member of the highest Kiowa military society, an honor gained because of his bravery in war. He'd taken many coups and slain dozens of the enemy in battle, and at Las Animas, on a night when thunder pounded the air and lightning raged across the shattered sky, he'd killed six of the white soldiers as they cowered in their tents.

There was talk about rounding up his people like horses and driving them to a place where they would be fed and watered by white men. They said these things to a man who once lanced twenty-five buffalo in one day. *Fed and watered by white men. Probably kept in a pen like a castrated horse. They might build a fence around my bones, but as long as my heart beats, there will be no fence around me.*

He'd taken his two sons, Satanta and Setimika, and fled before the troopers came. They were good young men; he was proud of them. *They are eighteen and nineteen and will never achieve my status, never truly be a Dog Soldier. But it is not their doing; it is the white man's fault. My people would have been content to roam the plains, hunting buffalo and stealing horses. But, no, the white man wanted to play with us like we were children chasing a feather through the air.*

Last month, up on the Arkansas River, Apiatan and his sons came upon the camp of a most peculiar group of white people. From the darkness, they watched as the slender men dressed in flowing cloaks, smeared their faces with paint, danced, and sang strange songs. Women and two small boys struck their hands together and laughed. The dancers even had a small bear, and he stood on his short hind legs and listened to the music of a strange instrument, his body swaying, his mouth muzzled with leather straps.

While his sons waited in the bushes near the river, Apiatan walked into the encampment, his hands outstretched. Initially, the dancing men were wary of the Indian. But when they saw he was unarmed, their fear dissolved, and they offered him a drink from a stone jug. It was against the warrior's belief to drink from something that had touched the lips of another man.

The dancers brought out a fancy stool covered with a soft, red cloth, and he sat, moving his hands in time with the music. One of the men made other pleasing sounds with the strange instrument by turning a crank on the big end, causing a low moaning noise. He fingered white teeth underneath the machine's belly. The sound made Apiatan smile.

The dancing men continued to drink from the stone jug. They giggled and pointed at the Indian. They drank again and soon fell to the ground, crawling on all fours, barking and raising their legs as if dogs peeing on a bush.

Apiatan stood, and his sons came from the bushes and filled the silly men and their families with arrows. The bear made snorting noises when the scent of blood reached him. Apiatan took the instrument and turned the crank. The low moaning came out, but he did not know how to press the teeth and make the melodic sounds that caused the bear to dance. The animal stood, back against a wagon wheel, tongue lolling through the leather muzzle, stringy saliva dripping onto its chest. Satanta paraded before the bewildered beast and danced.

The bear lunged against the chains securing him to the wagon and swiped at Satanta, front paws three times larger than a man's hands.

Together, they decided it would be an act of kindness to kill the bear, to set its soul free to wander in the timber to the north. Setimika emptied his quiver into the panicked animal. Soon, only the Indians breathed the early morning air.

After the Indians ate the silly men's food, they ransacked the wagon, tossing the costumes across the ground. They stripped the sequins from the cloaks and put them in a small sack. Their color and size gave them value in trade or perhaps as fetishes to ward off evil spirits. Apiatan took the cumbersome instrument, put it into a strangely marked black case, and tied it behind his saddle.

Satanta and Setimika wanted to drink from the white man's jug, but Apiatan forbade it and broke it against the ground. He did not want his sons to play the part of fools . . . did not want them to interfere with the bear's spirit as it left. He knew it would need to depart before the sun rose and cast golden arrows into its soul.

Four nights, the Indians followed Rule's wagon. Apiatan

watched the man, how he moved, how he handled his horses, how he walked. The Indian had known other such men, but they had all been Dog Soldiers, the very best of the Kiowa braves. *I am not afraid of the white man, but then I am not afraid of a buffalo bull.* Still, the buffalo was dangerous, and to kill one took great care and patience. It would be the same with this man.

The old man, the one who walks alongside the oxen during the day, presents no problem. I will let my sons kill him.

Apiatan admired the woman with the unusual hair. *She will be valuable, perhaps a dozen horses. The young child, maybe a boy, will have very little value.*

But the blonde girl. She could be a real prize. *If she has all her teeth, she could easily be worth two dozen horses and maybe three or four rifles.* Especially if she had never known a man.

His final concern was the dog. His people knew dogs had mighty spirits, and he felt the dog was aware of their presence. He'd watched the white man and the dog. If the white man was able to communicate with the dog's knowledge, it was not obvious.

But what if the dog warned his master about Apiatan and his sons? The Indian was sure they would prevail in battle against the whites. But he did not want to endanger his sons; he loved them deeply.

I will lure the short white man away from camp and kill him. Then when we do battle against the old man, the woman, and the children, there will be little danger of my sons being hurt.

But I must do this soon. He thought about the dog again. *I do not want the dog to find out my plans and conjure up the white troopers. There is a need for me to hurry.*

Apiatan tried unsuccessfully for three nights to lure the white man from the camp. Maybe he was turning the crank on the machine too slow. Tonight, he would sweep the grass in a larger circle and add more sequins to the mound—maybe the ones colored like the spring grass.

He studied the stars—the circular Councils of Chiefs—and believed the Chief Star was getting brighter. *It has always guided me northward; tonight it will bring the white man to me.*

His sons would wait at the foot of the bluff until he signaled by firing his gun. Then they would charge the white man's camp, trusting the eyesight of their horses as they raced through the darkness and across the uneven terrain.

Muuumm. Ahmuuumm. Muuumm. Ahmuuumm.

Frank held his breath; his pulse hammered in his ears. Point of Rocks. That was where the sound came from. Somewhere near the southern edge of the escarpment. He slipped from the bedroll, checked the shotgun, and jammed his hatchet and pistol under his belt. He moved carefully through the bedded cattle; even the bell steer paid him no heed.

The ragged outline of the bluff rose up before him.

He'd scanned the bluff with Hampton's field glasses that afternoon and found a narrow trail that led up to a ledge and then further upward to the top. Two buffalo-shaped boulders marked the beginning of the trail, and he marked these in his mind. Even now, their smooth outline stood etched against the darkness.

Apiatan swept the grass in a swirl and then mounded dirt over the sequins. The Indian knelt on the ledge, took the instrument from the case, pulled it against his chest, and vigorously turned the crank. He lowered his head and closed his eyes. *Tonight, this new medicine will lure the white man. Tonight the short white man*

will come to me. The Chief Star willed it so.
Muuumm. Ahmuuumm. Muuumm. Ahmuuumm.

Frank rose up in the darkness and, before Apiatan could stand, buried his hatchet in the Indian's shoulder.

Apiatan rolled to his side and pulled the knife from his belt. He was on his knees when Frank shot him with both barrels. The shotgun at such close range was devastating.

The Indian was hurled back against the rock wall, slid to a sitting position, and stared down at the dim campfire marking the white man's camp. He took a deep, shuddering breath. *Spare my sons, Councils of Chiefs, spare my sons.* His dimming eyes focused on the white man. *It is hard to believe I have been bested by such an enemy. My sons will take the blood of his family. We will never be defeated by the white men.*

Satanta and Setimika waited in the darkness, standing beside their horses, hands across their mounts' noses so they would not whinny. The first gunshot echoed off the wall of the butte . . . a heartbeat later, the echo of the second shot. It was confusing because they knew their father's rifle could fire only one shot before it was necessary to reload. But these two shots were close together. If their father had been successful in luring the white man into the trap, then perhaps he wrestled the man's gun away and used it against him. There was no other explanation. Their father had slain many warriors more formidable than the man who wore metal-rimmed glass in front of his eyes.

The two young braves swung up into the saddle and charged the camp, the pounding of their horses' hooves and their shrieks and whoops terrifying in the darkness.

Reyes rolled from beneath the wagon and stood, arthritic fingers clawing at his leather holster. He had not fired the pistol in five years, and now it felt clumsy and awkward. He raised the gun with both hands, but, before he could shoot, Setimika's horse slammed into him. The old man spun stiffly from the violent impact, fell to the ground, and the pistol slipped from his fingers.

On the opposite side of the wagon, Satanta leaped from his horse, slit the canvas top, and peered into the dim interior. Ellen swung a skillet at the Indian's head, but he warded it off with his forearm, then grasped the front of her gown and pulled her from the wagon. The two rolled on the ground, the woman screaming and clawing at the Indian's eyes. Finally, he sat astride her writhing body, pinned her with his knees, and pummeled her face with his fist. The cartilage in her nose snapped and blood gushed from it.

Screaming, Shirl came from the back of the wagon. She grasped the kneeling Indian's hair, dragging him until he stumbled backward and sprawled into the campfire.

Smoke rising from his singed hair, Satanta struggled to his feet, pulled his knife, and plunged it into Shirl's chest. She turned toward Ellen, howling, blood flowing from the gaping hole just below her heart.

Lips flattened against her teeth and with the guttural sound of something wild, something from another time, Ellen charged the warrior. Satanta struck her, and she crumpled to the ground, her body across her dying daughter.

On the other side of the wagon, Setimika slid from his horse and ran toward Reyes before the old man could stand.

The brindle cur, snarling in fury, came from under the wagon and sprang at the Indian, grabbing his leg and pulling him to the ground. The dog momentarily loosened his grip and lunged at Setimika's throat. The Indian screamed as the dog shook him like a terrier would shake a rat.

Satanta stood near the dying Ellen and Shirl and looked at his blood-covered hands. His father had told him of such violence, but he himself had never been involved in anything like this. He heard the dog growling and his brother screaming. And it came to him. *The dog warned the old man and the woman, and surely he alerted the short, fat man. Now I must kill the dog before it rips my brother's throat out. I need the help of my father; he would know how to overcome the evil spirit of the snarling beast.*

Satanta wiped his bloody hands on his leather breechclout, pulled the war ax from Ellen's head, turned, and took two steps toward his brother.

Frank Rule rose from the darkness, leveled his shotgun, and fired. Satanta stumbled, his knees gave way, and he fell face first into the dirt.

Reyes regained his feet, found his pistol, and fired once into the back of Setimika's head. Startled by the explosion, the cur loosened his grip and backed away, blood dripping from his jaws. Reyes cocked his pistol and waited for movement from the Indian. There was none.

Eleven days later and five miles out of Longsought, Ben Greer rode the shallow draws searching for stray steers. A thin cloud of dust rose from the prairie to the west. The rancher took his field glasses from a saddlebag and focused on the source. Two pairs of oxen pulling a covered wagon followed by a small herd of livestock were working their way along the trail toward him.

He took Frank Rule's heavily creased letter from his shirt pocket and read it again.

Mr. Greer

If everything works out me and the wife ought to be there before winter. You remember Shirl. She will be with us and little Joseph. Got an old man named Reyes. He'll be driving the oxen. A few horses and cows. Barely enough to get started. Be glad to see you. Frank Rule

Ben glassed the wagon. Nobody sitting in the driver's seat. Old man walking alongside the oxen must be Reyes. Riding drag at the back of the small herd of livestock, Frank Rule sat on a large bay, a little boy in the saddle in front of him.

Ben glassed the wagon again. No little girl. No woman. Nobody except the two men and the little boy.

He spurred his horse forward and in five minutes raised himself in the stirrups to shake Frank Rule's hand.

". . . and I just buried them right there at the edge of the bluff. Me and Reyes piled rocks on their graves so coyotes will never be able to get to them. I tell you, Ben, it was the hardest thing I ever done."

Greer turned from Frank Rule and dragged his shirtsleeve across his damp eyes. The pain of burying his own wife, Madelaine, was still fresh in his mind even after ten years. When he turned back, he said, "Damnation. Know it don't help you none, but I'd be a rich man if I had a dollar for every time I'd heard a story like that. We are getting close to cleaning up this country. Bet it'll be less than twenty years 'fore most of the buffalo are gone. Once that's took care of, we'll starve the Indians out. Put their mangy asses behind a fence somewhere, and they'll stay. Stop their runnin' around over the country killing white folks."

Frank shook his head. "Won't help me, Ben. Damn Indians run off with my boy, and I ain't seen hide nor hair of him since. They took my daughter and . . . well, you know that story, too. No need of me telling that over again. They took Ellen off and . . ."

Ben patted Frank's shoulder. "Ain't no need to go over that. I know everythin'."

"No, you don't. They took advantage of my wife. Awful thing. Awful thing."

Ben searched for a response. He had no words strong enough

to console the cowboy.

"You know, Ben, she never wanted to make this trip. I kinda pushed her into it. Might have been selfish on my part. Convinced her that she'd be safe while I hunted Billy. Now I've lost her and Shirl both. What kind of man does that make me?"

"Don't look at it that way. You was doing what you thought was right. Everybody makes mistakes."

Frank's voice was ragged. "Yeah, but I ain't . . . ain't everybody. I ought to have had more sense than to try somethin' like this. 'Specially with . . . with my family."

"Frank, we're gonna make it through this. You're gonna have a lot of help here. Longsought folks are caring and helpful."

"Ben, I appreciate you saying all these things. But I won't ever forgive myself. Nothing you can say that'll ever change that. Sometimes . . . sometimes, I feel like I'm going crazy."

Midafternoon and the village of Longsought was bathed in the early fall sun.

Frank found this country almost lush when compared to the dry range of his Rio Grande Valley homeland. Early settlers named the town Longsought after the stream that semi-circled the town on the east and south as it worked its way westward to the Arkansas River. The town wasn't near as large as Las Vegas, but it was the largest one Frank Rule had seen in weeks.

Ben Greer looked over Frank's meager herd of horses, steers, and cows. "Tell you what let's do. What say we take your livestock to the holding pens on the north side of town. I know the feller who runs the place, and I can get you a good deal on some hay and maybe a little grain. The trail you been on is powerful hard on stock. And from the looks of things, about as hard on the people."

Late afternoon, the livestock was safely corralled and feeding at the hayracks of the holding pens.

"All right, we got that done," Greer said. "Now let's go to work on where we're goin' to stable the people."

Frank shrugged. "That won't be a problem. We can camp down by the creek. That'll fit us pretty good. We been doing it for months—pretty much used to it."

Greer watched three-year-old Joseph playing beneath the wagon with the brindle cur. "Might work for you and Reyes, but it's gonna be pretty rough on the little boy. Winter will be here in a few weeks. You don't got any idea 'bout our cold weather—nothing like what you're used to down in the valley.

"So, we're going to handle first things first. Rose Cotton runs a little boardinghouse down at the corner of Washington and Second. Pretty good grub. Fact is, I like to pick up a bite of breakfast there when I can. Top of that, she's a widow woman and right pleasant to look at, if I do say so myself." Greer polished the surface of his fingernails against his shirtfront. " 'Course, not that I'd notice anything like that."

Frank ran his fingers through his beard and dislodged grass seed and a fragment of a leaf. "Not sure anybody would want us staying with them. We're purty tame, but we don't look much like it. Well, me and Reyes don't look like it. Joseph cleans up pretty good."

"Makes no mind; Rose has got a bath house out back. Dickie'll heat the water. Good scrubbin' will help everybody. And the woman that does the laundry for the boardinghouse will wash your clothes—and you won't hardly miss the money."

Frank followed Ben to his livery stable and parked the wagon on the downwind side of the barn. "Leave your things in the wagon and turn your oxen loose in my lot," Greer said. "Nobody will bother anything. I got a few things to take care of here. Take Reyes and Joseph and go on down to Rose Cotton's. Get you a room. Tell her I sent you. Can't miss it. Four blocks east and one block south. I'll be along directly."

Frank hefted Joseph up on his shoulders and, followed by Reyes and the cur, walked eastward on Lincoln Street past the school, the Emerald Isle Saloon, the newspaper office, the modest houses with scruffy front yards, and the bakery. They turned south on Second Street. Cotton's boardinghouse was on their right.

"Look at that," Frank said to Reyes as they stood in front of the two-story blue building. "Reckon it'll make us dizzy if we get a room on the top floor."

Two scruffy-looking men sat on the front porch of the boardinghouse, sharing an almost-empty bottle of whiskey.

"Well, would you take a gander at that!" the smaller of the two said. "Damn, Leo, I ain't never seen nothin' like that. Little short fat man growed 'nother feller on top of him. Looks like he's trying to make a normal size man—takes both of 'em and they still don't make it."

Frank looked away from the two men, pretending he did not hear them. The larger of the two stood and looked at Frank and Joseph.

"Why hell, Rupe, I do believe the little 'un sittin' atop the fat one is part Indian. Least he's some kind of mongrel. Half-breed of some kind. Reckon what he'll look like when he gets growed up?"

Frank lowered Joseph from his perch and handed the boy to Reyes. "Take 'im and go on inside. I'll be along in a minute."

"Wait a minute, Mex," Leo shouted, "don't take that thing inside. I don't live in this boardinghouse, but I might want to someday. And I'll tell you, I ain't sleeping in no place where a Indian has stayed. Even if it is only half Indian, or whatever the hell it is."

Rupe reached for the porch post and pulled himself to his feet. "And that goes double for me."

Leo was a big man and stood a head taller than Frank. "Hey,

Shorty, I'm talkin' to you. Tell that dumb Mexican to not carry that damn half-breed kid inside. Mrs. Cotton don't need no flea-carrying folks messing up her parlor. And probably stinkin' like a dead buffalo, to boot.

"And somethin' else. What kinda bitch whelped a pup that looks like that?"

It took Frank three steps to cross the porch.

"I'm tellin' you, it was the dangest thing I ever saw," Rupe said. He was a celebrity of a sorts that night because he was the only man in the Lucky Break saloon who'd witnessed the fight at Rose Cotton's boardinghouse earlier in the day. "Little fat man come after Leo like a bulldog after a range bull. Took Leo upside the head. Old Leo dropped to his knees, and that made the two men 'bout the same height. Fat man kicked Leo in the face. Teeth come outta Leo's mouth like corn outta a sheller."

"Leo's your buddy. You give him any help?" Rob Parker, the bartender, said and poured Rupe a drink.

"Help? Why, heck no. He got hisself into it with the fat man. I figured he was big enough to handle the job by hisself."

Boomduck Gentry quit playing the piano and came closer so he could hear the conversation better. "Well, did he? Handle it by hisself?"

Rupe drained his glass in two swallows and shoved it across toward the bartender. "Hell, no. Fat man had Leo down on the ground, stompin' his head like it was some kind of varmint."

Saloon owner Dab Henry nodded toward Rob. "Pour him another one. Do believe we got to keep primin' him if we ever want to get to the end of the story."

"Yes, sir," Rupe said, enjoying the attention. He held the whiskey up to the light so he could admire the clearness of the amber-colored liquid. "Little fat man stepped back, took off his glasses, and laid them by a porch post. While he was doin' that,

Leo got to his hands and knees and tried to crawl under the porch. Little fat man pulled him out from under there like a man pullin' a rabbit outta a hole and started beatin' on him again."

"Wait, wait," Dab Henry said. "Leo never pulled his gun or that knife he carries in his boot?"

"Oh, he pulled his gun all right. Fat man took it away from him—broke two of Leo's fingers doin' it. Took the pistol and throwed it up on the porch roof. Leo pulled that skinny knife outta his boot. Fat man took it away from him just like he did the gun. Stuck the blade down 'tween the boards in the porch. Snapped the blade off with one jerk."

"Wait a minute," Dab said. "Are you sure this was Leo? I never heard of anybody doin' Leo like that."

Rupe slid his glass across the bar. Dab nodded, and Rob filled it again. "Damn straight it was Leo. And if Sheriff Satterlee and Deputy McCormick hadn't come up and pulled him off, I believe the fat man would've beat Leo to death right then and there.

"Sheriff pulled his gun, cocked it, and shoved it up in the fat man's face. Look like there for a blink, fat man was gonna hit Satterlee. Then I reckon he saw the badge, and that sorta calmed him down a little."

"Aw, hell," Boomduck Gentry said. The piano player had taken a couple of whippings from Leo—something about not playing *Dixie* correctly. "I was hoping that man was going to finish the job."

Rupe swigged whiskey. "But then Leo had his second piece of luck. Judge McDonnel and Doctor Munro come walkin' down the street. Doc took one of Leo's arms, and the deputy got the other 'un, and they dragged him down to the doctor's office."

"Guess they arrested the fat man?" Dab asked.

Rupe looked into his almost empty glass and shook his head. "No, they never. Judge asked me if I seen what happened. I told him I didn't know what it come up over. Just looked like a regular fist fight to me."

"Hold on right there," Dab said. "You knew who started it. And Leo is your buddy. How come you lied to the judge?"

Rupe glanced at the saloon floor and shook his head. "Look, I got enough trouble of my own. Don't need to buy into somebody else's. I may never see that fat man again, but if I do, I want him on my side. Right here tonight, 'fore God and everybody, I ain't told nothin' but the truth. And I don't want nobody sayin' anything different."

Somebody at the bar asked, "You know how Leo is doing?"

Rupe shook his head again. "I stopped by Doc's office. He'd wrapped Leo's ribs up so tight he couldn't hardly take a breath. Splinted up his fingers. Sewed Leo's face up in a half-dozen places. Said there wadn't nothing he could do about Leo's teeth. Said he'd not be eatin' no more steak, less'n he could gum it."

A red-haired whore came downstairs still buttoning her blouse. Her hair was disheveled, and lipstick was smeared on one cheek almost to her ear. "I never heard much of the story, but he sounds like my kind of man," she said. "Right boisterous like. Vigorous. What did you say his name was?"

"He told Judge McDonnel his name was Rule . . . Frank Rule. Judge shook his finger in the man's face and told him to do his fightin' outside of town from now on."

"Reckon he'd like a little company tonight?" the whore asked.

Dab opened the till, and the bell chimed. "I'm gonna give you two dollars for your work today and a bit of free advice. Let that man alone."

Ben Greer turned the corner, stopped, and stared at the trio near the boardinghouse. "Thought y'all would already be inside eating fried chicken and stuff like that. What you doin' standing out here?"

Frank, Reyes, and Joseph looked back at him from under a scrubby tree across the street from Rose Cotton's place. Frank's face was scratched. A torn shirt pocket dangled like the ear of a disappointed dog. His knuckles were skinned, and he'd wrapped a ragged bandana around the more severely damaged hand.

Embarrassed, Frank examined his rapidly swelling knuckles. "There was . . . a bit . . . a little trouble out here, and I thought . . . thought it would be best if we waited for you here."

"Trouble? What kind of trouble?"

Using his teeth, Frank pulled a flap of skin from one knuckle. "Well, there was these two fellers sittin' over there on the porch, and they . . . they was saying stuff . . . saying things about Joseph. And . . . I kinda . . . kinda lost my temper and—"

"Whupped one of 'em," Reyes said.

"What did they look like?" Greer asked.

Frank described the men, and Greer nodded. "That'd be Rupe and Leo. Bet Rupe took off, and it was Leo you was fightin'."

"Didn't catch no names," Reyes said. "But anyhow, it'll be awhile 'til he starts any more trouble."

Making himself more presentable, Greer turned his shirt cuffs down and buttoned them. "Ah, Leo's a slow learner, but he's got a hard head. He'll be back soon as he heals up. Come on." He motioned the three to come across the street. "I've worked up an appetite just listenin' to you. Let's get inside and see what kind of vittles are getting cold."

"—and when you get finished, we've got custard pie for dessert," Rose Cotton said as she set bowls of fried chicken, corn, and potatoes on the red-and-white checked tablecloth. "So, you'll need to save a little room."

Two men sat at the end of the table. One wolfed food as if he had not eaten in days, and the other stuffed tobacco into a long-stemmed pipe. "Evening, gents," the smoker said. "I'm Doctor Jefferson Cantrell, best dentist in town. And this starving young man on my left is Dickie Dildine. We're regulars here. Always eat together; always set in the same place. I'm a paying guest, and Dickie is . . . well, let's just say Dickie is . . . jack-of-all-trades and food taster extraordinaire."

Dickie paused, loaded fork in mid-flight to his mouth, and nodded. "Miz Rose calls me her assistant and sometimes I—" The thought went away, and Dickie focused on the food balanced atop his fork before saying, "Gotta save room for pie."

Dr. Cantrell chuckled and nodded. "That's right, old friend. Save room for pie." He turned to Frank and quietly said, "Dickie is kinda . . . not right in the head. Life hasn't been kind to him. Mule kicked him 'tween the eyes some years ago, and ever since that, he's been . . . you understand . . . kinda troubled."

Greer left the table and returned with a pie plate and a coffee pot. "Talked with Miss Rose. Explained your circumstances. 'Bout your family, the boy, and all. She's got a vacant room on the top floor. Said you're welcome to stay long as you need to."

Frank sipped his coffee. "Then she knows—?"

Greer shoveled a slice of pie onto his plate. "She knows. She's a good woman. Her heart is bigger than your saddle."

Frank cornered the last of the potatoes with a piece of a biscuit. "You tell her we're not the kind of people that takes without giving back?"

"She says she is a little indebted to you already."

The potatoes conquered, Frank rested his fork on his plate. "How's that? Indebted, I mean?"

Greer slid the tin plate of custard down the table to Dickie. "She said she'd been trying all afternoon to get Rupe and Leo

56

off her front porch. Said you did it in 'bout half a minute. And she appreciated that."

The next morning was cool and crisp. "Fall is coming," Greer said. "Won't be long until the nights turn cold as a witch's tit at midnight." He had eaten breakfast at Rose Cotton's, and now he and Frank stood on the front porch of the boardinghouse waiting for Judd Snodgrass.

Snodgrass was the only land agent in Longsought. Years ago, he'd worked with the railroad peddling land they had gotten from the government in exchange for building the rail line. Snodgrass also kept up with claimed land after the owners' dreams had turned into nightmares, and they surrendered and returned to the more forgiving East. "Bet you I know where ever' boundary line and property corner is within fifty miles," he once bragged. No one challenged his claim.

Frank explained to Greer: "Like for Reyes to come with us, but he came down with a fever last night. Thought it best if he stayed in the room today minding Joseph."

The land agent arrived in a buckboard pulled by a matching pair of bay geldings. "Get in here," he said. "The Farnham place ain't more than four miles outta town. We'll be back way 'fore supper time." The three men squeezed onto the seat, and Snodgrass slapped the lines across the bays' rumps, "Maybe when we get back, might even have time to pick up something that's a bit tinged with alcohol down at the Eldorado. Cut the road dust off our tongues, don't you know."

The buckboard turned northward along the dirt road toward the Farnham place. Expressionless, Frank watched the rolling prairie slip past.

Ellen would have liked it here. Having neighbors. Being close enough to go into town Saturdays for groceries. Having somebody to talk to. A school for Shirl and, later, Joseph. But no, damn it, I kept

her out there in the edge of the desert. Then I let her die. And Shirl.
God'll never see my face, and I don't deserve it anyway.

The buckboard stopped. "Well, there you are," Snodgrass said. "Southwest corner. Property runs a mile north and a mile east. There's better land out here and land that is a whole lot worse. It's a full six-forty." He smiled and spread his arms wide. " 'Course, the price can't be beat. Might say it's free. Just keep the fences up, don't let the house and barn fall down. Get a government patent on it 'fore you know it."

They rode on north for a half mile and turned east down a line road. The farmhouse sat on their left in a small grove of elm and cottonwood trees. The men climbed down from the buckboard and walked across the front yard where buffalo grass competed with sedge and ragweed. Inside, their boot steps echoed hollowly as they moved through the barren rooms. "Dang good shape, ain't it?" Snodgrass said. " 'Specially considering nobody ain't lived here in two years."

Frank stood in the kitchen. Ellen's voice was clear.

We'll put the eating table over there. Put a cabinet in that corner.
Place for my dishes. I can sit out there on the back porch, churn,
watch you plow the garden. I've already looked at the back bedroom.
Come summer, we'll move our bed over by the window. Shirl and Jo-
seph can sleep on pallets. We'll be able to buy them beds by next sum-
mer. Who knows, we might need a bed for another child.

"Didn't know when you left the house," Snodgrass said when he found Frank leaning against the back of the buckboard. "Me and Greer was talking to you, turned around, and you was gone. What do you think of the place? Little bit of cleaning up. Make a nice home."

"It'll do," Frank mumbled.

Snodgrass stopped at Rose Cotton's, and Frank climbed stiffly from the buckboard. "Appreciate you showing me over the place, Mr. Snodgrass. Reyes gets done with whatever is ailing him, we'll take our livestock on out. Reckon you'll need to write and let the Farnhams know 'bout us moving in."

"I can do it," Snodgrass said. " 'Course, they ain't got no claim—less'n they come back. And I can almost guarantee you that they ain't. Mrs. Farnham liked to have went crazy livin' out there. Prairie life is hard on a woman. 'Specially if she ain't from around here."

Frank didn't respond. Head lowered, he walked away, hands buried deep in his pockets, dull eyes picturing a woman he would never see again.

Snodgrass didn't see any need to mention having a drink at the Eldorado.

Back at the livery stable, Greer thanked the land agent for his courtesy.

"Glad to do anything I can to help," Snodgrass said. "I don't know about that feller. I heard about the whuppin' he put on Leo. Rupe said it looked like Frank set out to beat Leo to death. Seemed like he was enjoying it. I'm just sayin' that—"

Greer put two forks of hay in a horse trough and turned to Snodgrass. "He's had a bad time. Lost his wife and a daughter few weeks ago. Just takin' him a while to get over it."

Snodgrass shrugged. "He left the house out there almost with us talking to him. In the same room, I mean. I found him outside. Just standing there in the yard. Bet I talked to him for two minutes before he even acted like I was in the world. I don't know, but I don't believe he's quite right. 'Course, I've never seen him before. Mayhaps he was always that way."

A week later, Waymon Pratt stood on the front porch of his hardware store watching Rob Gallagher unload the supply wagon from Wichita. Greer came riding down the street, and the merchant helloed the liveryman. "Say, there. You got a minute?"

The word around town was, Pratt was kinda underhanded in some of his dealings, but he'd always been square and trustworthy with Ben.

"Your buddy, Frank Rule, was in a couple days ago. Pickin' up some stuff. Thought I'd heered he didn't have no wife. That some Indians kilt her?"

"You heard it right. Out there close to Point of Rocks. Murdered his wife and daughter. You hear something different?"

Pratt marked off the last sack of flour from his shipping list and sent Rob back into the store to wait on a couple of women. "No, I ain't heard nothin' to the contrary. It was just that Rule came in and bought five yards of gingham. And about that much muslin. Ordered two dress patterns—one for a woman and one for a girl. Picked out a pair of pinkin' shears. Said he didn't have much money. Wanted to know if I'd take a quarter of beef in trade instead. Maybe run him a line of credit. We cut a deal. Said he'd be by purty soon with the beef. Reckon he'll pick up the dry goods then."

Greer pushed his hat back on his head. "Say anythin' else?"

Waymon recollected, forehead wrinkled like a newly plowed field. "No, pretty tight-mouthed, all inall. Oh, yeah, one other thing. He said his woman was a good seamstress."

Ben Greer rode out to Frank Rule's spread. A one-horse wagon sat by the edge of the yard near the back door of the house. Writing on the side of the wagon proclaimed: *Joseph Nash Fine Carpentry*. The signage was almost redundant because anyone observing the construction and finish of the wagon would have known the owner of the rig was either wealthy or an extraordinary craftsman. Nash wasn't the former but was certainly the latter.

Greer shouted through the open doorway. "You fellers need any help? I'm a fine hand with a handsaw, and I work cheap."

Nash came out onto the back porch, eyebrows speckled with sawdust, ample waist girded with a carpenter's apron. "Naw, Ben. We're just finishin' up. Frank had done most all the work, 'cept a couple of doors that was way outta plumb. Didn't take the two of us more than half a day to rectify that problem."

Frank came and stood beside the carpenter. "Glad you came by, Ben. Save me huntin' you up tonight. Gotta get my livestock outta them holding pens. Man there is giving me a good deal, but I swear my cows are eating like there ain't gonna be no tomorrow. Get 'em out here, let them start eating my grass instead of somebody else's hay."

Nash went inside to gather his tools while Greer and Rule sat on the edge of the porch. "I'll get by Rose's right after breakfast in the morning and give you a hand," Greer said.

"All right. I get a chance, I'm gonna bring my wagon out, unload my stuff, get things set up. Anyhow, see you in the morning."

The morning had not released its chill, and the roosters had not finished crowing, when Ben Greer tied his horse outside Rose Cotton's boardinghouse.

The dentist, Jefferson Cantrell, freshly shaven and sober, sat at the end of the table. Dickie Dildine sat to his right, loading a crabapple-size hunk of butter on the remainder of a biscuit.

"Mornin', fellers," Greer said. "Reckon Frank Rule ain't come down for breakfast yet?"

Dickie studied Greer over the top of the biscuit. "You backin' up if'n you're waitin' on Mr. Rule. He left just as I was getting to the table. Said he had some cows to move."

Surprised, Greer shook his head. "Why, hell, I come by to help him."

Dickie pointed his finger at Greer and laughed. "Looks like he don't need you. Said his boy was gonna help him."

Now it was Greer's turn to laugh. "You didn't understand him right. He ain't got but one child. That little boy. And Joseph can't be more than three."

"Jest telling you what he said. Told me that his boy was gonna help. Believe he called the boy Billy." Dickie stuffed the biscuit in his mouth and licked the escaped butter from his fingers.

Ben Greer followed the muddy trail northward from the holding pens toward Frank Rule's ranch. He crisscrossed the livestock's path, scrutinizing hoofmarks. He found the track of only one shod horse. If a rider was helping Rule move the livestock, he was riding an unshod horse—something no respectable cowhand would do.

Twice Ben saw Rule's livestock across the prairie, but then the rolling terrain would cause him to lose sight. While the herd was in view, he glassed the surrounding area, searching for riders. He made out Rule and his black hat—never saw another rider.

He rode northward along the line road, then turned eastward toward the house and barn. The livestock was grazing on dried grass along the shallow creek that diagonally crossed south of the house. Rule's horse, lathered and muddy from the morning activity, was tied to the garden fence. There was no other saddled horse in sight.

Ben watered his own horse at the wooden trough where a dime-size stream flowed from a creaking windmill. When the horse finished, he tied him to a post and walked toward the house.

Why, you've turned into a good cowhand, son. Couldn't have wanted for anybody better.

Pa, I learned from the best. You taught me everything I know. The Indians were good riders, but they didn't know squat about handling cows.

I tell you this. Your mama is gonna be mighty proud when I tell her about you running down that longhorn and her calf. You took off through that brush, limbs popping off your chaps. Sound like pistol shots.

Heck, wadn't nothing. I've seen you run down worse stock through a lot rougher country.

I was still proud of you.

You think Mama has got dinner ready? My belly button feels like it's growed to my backbone.

Come on, son, we ain't gonna find out setting out here on the front porch. Guess we ought to clean our boots off before we go in the house. Your mama will skin us alive if we muddy up her floor. Scrape 'em off on that stepping stone there.

Ben Greer stood behind the wind-whipped rose bush at the edge of the house and watched Frank laugh, then move to the stepping stone and knock the mud from his boots.

"Tell you, it was the scariest damn thing I ever saw." Greer sat in the Taylor County sheriff's office talking to Sheriff Satterlee and his deputy, Frank McCormick.

"It was just like Rule was talking to his boy. Sometimes he'd talk, then stop and act like he was listenin'. Talking about roundin' up livestock. Talking about his wife." Greer closed his eyes and shook his head in disbelief.

"How long did you say you've knowed him?" the sheriff asked.

Greer moved to the window and watched the gusting wind

huff tumbleweeds along the dirt street. " 'Bout a year. First time I saw him was when we was over in the territory trying to rescue all them women folks from the Comancheros. He was there by hisself trying to get his little girl outta that hellish camp."

Deputy McCormick was eager to show the sheriff his interrogation skills. "Then next time was a month ago, out west of town. Right?"

"Yeah. Indians had raided his camp. Killed his wife and daughter."

The sheriff added a couple of mesquite limbs to the fireplace, waited a couple of minutes, then swiveled the crane out across the hearth and lifted the coffee pot from the hook. He poured the brew into a mug and swished it around, watching the steam rise in thin, cloud-like streams, then took a swig and grimaced. "His little boy and that old Mexican still stayin' down at Mrs. Cotton's place?"

Greer nodded. "I talked with Rose a while ago. She says they are. Found out that many nights, Frank ain't around. She thinks he's staying out there in that house on his place. I don't see how he's doing it. Ain't a cookstove or stick of furniture in that house, much less a bed."

"Don't sound right to me. Stayin' out there in that empty house all by hisself," Deputy McCormick said.

The sheriff visited the coffee again and, once more, grimaced at its harshness. "Mayhaps, I'll try to see him tomorrow. Or maybe tonight. Be a good excuse to let my stomach profit from one of Rose's steaks."

It had been almost a week since Frank spent a night at Rose Cotton's boardinghouse. Reyes was recovering, and Mrs. Cotton, widowed and childless, joyfully became a second mother to Joseph.

"I'm short on money right now," Frank confided to Rose. "I can pay later. Or, if it's okay with you, I can drop off a quarter of beef. Might kinda make things even between us."

Joseph sat astride Rose's hip. For the first time in her life, she felt the joys of motherhood . . . even if it was temporary. "More than okay with me," she said. "And, since you aren't set up out at the ranch, just let Joseph stay around here with me. Only 'til you get settled, mind you."

"And if Reyes ain't no trouble, all right if he stays here, too?"

Rose shifted hips with the baby. "He's a kindly old man. Been helping bring in water, chopping kindling, and splitting stove wood. No trouble. None at all."

A bleary-eyed Dr. Cantrell sat at the end of the table, Dickie Dildine to his right. Sheriff Satterlee surveyed the T-bone steak before him, then tucked the red-and-white checked napkin between the third and fourth buttons of his shirt.

If the weather was at least halfway cooperative, the boarding-house table was crowded every Saturday night.

Dave Benteen sat at the opposite end of the table with three cowboys from the Crown-W. The cowboys had the smashed thumbs of men accustomed to roping but careless with the dallying; the creases along the outside edges of Benteen's index fingers were impregnated with grease, one sure sign of the gunsmith trade.

The final plate of custard circled the table and came to rest in front of Dickie. "Nobody else want them last two pieces, I'll take 'em," he said. Using the back of his knife, he swept the dessert onto his plate amid the remaining potatoes and gravy. There were no raised eyebrows, because Dickie always got the last two pieces of anything, regardless.

"Frank Rule ain't eatin' here at night no more?" the sheriff asked.

Dr. Cantrell nodded slowly, either in agreement or from the effects of his late afternoon consumption of alcohol—or, as he referred to it, "my allotment of jump-steady."

"You talking about that little short, bald man what wears suspenders?" the gunsmith asked. "Little round-frame glasses?"

"Yeah," the sheriff said. "You've seen him. Been round here less'n a month. Wife and little girl got killed out west of town. Took up out at the old Farnham place."

Benteen built a cigarette, lit it, and pulled the smoke deep into his lungs. "Kinda sounds like the same feller. 'Cept this feller . . . Frank, believe that's his name . . . come in the shop day or so ago. Said he was thinkin' about buying a rifle for his daughter. Said she needed to learn to shoot. Bought cartridges for his boy's little-ole peashooter Remington. He was in kind of a hurry. Said his wife was setting out in the buckboard. Said she was expectin' their fourth child, and he needed to get home so she could rest."

"Frank . . . Frank Rule said all those things?" the sheriff asked.

Benteen nodded. "I took him to be Frank Rule. He didn't introduce hisself." The gunsmith laughed. "I learned a long time ago, out here man usually has a reason for not giving his name."

"Gotta be the same man," the sheriff said. "Anything else?"

"No. Reckon not. Well, there was one thing. After he paid for the hulls, I followed him out to the porch. Kinda wanted to see what his wife looked like."

Sheriff Satterlee folded his napkin, waited for Benteen to continue. Finally, he said, "Well . . . go on."

Benteen drowned his cigarette in a cowboy's half-empty coffee cup. "Wadn't no woman. Old beat-up buckboard. Empty as Dickie's pie plate."

★ ★ ★ ★ ★

This is what I figure. Spring come, we'll do some fencing. Least fence off that quarter-quarter over there in the northeast corner. Get it so the cattle can spread out. Gotta have some cross fencing to keep the bull away from the cows. Don't need no outta-season calves.

I don't know. Maybe thirty or so more head. We've never gone through a season up here. I hear tell it can get pretty dry, 'specially if it's a windy spring.

I've been thinking about buying Shirl a horse. Need something that's well-broke. She's plenty old enough, don't you think?

'Course, when the baby gets here, Mama will need a bunch of help. So maybe we ought to wait 'til next summer to get the horse.

Yeah. Yeah. I know. It'll be different having a baby around.

Frank lay in the darkness on the floor of the empty bedroom. He'd covered himself with a horse blanket and pulled his hat over his face. The wind came just after sundown; pea-size raindrops were pelting the roof and bouncing through the windows where the panes were missing. He rolled onto his side and pulled his knees up against his body, unsuccessfully trying to cover his legs with the horse blanket.

Good to be inside on a night like this, isn't it, Ellen? Fire going in the fireplace. Antelope stew bubbling in the pot. I remember a time me and Reyes had gone over in the Panhandle and was bringing a herd back across the Canadian. Cold. Wind blowing. Spitting rain. Cows drifting ever' which way. Weather like this really makes a man appreciate a warm fire and a pretty woman.

'Course you're still pretty. Pretty as the first time I saw you settin' there on the banks of the Rio Grande mending a bridle. 'Member what your hair looked like. Curly. Blonde. I'd never seen anything like you.

Yeah, bet it did scare you when I asked you to be my wife. First time I'd ever seen you, and then just come right out and say something like that.

But our life has been smooth, hasn't it. Never had any problems. Not a single one. I'm glad you convinced me that moving up here to Texas would be such a good thing. Got these three good children, and now the baby comin' . . .

A brilliant flash of bluish light lit the room, and then a blast of thunder pounded the house. Frank Rule sat up, blanket and hat falling away, the acrid smell of ozone sharp.

It was getting more and more difficult for Frank to distinguish between what was real and what was not. It was comforting to have Ellen to talk with and hug at night—they'd always shared everything and now with the new baby . . . things were almost like they had been in the desert. And just to have Billy to help around the place, getting set up and all, was making his life easier.

The rain slackened, then abruptly stopped. The wind pushed the low-lying clouds eastward, and a pale, three-quarter moon cast an eerie half light over the prairie.

Barefoot, standing in the open doorway, Frank could make out the muted outlines of his cattle. During the storm, they had drifted southward and now milled around near the line fence. The herd bull was agitated, walking along the boundary, issuing a low, threatening challenge toward something or someone outside Frank's range of vision.

Frank, carrying his shotgun in his right hand, stepped off the back porch into the muddy yard. At the barn, he saddled his horse and then rode across the pasture toward his disturbed cattle. The bull walked along the fence, neck outstretched, nose and tongue testing the air.

Three riders driving four of Frank's cows before them came out of the darkness, moving slowly and deliberately along the road.

"Here, you sumbitches, what are you doing?" Frank shouted as he spurred his horse across the pasture. The two riders still in the saddle wheeled their horses and charged down the road, clumps of mud rising like startled night birds from the animals' hooves.

The rider at the gate swung up into the saddle, sawed on his horse's reins, and turned to follow his companions. Frank fired the first barrel of his shotgun, and the rider seemed to rise up in his saddle, pitching backward. Frank fired the second barrel. The rider's hat lifted from his head as if snatched by an invisible hand. This time, he lurched forward and lay flat against his horse's neck. The frightened animal bolted after the other horses and disappeared into the darkness, its rider swaying forward and backward like a rag doll.

The four cows, startled by the gunfire, stampeded in the opposite direction from the horses, mud splattering up on their wildly swinging udders.

"Don't know what the hell was wrong with 'em." Frank Rule stood outside the sheriff's office, talking with Deputy Frank McCormick.

"Would you know 'em if you saw them again?"

Rule shook his head. "Don't know. But one of them is gonna need to see a doctor. I shot him twice. Danged near knocked him outta his saddle. 'Spect he's purty heavy loaded with buckshot. If'n he don't die first, Doc is gonna pick a double handful of shot outta his worthless hide."

"You just come up on them, out at your ranch last night?"

"Yeah. Stayin' out there most of the time now. Settlin' in. Wife got the new baby and all. Shirl is helping just like she was a grown woman. The country is suiting little Joseph; boy is growin' like a weed. Me and Billy gonna start fencing pretty soon. Things are going fine. Just fine."

The deputy nodded. "Good to hear all that. Family is awfully important."

"Yeah. You got that right. We've . . . we've always been a mighty close family. Gonna fit right in here at Longsought. Maybe next time I come into town, I'll bring them with me. Give you a chance to see how special they are."

Frank took a cup of yesterday's coffee to the back porch, where he stood looking toward the pasture and, beyond that, the road where the rustlers attempted to steal his cows night before last. Exactly what had taken place was unclear in his mind. Were there three or four rustlers? Had they cut the fence or opened the gate when they were taking the cows?

He drank the last of the coffee, pulled his hat onto his bald head, and crossed the pasture toward the road. He counted the cattle and horses—they were all there. The pasture fence was undamaged. The wire that fastened the gate remained in place, the tie and wrap his just as much as his signature would have been.

He parted the barbed wire and stepped out into the muddy road bordering his pasture. There were no hoofprints—from either horses or cattle—and the muddy road's surface was smooth, undisturbed. He walked along the side of the road a hundred yards in both directions. Nothing. No prints and no sign of blood from the rider he'd shot.

He turned and crossed the pasture toward the barn. The livestock continued grazing and paid him no mind.

Frank Rule sat on the edge of the water trough, the morning sun combining with a windmill leg to cast a vertical shadow across his body. And for the first time he wondered if none of the things he remembered about the rustlers were true, if a dark shadow lay across his mind, and if, in time, all his mind might go dark.

★ ★ ★ ★ ★

THE DRAGON'S TAIL

★ ★ ★ ★ ★

Frank Rule sat on a rusted bucket at the corner of his barn, watching nighthawks playing their acrobatic aerial games at dusk—that hour when daylight and dark wrestle for control of the earth. He found himself at the barn more and more after the sun sank beneath the horizon; something about the gentle movements and muted sounds of the livestock was soothing.

He'd put off bringing Joseph and old man Reyes out here; they were happy at Rose Cotton's boardinghouse. Reyes enjoyed the dining table, and Rose treated three-year-old Joseph as if he were her own offspring. Maybe better.

But the most important reasons were the conversations he had with Ellen and Billy. Billy seldom said anything, but Frank did enjoy talking to him. A man needed a son to talk with, make plans, pass along what he himself had learned. But with Ellen, he mostly listened. Her sweet voice was comforting. Helped him through the empty nights. Gave him hope that someday he might see her again. Living by himself was lonely, but what would happen if others were in the house when she came and talked to him? What if her spirit did not want to share? It was a risk he could not take—not until he got his mind straight, anyway.

Frank still showed up at Rose's twice a week—just checking on things, he told himself, but he was really putting salve on his shame because of the self-imposed desertion of what remained of his family.

"I'm gettin' fat, Frank," Reyes said. "Gonna have to quit buttonin' my shirt if I keep eatin' like this."

Joseph liked to sit in his father's lap after supper. But it bothered Frank that the boy kept sliding away and running into the kitchen to "see what Aunt Rose is doin'."

After the boarders and other guests finished their meals, Rose brought a cup of coffee and a slice of apple pie from the kitchen and set them on the table in front of Frank. "Thank you for taking up the slack in my life," Frank said, "looking after Reyes and Joseph. I'm kinda having a problem getting things straight in my head. Losing Ellen and . . ."

Rose removed her apron and sat across the table from Frank. "I know. Mr. Reyes told me the story. Indian raid in the New Mexico Territory. Tracking your daughter down in that den of outlaws and rescuing her, but then never finding Billy. How old would he be now?"

Frank furrowed his brow and dragged his thumb across his unshaven chin. "Near as I can figure—close to eighteen. 'Bout grown, I reckon."

"Then, I know about Joseph. Know that Ellen . . . didn't make it. Know that Joseph's father was an Indian."

Frank stirred his coffee and watched the dark vortex diminish in the cup. "Yeah. Killed that sumbi—rascal a couple of days after he took advantage of her. The last straw was later when the Indians killed Ellen and Shirl out west of here at the Point of Rocks. It's like I wadn't meant to have a family. Couldn't take care of one."

Rose went to the kitchen and came back with more coffee. "You're being too hard on yourself, Frank."

"No. That's not right. I've got good folks behind me. Good blood. One of my grandfathers way back was a Catholic priest from Spain. Not right sure what that says about him, being a grandfather and a priest, but he was both." Frank wiped his glasses with a napkin and continued. "Ma's folks were Tohono O'odhams from the desert country over in the Santa Cruz Valley. They looked after their people."

"But sometimes—things are different now."

"Appreciate what you're saying. Still think everything is my fault—one way or the other. All I got left is little Joseph and a red-haired son who is probably thinking like an Indian brave right now." Frank stood and slurped down the last of his coffee. "I'll die a hainted man," he said, adjusted his hat, and left without saying anything else.

When he was younger, Bloody Stone had been a Comanche Dog Soldier. He was fabled in the tribe as a horse thief. His herd greater than a hundred. But his ability to steal horses came second to his bravery. When Bloody Stone and the other warriors returned victorious from battle, there was always a great ceremony with women dancing, storytelling, and feasting. Often, the braves told tales of Bloody Stone's fierceness. His coup stick was heavily notched, and it was whispered that he had taken more than three hundred scalps.

But his most daring exploit took place on a cold day when snowflakes the size of bird feathers danced through the frigid air. Attacking Cheyenne swarmed the plains as thick as fleas. Bloody Stone pinned the rear apron of his long breechclout to the ground with a sacred arrow, and, challenging enemy warriors, he stood atop a small hill as the battle raged about him. It was accepted that only one enemy at a time could take up weapons against a tethered warrior. On that day, eleven Cheyenne died by his hand. Comanche women killed six other warriors he mangled so seriously they could not escape the women's wrath.

That was years ago. Bloody Stone was now called Gone Arm.

His name changed after his left arm was mangled in a buffalo hunt. Although he had many wives, all except one were barren. After he was forty-five, this woman bore him two sons. He taught them everything he knew about warfare, stealing horses, and bravery. When they were in their late teens and during the *tahma mua,* or summer moon, he allowed them to accompany a party of hardened warriors led by Sharp Point on a raid in the New Mexico Territory. North of the Mexican border, his two sons died in battle against a demon disguised as a short, fat man who wore glass in front of his eyes.

But Sharp Point made off with the fat man's children, and as tribute to Gone Arm's sons, the old man was given the white boy. Because of his yellow-reddish hair, he was called Burning Stick.

It's easy for a boy to fall into the ways of a Comanche. The freedom of the plains and the Indian lifestyle suited more than one white lad who ended up in the hands of Indians. If the youngster survived the cruelty of his early years in captivity, he was accepted into the tribe and usually adopted as a replacement for a deceased relative and treated as a true son. Some of these survivors ripened into fierce warriors who raided wagon trains and warred constantly against other Indian tribes and the white devils.

It was a drippy spring day with the temperature waffling between the need for a coat or just a long-sleeved shirt. Frank walked past the Lucky Break saloon twice before he gave way to the laughter inside and the bouncy sound of a piano. He had never been a drinking man—it's easy to be a teetotaler when you don't have money—and it would be a couple of hours before the blacksmith got his mule shod. And, he reasoned, he had nothing better to do.

Dab Henry, the saloon owner, stood at one end of the bar

talking with two cattle buyers. Mid-bar, Rob Parker combined whiskey from four almost-empty bottles with one half full. Boomduck Gentry was trying to coax a melody from the old piano that neither of them was capable of producing. Three soiled doves shared a joke on the stairs leading up to their roost. Judge McDonnel and Doctor Munro sat at a round table near the stove playing a game of pitch.

Frank had started to the vacant end of the bar when Judge McDonnel called to him. "Say, aren't you Frank Rule?"

The cowboy turned toward the two men and nodded.

The judge said, "Come over and sit with us a spell. I got a question."

Frank stood mid-floor and looked at the two seated men. "Hadn't been in no trouble. Reckon you must have me confused with somebody else."

The doctor folded his cards, grinned at the judge, and said, "Here, let me try." He turned toward the cowboy and said, "Mr. Rule, we'd like to buy you a beer."

There are no magic words, but these were close.

The doctor slid a chair out from the table with his foot. "Sit here, Mr. Rule," he said, then got the bartender's attention and held up three fingers.

Judge McDonnel looked at Frank and smiled. "Believe last time I saw you, you'd been beatin' up on Leo. Cautioned you about that, didn't I?"

"Yes, sir. Not been in no trouble since then. None to speak of, I mean."

Doc Munro took a drink of beer, belched, and wiped the suds from his mustache with a shirtsleeve. "Best I recall, Leo hadn't been in any trouble either. Fact is, I ain't seen him since I patched him up. I believe he was not acquainted to being treated like that—butt whipped, I mean. You seen him, Judge?"

"No, but I haven't been lookin' for him, either."

Doc Munro made circles on the table with the bottom of his damp glass. "You live up north of here, don't you, Frank? On the old Farnham place, I believe."

"Yes, sir."

"Live by yourself?"

Frank shifted in his chair. "Part of my family is stayin' over at Rose Cotton's . . ."

The doctor waited for Frank to finish and when he didn't, said, "You got more people?"

Frank nodded. A free beer was not worth this painful interrogation. "Yes. They're kinda scattered."

The doctor's eyebrows raised. "Scattered?"

Judge McDonnel watched Frank's discomfort, then with his foot nudged the doctor under the table. "Reason we was askin' about your family and where you lived, woman brought her husband in to see Doc Munro here couple days ago. Doc had to dig an arrow outta the man's leg."

Frank set his beer on the table. "Where 'bouts did he live?"

"Man lived somewhere up close to where you live."

"He gonna be all right with his leg?"

The doctor nodded. "Yeah. But it was the second time in two weeks. 'Nother man came in earlier. He'd been shot in the shoulder. Seems like it might have been the same two Indians. Tryin' to take his horses. Said one of them was an old man with a crippled arm. The other man younger and—if this ain't the dangest thing I ever heard of—had yellow hair. Maybe dyed with some sorta mud, I'm guessing."

The thought of an Indian with yellow hair rumbled through Frank's mind like a runaway stagecoach.

An hour before midnight and after a ride through a steady rain, Frank stabled his mule. He walked to the house and shed his wet coat. A cup of coffee would be good but wasn't worth the trouble of starting a fire in the kitchen stove. On the bottom shelf of the corner cupboard, he found a tin of apricot preserves and opened it. He got a spoonful and moved to the front porch where he stood licking the sweetness and watched the clouds breaking up, allowing skimpy views of the moon.

Frank, you've got to take care of yourself. Be careful traveling through the dark. You've got a family to protect.

Frank dropped the spoon of preserves—Ellen's voice had never been this clear.

I worry about you. Living out here by yourself. You could be bucked off a horse or hooked by a cow. It might be days before anyone found you—if ever.

He remained still, scarcely breathing, straining to hear each word.

There is something I have a bad feeling about. Today, the judge and the doctor talked about an old Indian man. And what might be a yellow-haired boy with him. I felt an unnatural coolness creep over me when I heard that. I'm uneasy, Frank, just uneasy.

Frank waited. The clouds no longer sheltered the moon, and a coyote howled in the distance. He did not hear the voice again, and a wetness gathered in his eyes.

Frank Rule was raised in the dry country of Arizona and New Mexico. There, he'd witnessed an occasional hailstorm, but the weekly squalls and infrequent tornado-producing thunderstorms on the High Plains in the spring mystified him.

Once the ground warmed this year, he had put out an early garden and took pride as the squash and cucumber vines crawled across the ground and spread their broad green leaves. A two-minute storm not only shredded the plants' tender leaves but left the ground blanketed with Indian-head penny–sized hailstones.

Old plainsmen told tales of Indian villages and buffalo

hunters' camps leveled by tornadoes and debris scattered for miles across the prairie. He had never witnessed anything like that, but still he had a morbid curiosity.

The half-dozen chickens that lived in his barn seemed to have a sixth sense about approaching hailstorms and took shelter long before the appearance of the foul weather. He found it embarrassing that he'd started relying on the wisdom of chickens.

Frank leaned in against the lever-pole to tighten the garden fence before nailing it onto a crooked mesquite post. He stood erect at the sound of a horse running toward him on the road. Everett Holley, brim of his hat blown back against the crown and coattail flapping, approached from the west. He reined his horse to a stop and slid from the saddle.

"Bad news, Frank," he said. "Rose . . . Rose Cotton's place burned to the ground last night. They sent me to tell you."

Frank stepped away from the fence and grabbed Everett by the shoulders. "Joseph and old man Reyes—they all right?"

"Don't know. Some folks got out, but Sheriff Satterlee sent me to get you. They was still digging through the ashes when I left."

Rose Cotton's boardinghouse was reduced to irregular rows of gray ashes and still-smoking, charred wooden beams that stood like motionless ebony fingers reaching toward the sky. Both brick chimneys had collapsed, one scattered across the remains of the kitchen stove, the other littering what had once been the parlor.

Rose sat on a chair Oscar had brought from the saloon. Consoling women gathered around her, rubbing her shoulders and holding her hands as she wept.

At the side of the smoking ruins, Reyes was on his knees, surrounded by Boomduck Gentry, Jud Snodgrass, Deputy McCormick and Sheriff Satterlee, and saloon customers. Doctor Munro stood before the old man applying ointment to silver-dollar–size blisters on his face and hands.

Frank elbowed through the group of men, shouting, "Where's Joseph—where's my boy?"

Reyes wobbled to his feet and held his hands out. "Frank, I couldn't get to him in time—couldn't find him in the smoke. And the fire . . . hot . . . just too . . ."

"Where is he?" Frank yelled, his voice coarse and ragged.

Reyes's hands dropped to his side, and his body fell slack. "I done the best I could, Frank. The boy's gone."

"I left him with you to look after," Frank screamed, cords and veins standing out in his face and neck. He backhanded Reyes, and before the old man could fall, struck him twice in the face with his fist. The sheriff and his deputy wrestled the cowboy to the ground, and bystanders helped restrain his thrashing body until the madness left and a great sobbing set in.

". . . and this is the best we can figure out what took place," Sheriff Satterlee told the men gathered outside Charlie White's grocery. "Old Doc Cantrell here," the sheriff nodded toward the dentist, "was coming home the other night from the Emerald Isle saloon—three sheets to the wind, as usual. It was just before daylight, and he had spent part of the night passed out behind the livery. He came around the corner of the barn, and there was an Indian standing there with a bridle in his hand. Doc asked him if he was lost, and the Indian kinda grunted."

Cantrell raised one hand like a schoolboy needing permission to go to the toilet and took over the story. "A fierce lookin' old feller—don't believe he had but one arm. Didn't have no horse, just a bridle in his hand. I had a little liquor left in the bottle and offered him a drink. He kinda backed up against the barn and glared at me like I'd done somethin' wrong. And then . . ." Doc stopped and screwed up his face like he was trying to get the facts straight.

"Go on," the sheriff said, "it's your story."

"Uh. I was still pretty tipsy, and it . . . it offended me."

"Go ahead, tell it," the sheriff urged.

"Well, this part I'm fixin' to tell don't make me too proud. I . . . uh . . . I took a shot at him."

"Yeah, makes a lot of sense," the sheriff said. "The Indian wouldn't take a drink with you, so you got mad and shot him."

Several men in the crowd turned and looked at Doc Cantrell, and there were lots of "damns" and "crazy old coots" mixed with some really demeaning words.

Doc grew defensive. "Well, it wadn't like I was tryin' to kill 'im. Shot him with a little old .22 derringer. Hit him in the side of his ass. Probably wadn't no more than a bee sting."

"Go on."

"Well, he wobbled off 'bout fifty feet, stopped, and started cussin' me. 'Least that's what I think he was doing. I don't know many Indian words, but it sounded like cussin' to me. So, I shot at him again. But I don't believe I hit him this time 'cause he was too far away."

Sheriff Satterlee made jerky lifting-up motions with his hands, urging Doc Cantrell to continue. "What happened?"

"I got kinda scared. The derringer was outta bullets. And the Indian was standin' there lookin' at me. Cussin'. I figured I'd get on back to Rose's place. Maybe get some help, case I was 'bout to get in trouble. Old Indian followed me down the street. He was shuffling some, and I started to wondering if I'd hit him with the second bullet. Toward the end, I trotted best I could. 'Course, there wadn't anybody still up at Rose's, but she'd left a lamp lit in the parlor for me."

The dentist rummaged through his pockets as if he were hunting for something. "Took the lamp out and set it on the porch. Figured the light would scare the Indian off. Figured he'd not want anybody to see him. I went back in the house and to the kitchen to get a drink of water. Hadn't hardly got the dipper to my mouth when the lamp come busting through the front window."

The sheriff nodded again. "And that's what started the fire?"

"Yeah. Coal oil goin' everywhere, and 'fore I could even start to pour water on the fire, looked like the whole downstairs was blazing. I run through the house hollerin'. 'Bout everybody got out all right."

"About everybody," the sheriff said. "Not everybody."

"Yeah, well, I done the best I could."

"You know Frank Rule?" the sheriff asked.

Doc Cantrell said, "Yeah, I see him every once in a while when he . . . when he used to come by the boardinghouse to see his little boy."

"Well," the sheriff said, "I got him locked up down at the jail. Waitin' for him to cool off. Be lettin' him out pretty soon."

Judge McDowell stepped from the crowd and placed his hand on the dentist's shoulder. "You haven't committed a crime. Nobody begrudges you shooting a damn Indian. But I suspect Frank will hold the boardinghouse burning down against you. You didn't do it, but in a way you was the cause it burned." The judge lifted a heavily chained gold watch from his vest pocket and looked at it. "There will be a stage through here in less than an hour. If I was you, I'd be getting my stuff together and packing my grip."

"Thank you, Sheriff. I was plumb outta my skull. Didn't have no right to hit Reyes. I kinda lost my head. Gonna find the old man and apologize. We've been good friends a long time. He came with me from the valley, you know."

Frank and Sheriff Satterlee stood in the jail office, the open cell door behind them.

The sheriff nodded. "Understand how a man can lose his mind every once and a while. I'd probably of done the same thing."

"I feel pretty bad about it. Reckon it'll be all right with Rose if I get some ashes from about where Joseph was sleeping? Bury them out behind where the boardinghouse stood—maybe put up a little wooden cross with his name on it?"

Satterlee looked at the man he'd just discharged from jail: haggard, red-eyed, disheveled. "Yeah," the sheriff said. "I'll tell her. Don't see how she'd care."

"What about the Indian?" Frank asked.

"What about him?"

"You know what he done wadn't right. Some folks might overlook that he was tryin' to steal a horse. But not burnin' down Rose's place. Took the life of an innocent. My little boy."

Satterlee shook his head. "No telling where he is. Me and Deputy McCormick got out and looked a while this morning. Didn't see him. Didn't even find any horse tracks that looked unusual."

"I'll find him," Frank said. "Me lookin' and you lookin' is different."

Frank dug a hole and put a can of ashes in it. He nailed two wooden stakes together, carved *Joseph* with his knife on the crosspiece, and pounded the cross into the ground with a brick.

Rose and two women came and stood beside the still-kneeling Frank. "I loved the boy like he was my own," Rose said. She placed her hand on his shoulder, and Frank covered her hand with his. "I wish there was something I could do, something I could say."

Frank stood and nodded, without looking at the women, then crossed the yard to his tied mule.

One of the women said, "Why, he didn't even act like we were here. Never said a thing."

Rose shook her head. "No, that's not right. He said a great amount for him."

At his ranch, Frank stood staring across the plains before gathering his Sharps buffalo rifle and L. C. Smith double-barreled shotgun. He put coffee, a small skillet, meal, and a packet of grease in his saddlebags, then tied a ground cloth behind his saddle. In the off-side saddlebags, he put his binoculars, coffee pot, and two dozen shells for each gun.

He slept in the barn that night, waiting for Ellen's voice. Dawn was beginning to pass through the barn cracks when she came.

You be careful, Frank. Don't get caught in some kind of ambush. One other thing: I dreamed of the yellow-haired boy again last night.

Frank rode northward from Longsought and camped. He reasoned that the Indian would have traveled in this direction after causing the fire at Rose Cotton's. It was not likely he would have traveled southward toward Oneida, the largest town on the plains. To the east lay the edge of the Caprock and roving bands of hostile Kiowa. To the west lay the vast lands ruled by scattered bands of Comancheros who declared war on everything and everyone who came into their territory.

From his camp, he walked the prairie in ever-larger crescents, looking for matted grass or broken mesquite limbs. He found signs of a solitary buffalo bull, a small herd of antelope, and a spot where jackrabbits had taken their daily dust baths. Half of the sun had slipped below the western horizon in a large fiery ball when Frank found the sign of an unshod horse paralleling the footprints of a walking man. He'd thought he was only trail-ing the Indian. Now he reasoned there were two people—one mounted and one not—and as he figured, the trail was tracking a line straight north.

At day's end, he made a small pot of coffee, then mixed grease and meal and heated them in the skillet. Somewhere up to the north, he figured the folks he was tracking were laying up for the night.

After eating his meager supper, he lay curled up in his ground cloth wondering what tomorrow would bring. To the west, faint in the glow of a half moon, a ribbon of clouds layered along the edge of the horizon.

Frank woke to a light coating of dew and a stiff back. He saddled up, checked his guns, and rode north. The people he followed had apparently made no effort to hide their trail; otherwise, they would have stayed away from sandy patches and remained on hard ground that would have shown no hoofmarks.

Noon came, and the clouds from the west thickened, rising from the horizon like ever-shifting purple and black, smooth-topped mountains. At the base of a slight rock outcrop, Frank found a campsite and ashes from a small fire. By the tracks, he was now confident he trailed two people. Two people and one horse. This explained why the Indian was trying to steal a horse from the livery stable in Longsought. Now, the only remaining question was the identity of the second traveler. He took binoculars from his saddlebags and glassed the prairie to the north. Nothing except grass convulsing with the gusty wind.

As dark came, Frank found more hoofprints in a patch of barren sand. Off to the side, the prints of a walking man. Both sets of prints were fresh, and the wind had not shifted the shape of either of the markings. He was getting closer. He would wait for daylight.

Morning came gray, the air heavy enough to drink. To the

west, thunder rumbled like the growling guts of a giant. On foot, Frank moved forward, believing his quarry was unaware of their pursuer. He topped a low knoll and squinted through the gauzy light. Less than a hundred yards away, a narrow blade of wind-whipped flame danced. He raised his binoculars and studied the meager camp. A gray-haired man with a withered arm stood near the fire warming his backside, talking with someone seated on the ground. Cautiously, Frank moved forward ten yards and enhanced his view. He glassed the camp again. The standing man, poorly dressed and gaunt, was an Indian. The seated person had reddish-yellow hair pulled back into a single plait. The Indian stood looking at the approaching storm and making circular movements with his hand.

To the west, the leading edge of the storm absorbed the daylight. A curtain of heavy rain dropped, and lightning spewed from the clouds, jagged bolts zigzagging toward the earth, seeking anchor. Frank dropped to a sitting position, legs pulled in tight and crossed at the ankles, elbow resting on one knee.

A heavy blanket of dead air enveloped everything. Complete silence. Nothing in nature moved—not a blade of grass, not a leaf, not a breath of air. Nothing.

Frank tucked the stock of the heavy buffalo rifle against his cheek, aimed, and pulled the trigger.

With the gut-churning roar of a dozen trains, the cloud lowered its long dragon's tail, and it swept through the Indian's camp. Frank flattened on his stomach, fingers digging into the ground, teeth clenched. The tornado raged another mile to the northeast. Then, as quickly as it appeared, the tail broke away from the clouds and fragmented into a lazy whirlwind of grass, limbs, and dirt. The silence was shocking.

Frank rose to his knees. The grass between him and the Indian's camp lay flattened. He chambered another round into the Sharps, stood, and walked forward. Nothing remained. The debris field was less than fifty yards wide, and he followed the path. The grass swirled in meaningless patterns, and in some places, clumps of it were pulled from the soil, leaving patches of naked earth. He found the horse first, three legs broken and neck tucked underneath its body in an unnatural position. A quarter of a mile later, he found the body of the Indian, on his back, sightless eyes staring up at the slate-gray sky. One leg was broken, and his single once-healthy arm lay peacefully across his chest.

Frank followed the storm's path until it lifted from the ground and faded. He found no other objects save a frayed blanket and a tin bucket. He turned back toward the camp, and when he reached the Indian, he squatted and examined the corpse again. The body was cut, bruised, and mud-splattered. There was a penny-sized hole under the left eye and, halfway around his skull, a hole the size of a hen egg where the .50-caliber bullet exited.

At the camp, there was no sign anyone had ever been there: no fire pit, no food remnants, nothing.

He spent an hour circling what had been the camp looking for footprints in the mud. Nothing. There was no trace of the reddish-yellow–haired person or anyone else that might have been in the camp; it was as if that person's body had gone away to wherever spirits go.

"Hello, Frank," Sheriff Satterlee said. "Been three months since I last saw you. Right after Rose's place burned and them folks . . . sorry 'bout that, I forgot that—"

"I know; you don't need to call his name. He was pretty much the last of me. I reckon that when I die, there'll be no more folks named Rule in this part of the country."

The sheriff leaned against the hitching rail in front of the jail. He looked up at the hollow-eyed man sitting on a red mule.

The animal was lean and his coat brushed, mane and tail trimmed. The sheriff thought you could tell a lot about a man depending on how he treated his riding stock. It was obvious that Frank took care of what belonged to him.

"Don't reckon you was affected by that big storm, was you?" the sheriff asked. "The one that come through back in the spring."

"No. It went north and east of my place."

"Yeah, talk in town was that it was pretty bad. Said it didn't stay on the ground for no distance but it was rough while it did. Changin' the subject. We was talkin' the other day 'bout that Indian. Feller that threw the lamp through the . . . Don't reckon you've run across him, have you?"

Frank stepped down off the mule and tied the beast to the hitching post. "Yeah, I did."

"You did! Hope somebody killed the sumbitch."

Frank did not answer. Instead, he crossed the dusty street toward the hardware store.

Sheriff Satterlee mumbled, "Well, I guess that's about all I'm gonna get out of him about that. The man shore ain't much for talkin'."

★ ★ ★ ★ ★

THE PREACHER'S WIFE

★ ★ ★ ★ ★

After the death of his family, Frank lived the life of a loner on a windswept tract of land in a ramshackle house. He liked it that way, and most folks who knew of his temper and strange ways were in agreement with his lifestyle choice. On his infrequent trips into Longsought, Sheriff Satterlee and Judge McDonnel avoided the cantankerous rancher as if he were a barbaric throwback to a time when only the toughest men survived. Even the testiest patrons at the Antelope Flag Saloon gave Frank considerably more than just elbow room at the bar.

It had been years since his wife's death. He could not forgive himself for leading her and the children across the plains and for his inability to protect them from the Indian attack. She was the first and only woman he'd ever loved. She still came to him at night—not in dreams, but in that sleepless state when he wrestled with his madness and fought his demons—and whispered how much she loved him.

Knowing that she would come, yet he could not touch her, was slowly driving him insane. However, the thought that she might stop coming drove him even wilder and caused him to look bitterly at the world.

Her death was an open wound on his soul that time had not even commenced to heal.

The fiery death of Joseph was buried in the most remote part of his mind where it would smolder forever.

He shaved when the seasons advanced. The rim of hair that

defied his baldness grew to shoulder length and was pruned with a knife in early summer. He eschewed horses and handguns but owned three mules—ugly creatures that could endure long trips across the Llano Estacada that left horses reduced to heaving sides and disorientation. Most times when he stepped out of his house, a double-barreled shotgun swung by a leather strap from his shoulder. If he was in the saddle, armament was a .50 Sharps or a .44 Henry. And, at times, both.

Frank Rule was a man easily remembered.

Terrified of guns, Duncan Clark was diametrically different from Frank Rule in every sense. His thin body, light hair, and pale skin were not compatible with the harshness of the plains. Nevertheless, the ministerial leadership in St. Louis convinced him there were souls in the Great American Desert deserving of salvation.

The brethren were happy to see the inept Clark leave. But they would miss seeing Cécile, his Louisiana wife, an attractive young woman with red hair and a timid smile. The Clarks had been married longer than two years, and there had been no children. Whispering lecherously behind their hands, several of the leadership confided that they would be delighted to assist Duncan in his husbandly duties.

Sweat accumulating between his shoulders and soiling his vestment, Duncan Clark waited next door to the Antelope Flag until Frank Rule came out. "Sir, might I trouble you for a few minutes?"

Rule turned to the smooth faced preacher and scowled. It had been years since he had been this near a minister. "Me? You want to talk with me?"

Perspiration gathered on Clark's upper lip and forehead. Rule was the most evil-appearing and intimidating man he had ever seen. "Yes. I mean, yes, sir. If you could just follow me to the church. I won't detain you more than a few minutes."

Rule stared at Clark. "I'm not a church goin' man. Hadn't been in one of them places in years. Not since my family . . ." Uncharacteristically, Rule's tone softened and trailed away. "Ain't got but a minute," he continued. "Let's get on with it."

The two men sat separated by a scarred, wooden table, Rule peering from beneath his hat brim, Clark delicately mopping his damp brow.

". . . and Cécile just didn't return," Clark continued. "I found her empty bucket at the plum thicket but not her gloves. Her horse was gone. I'm not a tracker. I can barely find my way from my house to the church. I . . . I waited a day and a night. Didn't want people to know that . . . that I was so useless. I prayed that she would return, but . . ."

Rule's eyes burned into the innocence of Clark's face. "Shit, feller. Whatta you mean, you waited? Your wife was gone, and you waited? What the hell you waitin' for? God to deliver her to you in a buggy?"

Clark covered his face with his hands. Tears leaked from between his fingers, rolled to his wrist, and darkened his shirt cuffs. His voice was muffled. "Can you help me? Dear God, can you help me? I don't have much money, but I can get some from my parents. At least fifty dollars. It's my wife. Can't you understand?"

If Clark had mustered the courage to look at Rule's eyes, he would have seen the fierceness soften. "When did she leave?"

"Yesterday. Yesterday morning. Not sure what time it was. You see, we've not shared a bed in—"

Frank Rule shook his head. "Don't want to hear 'bout that. Take me out to where you found the bucket."

The preacher sat in the buggy while Rule slid from his mule and examined the hoofmarks around the plum thicket. Last night's dust storm had nearly wiped out the markings, and a less-skilled tracker might have been confused. Rule stood and looked northward. "That-a-way. Yonder toward the river breaks. Mayhaps fifty miles. Most likely where she went."

Clark had no idea how long it would take to span fifty miles across the High Plains. "I'll go with you," he said. "I'll need to stop by the house and get my coat. And I suppose I should try to borrow a pistol. Just in case there is . . . trouble, you understand."

Rule didn't acknowledge this, just climbed on his mule and moved out at a trot. He looked over his shoulder only once, and his scowl had returned.

The preacher knew he would not be welcomed on the search. And that his days in the West were numbered. And that his days as a husband might be even fewer.

Twilight came as Frank followed the tracks into an arroyo. He tore a rag from his shirttail and tied it to a mesquite bush, marking the trail, then turned eastward toward the rising moon and his ranch.

In the faint light of a kerosene lantern, he stuffed ammunition for the shotguns and the Henry into his saddlebags. He put coffee and a battered coffee pot, five cans of beans, meal, and a jar of bacon grease into a sack and wrapped everything in a strip of wagon sheet.

Frank took off his boots and lay on the wooden floor of the room that was to have been their bedroom. Night noises grew: a coyote howled, and one farther north answered; a cricket chirped in another room; the *barrouppp* of a nighthawk at the end of its dive echoed through the darkness. The relentless prairie wind stopped its restless movement. Now there was only loneliness.

He lay sleepless in the stillness, listening for the whispers of his long-dead wife until the grayness of dawn silently entered the room.

Riding one mule and pulling another loaded with a packsaddle, he found the strip of shirttail on the mesquite bush and turned northward, following the faint tracks. Some forty miles ahead lay the river breaks and, beyond that, the domain of the Comancheros. He hoped he would find the woman before reaching that desolate country. Nothing good had ever happened to him in that part of the plains.

The horse tracks were becoming clearer now. Occasionally other tracks crossed them, and once a single rider had ridden parallel for a half mile before apparently losing interest and drifting to the west. But mostly just the single set of tracks. Rule had trailed kidnappers and marauders before, but never just one set of tracks. The more he thought about this, the more perplexing it became.

Two days south of the river breaks, Frank Rule saw the first dead Indian. His mule detected the sour-sweet odor of a decomposing body, pricking its ears forward and snorting loudly. Three turkey vultures rose in a staggered pattern, great wings frantically fanning in the midday heat, crusted, reddish heads moving jerkily with the exertion of flight.

Frank dismounted and advanced cautiously toward the body. He knew Comancheros had used dead people as a ruse to dupe unsuspecting victims into an ambush. The rancher stopped ten feet from the corpse. The buzzards had stripped much of the flesh from the carcass and destroyed any sign of the nature of the death. No arrows protruded from the body. So perhaps this was a killing by revenge-seeking ranchers or white scalp-hunters.

Late afternoon, Frank crossed a dry streambed. An Indian child and woman lay under the shadow of a honey mesquite, faces swollen and poxed with once-weeping sores. Just beyond that, a lifeless old man slumped against a rock outcrop. The patrolling vultures had not yet discovered these bodies.

Within the next two miles, he came upon four more Indians, and still, the tracks he had followed for three days advanced northward.

That night the wind changed and blew southward, and he could smell smoke—not a prairie fire but a campfire—and the stench of burning cloth and hair and flesh.

Dawn moved silently across the plains, its light subdued by an uncharacteristic ground fog.

Frank fed the mules, saddled and hobbled both. He hoped it would not come to a race of mules against Indian ponies—odds of survival in this type of contest were not good. He sipped a cup of bitter, leftover coffee and ate a mixture of bacon grease and meal.

He walked warily through the fog, a battered binocular case swinging from his neck, the Henry in his left hand, the shotgun in his right.

Without doubt, he was within a couple miles of Cécile. Her horse tracks went unerringly northward and were heading directly into the place where smoke was still rising. She couldn't have passed through without being detected, and the tracks were fresh. The most important question: was she dead or alive?

Frank lay on the low bluff, studying the narrow creek bottom. The Indian encampment contained fewer than a dozen tepees, their coverings wind whipped, torn and sagging. At the edge of the camp, nine Indian ponies and a horse wearing a white man's saddle grazed on the parched grass. Emaciated dogs, curiously sniffing at still forms, roamed the camp. Two children wandered the barren ground, listlessly searching for food—or maybe parents. He counted seventeen bodies.

A wind howled through the encampment, propelling narrow dust devils with their cargos of twigs and grit. One swept past a gray-shrouded figure feeding a slumped man near a smoldering campfire. Its errant gust blew the head covering aside, and the copper hair contrasted sharply with the dullness of the death camp.

Cécile! He'd found Cécile.

She stood, wiped her inflamed eyes, and stared at the devilish man standing near the edge of the camp. "Don't come any closer. They've got the pox. They are dying. All of 'em." Cécile shaded her eyes and looked wildly about. "If there are any other white men with you, they need to leave. And you need to go."

"Duncan sent me," Rule said. "I aim to fetch you back."

"I can't go." The woman shook her head. "I didn't think he could find me."

"I don't reckon he could. That's why he sent me."

"But you don't understand."

"No, ma'am. You don't understand. I'm to carry you back with me. I can tie you on my pack mule, but I expect you'd be more comfortable ridin' your saddle horse. But I'll tie you, if you make me."

"But can't you see these people are being taken with the pox? If I went back with you, I would spread it—"

"You wouldn't spread it nowhere. I ain't known a white man to catch the pox in twenty-five years. Least, not the kind these Indians have."

She moved toward Rule and stopped ten feet away. "I have something more evil than pox. It's—it runs in my family. My

Louisiana grandmother had it. Mama didn't; it skipped a generation. I believed we were through with it. I wouldn't have married if . . ."

"You're just makin' excuses. You don't want to go back to that preacher."

The woman clasped her gloved fingers and raised them to her chest. Her breathing was ragged, raspy, a deep, decayed growl. "That's not true. I love Duncan more than life itself. I can't do anything to damage him."

Rule took a step forward. "Then let's go."

"No," Cécile screamed. She grabbed the front of her dress and ripped it open to her waist.

Rule left the village of the dying, by himself, traveling southward toward Longsought and Duncan Clark.

If he lived to be a hundred, he would not forget what he'd seen. Cécile's breast and stomach were covered with whitish, hand-size lesions. She took off her gloves, and flesh hung in shreds from the tips of her fingers. "It's leprosy. I watched Grandmother die from it. I don't want Duncan to see me go through that. I thought I would just run away. Get out here somewhere and die by myself. Maybe this terrible disease would die with me. Then this . . . this misery . . . these poor people . . . all dying . . . the least I could do was try to . . ."

He would have to tell the preacher—something. But there was no way he could explain the hideousness of the nightmare he'd witnessed.

However, Frank Rule was not a man given to lying. Perhaps tonight his dead wife would whisper the right words to him.

100

★ ★ ★ ★ ★

FRANK'S MULE

★ ★ ★ ★ ★

Oh, I wish I had a smoke or even a chaw.

It was another miserable night for Frank Rule. He lay on the wooden floor waiting for sleep, and just as the pale light of dawn crept softly through the cracked windowpane, Ellen arrived. Dead for all these years, she still called on him. It was difficult to separate the vision of the woman he'd married from the woman he'd buried out on the prairie, her face disfigured by the Indian's war ax. If he could have his choice of images, he would choose the face he had first encountered when swatches of sunshine danced across her blonde hair alongside the Rio Grande twenty years ago.

But he was not the master of his choices, and Ellen came with the face the nightmare chose.

The agony of losing her was pushing him into insanity. He realized this. He also recognized it was something beyond his control, but that did not make going crazy any easier.

I'd settle for a drink of likker and a game of craps. Hot dang, smoke coming off the dice like my hands are on fire.

Frank fed gnarly mesquite into the cookstove and set a small bucket of water on the eye. Once the water boiled, he opened a wrinkled sack of Arbuckles and dropped a half-handful of coffee into the bucket. By necessity, he was a frugal man, and he let

103

the grounds accumulate in the bucket for days.

Last night, he'd cooked a skillet of beef and made biscuits. Cold food was tolerable if he had hot coffee. And apricot preserves. Last fall, Frank traded a handgun to a cavalry trooper for a stolen case of tinned apricot preserves. Now, he ate apricot preserves every morning, and even if there were no leftover biscuits, he ate the sweets with a spoon.

A blue norther swept through two days ago and dropped something less than twelve inches of powdery whiteness. Yesterday the wind blew steadily from the north. This morning, the upwind side of his stable was almost clear of snow, but a triangular drift taller than a man snuggled against the other side, blocking the door.

First order of business today was to clear the snow away from the door so the mules could leave the stable and get water. To combat the chilling wind, Frank tied a strip of worn saddle blanket around his head, leaving his mouth and eyes uncovered. He shouldered his shotgun, pulled the wooden-handled shovel from under the back porch, and crossed the mule lot.

'Bout damn time you got out here. I'm freezing, and I'd kill two men and a nanny goat for a cup of hot coffee.

Frank jabbed the shovel in the snowdrift in front of the stable. He had heard this voice for most of the month. It was nasal and raspy, and sometimes the words were cruel and profane.

He was not a man who tolerated cussing in his presence, unless it was him and he found it absolutely necessary, especially not after his marriage. Whether out of respect or fear of Frank, the scratchy voice was silent during the dreamtime he spent with Ellen.

Don't act like you don't notice I'm in here. 'Cause you know you ain't ever heard a damn mule talk. Get that door open! Old Scratch wants outta here.

Frank shattered the ice covering the water trough, and once the snow was cleared and he freed the stable doors, the mules trotted out into the lot for their first drink in two days. They stood in the corner of the lot after they had their fill, steam flowing from their nostrils like miniature steam engines, and waited to be fed.

Shotgun resting across his forearm, Frank stepped through the open door and into the stable. Nobody. Nothing. The only movement, a thin vapor rising from a remarkably large pile of warm mule dung. Twice, he came from the stable and circled the building, checking for footprints in the melting snow. Only a hopping crow and a coyote's tracks marred the bluish-white landscape.

After shoving his shotgun into the loft, Frank climbed the ladder and looked out the hay door. The mules moved from the edge of the lot and stood at the barn looking up at the rancher. He forked grass hay from the door, and they ate as if they had not seen food in a week.

Yeah, feed them damn mules. Leave me sitting here. My guts would be growling if I had any.

Frank released the pitchfork as if it were a snake and scrambled for the shotgun. He took a step backward, cocked both hammers, and leveled the gun toward the corner of the hayloft. His abrupt movements caused two pigeons nesting in the rafters to take flight. Startled, Frank turned the shotgun and fired both barrels at the panicked birds. Bird guts and gray feathers rained down into the hay.

Whoa! Helluva shot, Frank, helluva shot. Bet there ain't enough left of them birds to make a decent stew. And I do believe you've done considerable damage to the barn roof.

Searching for the source of the voice, the rancher attacked the meager pile of hay with the pitchfork, slinging fodder across the rough floor and causing the cold air to come alive with dust motes. He found nothing except a chilled field mouse and the shed skin of a chicken snake. Exhausted, Frank reloaded and leaned against the wall, the shotgun clutched in his work-worn hands. He waited for the voice, but except for his labored breathing, there was only the moaning of the north wind as it sliced its way between the cracks in the stable wall.

Skiffs of dirty snow remained on the ground for a month and a half. Advancing a hundred miles a week, Spring finally came to the High Plains and moved northward past Frank Rule's ranch. The mules shed their winter coats. Using a Bowie knife, Frank shortened his own hair and beard by three inches.

In three months, he had only seen four live people and one dead man. Although he enjoyed his own company, Frank wondered if anything exciting had occurred in Longsought. Or if the dreary little town even continued to exist.

After a breakfast of warmed-over coffee and a spoon of apricot preserves, the rancher saddled his favorite mule, Red, and set out down the dirt road to Longsought. There was no sign of life at the old Mallory place, no smoke rising from the chimney, no livestock in the lot. The first human he saw was at Everett Holley's ranch. June Holley, wearing her husband's coat and trailed by a yellow cat, came from the cowshed carrying a milk bucket. She stopped at the yard gate and waited for Frank.

"Morning to you, Frank," she said. "Been wondering how you fared the winter."

"Survived," Frank said. "How's things around here?"

"Been having a hard time. You knew Everett passed the day after Christmas?" she said matter-of-factly. "Me and the kids are hanging on. Just hopin' for a better year and greener grass."

Commiserating was not one of Frank's strong points. "Well . . . reckon we all have our troubles. I . . . uh, better get going. Call on me if you need help."

June Holley tucked an errant sprig of hair under her head-scarf. "Might do that. 'Specially when branding time comes around."

Frank nodded and touched the brim of his hat with a thumb and first finger. "Send your boy to get me." He heeled his mule and did not look back, mostly because he feared she would still be standing at the gate, staring at him.

Whoa! What about that? Widow woman! Did you see her? Primping! Shoving hair under her scarf. Might need a little help! Get old Frank a bit of female companionship.

It had been a month since the day at the mule shed when the devilish voice hectored him about food and the dead pigeons. Perhaps the voice—self-identified as Old Scratch—was staying away because of Ellen. Maybe her nightly dream visits made Old Scratch uncomfortable, or perhaps there was not enough room in his mind for both voices on the same day.

Join her place up with yours. Make a respectable spread. Move you up in the world. 'Course, 'fore any of that could happen, you'd have to shave regular. Take a bath more than once a month. Bet she can cook biscuits better than yours.

Frank ran his fingers over the shotgun housed in the leather scabbard under his saddle and looked straight ahead.

Old Scratch got your best interest at heart, don't you know. Wouldn't want to be putting any ideas in your head or nothing like that.

Both hitching rails at the Antelope Flag Saloon were full of cow-horses, and Frank tied Red to the wheel of a wrecked buggy occupying a permanent position at the side of the building. The rancher unsheathed his shotgun and carried it across the crook of his arm into the bar.

Inside the building, the odors of whiskey, tobacco smoke, and unwashed bodies were mixed and pungent. Cigarette burns had tattooed the wooden floor, and the spittoons were nearing overflow. Wall-mounted kerosene lamps cast a warm light across the perpetually dark room but allowed deep and, sometimes, sinister shadows. The hardwood bar ran half the length of the back of the room. Behind it, whiskey bottles sat on wooden shelves in front of a mirrored background that falsely doubled their count.

A dozen battered wooden tables—tops stained and scarred— were randomly placed and surrounded by equally worn chairs. Chair occupants ranged from a grizzled, broken-down buffalo hunter to a sixteen-year-old who had escaped an overbearing St. Louis stepfather. Most of the occupants were cowboys from Panhandle ranches who had ridden at least twenty-five miles in the hopes they might get to spend a little time upstairs with one of the five women who plied their trade on soiled and wrinkled sheets. Three men, hats shoved back on their perspiring foreheads, were losing their winter wages to a dapperly dressed card shark—known only as the Gambler—in the center of the room, while a relief stagecoach driver, a jackleg range veterinarian, and a cavalry lieutenant waited their turn to get fleeced. An unattended piano nearing the fiftieth anniversary of its birth sat between a shallow performance stage and the building's side door.

A thousand western saloons qualified as twins to the Antelope Flag.

Frank Rule moved to the end of the bar where the shadows were deepest and rested the shotgun muzzle on the floor while the scarred stock leaned against his leg.

He knew the bartender, Oscar Parks, as much as any man can know another whom he sees only four times a year. "I'd like a touch of your cheapest skullpop," Frank said, reaching for a wooden bowl of thrice-picked-over peanuts. "It's still a nickel, ain't it?"

"Ain't gone up in two years, and it don't taste no better either," Oscar said, setting an almost-clean glass in front of Frank and pouring three fingers of what passed for whiskey in this country. "Ain't seen you in a while."

Frank blew the partially loosened skin from a peanut, took a drink of the vile whiskey, grimaced, and said, "About as often as I see you."

The batwing doors burst open, and two cowboys from the Box 7 Ranch swaggered into the saloon. One of them had finished second in a knife fight, and a red scar extended from one ear to the corner of his mouth. The other had the hunched shoulders of a poor-postured man who had spent too many years horseback. Pistols resting in low-slung holsters tied to their legs, they moved to the bar with a great jingling of spurs and voices too loud for the room.

Oscar shoved two glasses across the bar and poured each half full. "Two bits before you swallow," he said.

Hunch Shoulders dug a coin from his vest pocket, nestled it in the crook of his index finger and flicked it with his thumb. The coin spun across the bar and fell to the floor. When Oscar stooped to retrieve the coin, Scar Face took a quick drink straight from the bottle. The two cowboys guffawed as if they had pulled off a train robbery.

Oscar refilled their glasses and, this time, caught the spinning coin before it reached the edge of the bar.

Scar Face rested his forearms against the bar, reformed the edges of his mustache with a dampened thumb and forefinger, and admired his reflection in the mirror. "Oscar, you must run the best saloon in town. So damn busy, wadn't room at the hitching rail to tie our horses. Some jackass had tied his mule to that old broke-down buggy. Kinda got our goat that a mule rider would do such a thing, so we set the mule loose and tied up our horses to the wheel. Reckon it's our day to give a free lesson in manners."

Hey, did you hear that? Man called you a jackass. Turned your mule loose. Looks like we gonna have to walk home.

Oscar refilled the Box 7 waddies' glasses. "Turned the mule loose?" the bartender said with disbelief.

"Yep," Hunch Shoulders said. "I cut him a good 'un across the ass with my quirt, and he went runnin' down the street fartin' like he'd eat a fifty-pound sack of pinto beans."

Well! Reckon that sews it up. Guess we'd best get started walking if we want to get home by dark.

Frank turned and faced the two boisterous cowboys. "Fellers, I do believe, the way you are describin' things, that was my mule."

"Would you look at that," Scar Face said. "It does appear that we are in the presence of a *gen-u-ine* cowhand. He's wore out so many horses, he's had to take to ridin' mules."

Whoa. Gen-u-ine!

Frank lowered his hand and felt the wooden stock of the shotgun. "I'm guessin' it won't take you more than ten minutes to find the mule and tie him up back where you found him."

Hunch Shoulders grinned. "Why would we want to do that?"

"So as I wouldn't have to get blood all over Oscar's floor."

Scar Face laughed. "Okay, mule rider, you want to wipe your blood on the floor, go ahead and do it."

Frank took a step toward them and raised the shotgun. "Not talkin' about mine. Talkin' about yours."

Scar Face stopped laughing as if a sandbur had lodged in his throat.

Hunch Shoulders took a step away from the bar and flexed his gun-side hand.

"Hold on, fellers," the bartender said. "I've got a good idea.

Y'all go round up Frank's mule and tie him up where you found him. Save everybody a whole bunch of trouble, and, bad as I hate to, I'll stand a round of drinks for the house."

Scar Face did not take his eyes away from Frank's shotgun. "We didn't come here to be a part of a mule roundup. If he wants his damn mule, he'd best get after it hisself."

The Gambler left his table, moved to the bar, and stood between the Box 7 cowboys and Frank Rule. "I've been watching and listening to you cowboys about to let your mouth overload your ass. This is not the first occasion I have observed a conflict in which Mr. Rule was involved. I fear you are about to make a fatal mistake. And you are costing me money by interrupting a very profitable card game in which I've invested several hours."

"Don't know what you're talkin' about," Hunch Shoulders said. "And you're standing right in the middle of what is about to be a serious gunfight."

The Gambler nodded. "I know you think that. But you're wrong. There is gonna be two men die, and Frank Rule is not one of 'em."

Hunch Shoulders added, "You don't move your fancy ass, you might be the first one."

The Gambler smiled, teeth white as piano keys. "I make a living wagering." He took a fat wallet from his left inside coat pocket and a buckskin bag of coins from the right pocket and laid both on the bar. "Oscar, would you kindly verify that there are over five hundred dollars in the wallet and at least that much in gold coins in the bag?"

The barkeep riffled the bills in the wallet, then emptied the sack containing the gold on the bar. He arranged the coins in stacks of five and nodded his head as he calculated. "Best I can tell, there's twelve hundred and some odd dollars."

The Gambler smiled again. "Why, Oscar, you ever give up

the saloon business, I believe most banks would hire you in a hot minute."

The sound of the gold coins clinking on the bar had drawn a small crowd, and a dozen bystanders stood in a semicircle around the would-be shooters.

Damn! Look at all that money. Why, if you had all that we could go up to Dodge and open a whorehouse. Wouldn't have to borrow a dime or answer to nobody.

The Gambler leaned back against the bar and hooked the heel of a polished boot behind the brass rail. He took one of the coins and manipulated it between his fingers. "I am a daring fellow but not one accustomed to taking uncalculated risk. Without consulting Mr. Rule, I'm willing to bet that he will kill both of you before your pistols clear their holsters. Should you best Mr. Rule, all the money is yours . . . or whichever of you two that survives."

Hunch Shoulders looked at Scar Face, then back to The Gambler. "Well, hell, what are we bettin'?"

The Gambler added another coin, and now the second coin traveled between his fingers, pursuing the first. "Oh, sorry. I thought you understood. You would be wagering your life. And, of course, the guns and horses that you would no longer need would become the property of Mr. Rule, should he, and he surely will, be the winner."

The Box 7 cowboys glanced at each other, then at their adversary, who had not wavered during the Gambler's presentation. Rule's thumb still rested across both hammers of the shotgun, his eyes unblinking.

Good gracious, just go ahead and shoot them. The world would be a better place, and I need folks like them in Hell. I'll get them a job shoveling coal and aggravating people.

A cold sensation swept across Scar Face's shoulders, followed by a drop of sweat that slowly slid down his spine and continued its journey through the cleft of his buttocks. "And if we decide to not accept your bet, then what?"

The Gambler shrugged. "I was about to get around to that. You see, Mr. Rule believes you've done him wrong. A considerable injustice. You've . . . you've hurt his feelings, vexed his manhood, so to speak. Although you probably cannot tell by looking at him, Mr. Rule is a very sensitive man. He treasures his privacy and his livestock. I believe, and, of course this is depending on his approval, he might be willing to forget this entire unpleasant happening—provided you retrieve his mule and restore it to its former place at the old buggy. And, naturally, he would also want you to leave this saloon."

"No. We're not going to do that. That would be belittlin' *us*." Hunch Shoulders looked at Scar Face and was surprised by his concerned expression.

"All right," the Gambler said. "I see no other way other than for us to step back and let you two get shot."

"No, wait," Scar Face said. "How would we do this? I mean, how would Frank . . . Mr. Rule . . . know we'll bring his mule back once we leave this bar? What if we kept on goin'?"

Yeah, what if these two turkeys run off once they get out of here? Just get-it, get-it, get-it right on down the road.

The Gambler stroked his chin, as if in deep thought. "There might be a solution. A way to get both of you out of here alive and not be fugitives from Mr. Rule's wrath. Take your guns and put them on the bar. One of you go search for the mule. I believe the mule is named Red, is that right, Mr. Rule? It is Red, isn't it?"

Frank nodded almost imperceptibly.

"Okay, there you are. You two decide who goes and gets Red. The other stays here. Consider it like an insurance policy. Mule comes back; man in the bar leaves alive. Sound fair?"

Very carefully and with a deliberately slow hand movement,

Hunch Shoulders wiped a bead of perspiration from his forehead. "What happens if whichever one of us goes to get the mule don't come back?"

"Yes. I've thought about that," the Gambler said. "I believe it would be Mr. Rule's obligation to shoot the insurance man in the head. Of course, that would be his decision, but, knowing him, I think that's what he would do."

Yeah. Bam, bam. Good bye, Sam—or whatever your name is.

"Of course, Mr. Rule would probably feel it necessary to hunt down the man who'd gone for the mule but then deserted his partner. Mr. Rule has the reputation of having exceptionally high expectations from his fellow man."

Oscar moved the stack of coins to rest beside the Gambler's over-stuffed wallet. "What's it going to be, cowboys? You gonna pull on Frank? Or is one of you gonna go search for his mule? It's put-up or shut-up time."

The crowd, or at least the ones standing near Scar Face and Hunch Shoulders, gave the first option considerable consideration and moved away from the two cowboys. Everyone knew Frank Rule loaded his gun with double-ought buckshot, and while the pattern would not spread much at this close range, there was no reason to take a chance on being struck by an errant projectile.

"I'll go get the damn mule," Scar Face growled, attempting to maintain his rough image.

"No. I'll go," Hunch Shoulders said. "I know I'll come back, but I ain't so sure you would. You ain't gonna leave me as insurance on a bad damn risk."

A spirited, acrimonious debate ensued with both Box 7 cowboys insisting that they be the one to go fetch Red and the other be left behind as a guarantee. Eventually, Oscar flipped a coin, Hunch Shoulders accurately predicted the outcome of the toss, and he became the mule searcher.

114

"Just be damn sure you come back," Scar Face threatened Hunch Shoulders, "or I will come after—" It was sinking in that if Hunch Shoulders did not return with the mule, Scar Face might not be doing anything to anybody. "Promise me, that's all I ask."

The two Box 7 cowboys unbuckled their gun belts and placed them beside the Gambler's money. Oscar dragged a chair to the end of the bar. Scar Face sat on it, started to cross a leg over the other, changed his mind, and kept both feet on the floor.

Look at him. Give him half a chance and he'll run like a scalded dog. Why don't you just go ahead and shoot one of his feet off? Take his mind off escaping. You probably gonna get to shoot him anyway.

Half of the saloon's patrons followed Hunch Shoulders out onto the front porch and watched him disappear down the dusty street. The remaining half of the crowd pulled chairs away from the tables, sat, and watched an uncomfortable Scar Face. Side bets arose in the crowd: two dollars would get you one dollar that if Scar Face ran, the odds of Frank Rule killing him before he reached the door were so great that there were no takers— even at the four-bit level.

It was a profitable afternoon for Oscar with whiskey and beer sales exceeding even that on July Fourth. The Gambler bought Scar Face three beers, and the cowboy desperately needed to pee but feared Frank Rule might misconstrue his predicament as a ruse to flee.

Three hours of sunlight left. The sixteen-year-old St. Louis escapee charged through the batwing doors, yelling, "They're a comin' up the road. The cowboy and the red mule. Be here in a minute."

Frank Rule did not change position or take his eyes off Scar Face. "Is he ridin' the mule?"

The kid ran back through the doors out onto the porch, then reappeared before the doors swung a third time. "Man is walking in front of the mule, just got a halter and a lead."

Frank almost smiled. "Good; wouldn't want him ridin' Red. Wouldn't be fair to the mule. Sorry man like that ridin' such a fine mule."

Drat. Looks like you are not going to get a chance to shoot either man. That's too bad. I was counting on a touch of excitement. Why don't you go ahead and shoot Scar Face just for the fun of it? Maybe in the arm so's he can still run around and holler.

The group that had been observing Frank Rule watch the hostage—most of whom were secretly disappointed when it appeared no blood would be shed—moved through the side door and out to where Hunch Shoulders would be escorting the mule to its final destination. They arrived simultaneously with the group that had been standing in the street. Never in the history of Longsought had so many people been interested in seeing a mule tied to a buggy wheel.

"All right, there you are," Hunch Shoulders said as he straightened from knotting Red's lead line. "Lived up to my part of the deal. Now I want my gun, and then I aim to bid this dump a fond *adieu.*"

BLAM. BLAM. Two shotgun blasts. Panicked, the crowd of men who had witnessed Hunch Shoulders's final declaration stood still for a millisecond and then stampeded like a buffalo herd under Comanche attack.

Boogered by the surrounding insanity, the red mule lashed out repeatedly with its back hooves, wounding a sheepherder, a stable boy, and addling an overaged prostitute who had just come on duty.

Only the Gambler had witnessed the entire madness. Scar Face, followed by Frank Rule pressing the shotgun against the small of the cowboy's back, came through the saloon's front door.

Frank turned Scar Face until he faced west. "When I tell you to run, I expect you to run and not look back. You savvy?"

Scar Face had not even finished his first nod of understanding when Frank rested the shotgun against the top of the cowboy's head and fired both barrels.

"Old Scar Face stumbled on his first step, caught his footing, and, I'm telling you fellers, I never saw a man run as fast in my life. His shirttail even come outta his britches and was sticking out so far, you could have played a game of poker on it." The Gambler stopped his narration and spasmed with laughter. "Well, reckon the other cowboy was pretty damn fast, too. He broke out of the crowd and turned east toward the creek. He was running so fast, his hat blew off. There was a little feist dog that was running alongside of him, barking. He ran off and left that little dog like it was a broke-legged chicken."

The Gambler relit his cheroot. "Don't know but, if I was a wagering man, I'd say those two won't be back in Longsought for a few years. I'm gonna keep their guns and horses as kinda' a fee for putting the whole shindig together. Mr. Rule did not want them. Oscar and I talked it over, and it was all right with him. After all, I'm pretty much responsible for keeping blood off the floor and buckshot outta the walls."

Well, I hope you are satisfied. We are leaving town with two bits less than when we got there. Didn't shoot anybody. Didn't spend any time upstairs with them women, and I thought that little skinny blonde was kinda special.

You know, you've got a reputation to maintain. Word gets around that you let folks call you a jackass mule rider and get away with it, won't be long 'til little kids start inviting you on Sunday school picnics. Deacons be wanting you to lead singing at church.

Wait, wait. Whoa. Stop. There's Widow Holley coming from the chicken house. Maybe you ought to rest your mule by her front gate— give her a chance to . . .

John Neely Davis

Dang it, just ride on by like you was deaf and blind. You ain't listened to a damn thing Old Scratch has said all day.

And another thing . . .

118

★ ★ ★ ★ ★

BEERSHEBA'S MILK COW

★ ★ ★ ★ ★

To describe Frank Rule as ornery-as-the-devil would have painted an unkind picture of Satan. On his very worst day, the day he mortified Job, Ole Lucifer would have been terrified of Frank and hidden behind the nearest brimstone mountain.

The groundwork for his foul reputation became established when, on his first visit to Longsought, he had whipped the town bully from one side of the street to the other—twice.

On the northern outskirts of Longsought, grass widow Beersheba Mounds lived in circumstances similar to but somewhat better than Frank's. In contrast to Rule's house, Sheba's windows were intact. Dirty, but intact.

Sheba—Beersheba's preference—while still lusty at heart, was approaching that indeterminable age women reach when wrinkles deepen and the backs of their upper arms commence to resemble wings. Her disposition, which was never rosy, totally soured after her husband Melvin disappeared. He went out to check on the windmill one afternoon and never returned. Sheba did not suspect foul play; she had watched his face at night when the train whistled for the crossing and saw his eyes glaze. She figured the coward had hopped an eastbound freight.

Now she lived alone with three tomcats, a barren sow, and Hannah, a cow of mixed lineage. However, Sheba never got any milk from the cow. The animal had a despicable habit; she nursed herself. Oh, there was plenty of milk, but Hannah got it

121

all. She was fat, and her coat glistened. This was in sharp contrast to the gaunt sow that rooted for grubs in the lot behind the barn. Had the sow been as fat as Hannah, Sheba would have hams and sausage hanging in the tack room.

East of town, out where the Caprock started to crumble and the land commenced its southeastern slope, two brothers lived in a soddy, a house burrowed back into a dirt bank much like a terrapin withdrawing into its shell. Bill Barksdale and his brother, Booger, had occupied this dugout for years—ever since their father got caught in a hailstorm in 1859. Their old man had taken refuge under an elm that succumbed to a blue norther earlier in the year. He poked his head from under the tree trunk to see if the storm was over. It was not. A solitary chunk of ice slightly larger than a can of condensed milk hurtled from the sky and took the old man in the left temple. Bill and Booger found his body two days later when they went to investigate a flock of magpies scuffling over what the young men took to be a bundle of rags.

There was limited mental stability in the Barksdale family, reaching back at least ten generations. The older brother, Bill, had developed the ability to drive steeples in fence posts and herd cattle—for limited periods. On the other hand, Booger was prone to spending long days sitting in the creek staring at clouds and rubbing his cat, Kitty. The cat rubbing abruptly ceased when a bitch coyote engaged Kitty in a fifty-yard dash and was victorious. Without a pet to boost his morale, Booger lapsed into a permanent case of glumness.

". . . the sorry sumbitch has stole my cow." Sheba stood like a spavined horse by the edge of Frank Rule's mule lot. She wore a pair of her former husband's faded pants; the patches had come loose at the knees and flared open to resemble an extra set of pockets. She'd put on one of his shirts, and the lower three buttons were not fastened, allowing her belly button to peep out when she swung her arms. Frank tried to ignore the row of dark hair that emerged from the top of the pants and circled her navel.

"What he is doing is taking advantage of a pore, defenseless widow woman," Sheba said and mopped the sweat that escaped her hat and coursed through the red dust accumulated on her forehead. "If I had a man at my house, that Booger Barksdale, sorry sumbitch, wouldn't have stole my cow."

Frank stared above the woman's head and off into the distance. "Why are you tellin' me all this?" he asked.

Sheba swiveled to look in the direction Frank was staring and, not seeing anything, turned back to face the rancher. "Want you to go with me to fetch Hannah."

"Hannah? Thought you said it was a cow."

"It is. Her name is Hannah."

Frank wished he had hidden when he saw Sheba coming across his pasture. "You don't need nobody to go with you just to get your damn cow."

"Do, too. I was out there to the Barksdale place yesterday. Booger, he's the idjit brother, told me he didn't have my cow. Hell, I trailed her all the way out there and was standin' there lookin' at her. She was knee deep in the creek. He was standin' right there beside her, pourin' a bucket of water on her, washin' her with a croaker sack."

Frank Rule shook his head. "I don't want to get in this mess."

"Scared, ain't you? Scared of them Barksdale brothers. You a coward jest like all the men 'round here."

Sheba did not know it, but she had said two magic words— *coward* and *scared.*

Fifty yards from the Barksdales' soddy, Frank Rule and Sheba

123

got off their mules and tied them to a mesquite bush. He handed
her his shotgun and pulled the .50 Sharps from its leather scabbard.

She checked the shotgun to see if it was loaded. "All right.
Let's go get my cow."

"Let's stand around here for a few minutes," he said. "Kinda
get the lay of things, see if anything's going on."

"I ain't leavin' without my cow. Don't care what's goin' on."

Frank did not want to argue with her . . . or even look in her
direction, just in case her shirt might have ridden up on her
belly again. "We've come for the cow. We'll leave with the damn
cow. But we'll do this my way. You best know, I don't tolerate
no smart mouth. Understand?"

Sheba thought of several things to say, but she was not going
to say any of them to Frank.

They waited ten minutes, Frank staring at the house, breathing through his mouth, not moving. Sheba sat cross-legged in
the sand, peering through the bushes.

The door to the soddy opened, and a barefooted Bill came
out. He moved along the narrow dirt path to the woodpile and
gathered an armload of mesquite branches, then went back into
the soddy. There was no sign of Booger.

"Ain't you gonna shoot 'im?" Sheba whispered.

Frank did not look at her. "Shut up, woman! I have been in
more situations like this than you have. I know what I'm doin'."

He levered a shell into the Sharps, aimed, and fired at the
soddy's doorway head-sill. Bits of the sill splintered and fell to
the ground. A small cloud of dust rose from the sod roof. He
reloaded and fired a second time. The remainder of the sill fell
to the ground, and more dust rose from the roof.

"What are you doin'?" Sheba asked.

Frank jacked another round into the gun. "Getting their attention."

The door opened six inches, and a broom handle emerged, topped by a single gray sock. Then a wavering voice: "What do you want?"

Sheba stood and shouted, "We've come for the . . ."

Frank fired a third time. This time the iron stovepipe extending through the soddy's roof spun and fell into the dugout.

The gray sock waved in a wider arc. "Damn. Fellers. Quit shootin'. Ain't neither one of us armed. Well, we got a gun, but we ain't got no shells. Swear to God."

Frank fired again, and the broom handle splintered. "Both of you. Come out with your hands up in the air. And if either one of you come out with a gun, I'm gonna shoot both of you 'tween the eyes. You hear me?"

"Yes, sir. We hear. We're comin' out. Don't shoot no more."

"No, ma'am. I don't know nothin' about the cow. Been doin' some work over at the Bates ranch. Just got home 'bout midnight. I ain't even talked with Booger more than just to say hello. If we got your cow, I guaran-damn-tee you it'll be back at your house 'fore dark."

Tears were streaming down Booger's face, and he was making huffing sounds. "No, Bill, don't say that. I . . . I . . . need the cow. Need something to pet and look after."

"Damn, Booger, act like you got a little sense. Mrs. Sheba, we don't want to put you out none. I'll find the cow, and she will be back in your lot quicker than you can blink your eyes twice."

Frank slid a shell into the Sharps. "You boys ain't gonna do nothing to cause us to come back out here again, are you?"

Almost as a duet, the Barksdales said, "No, sir, you ain't gonna have to come out here no more."

Sheba and Frank rode away from the Barksdale place. After a

mile, Sheba said, "Well, it'll be a relief to have Hannah back home in the lot." They rode a bit farther, and she turned toward Frank. "I'm thinkin', that feller Bill, up close, he's right good lookin'. And way closer to my age than I figured."

Frank grinned. "He did look some better when he stopped shakin'. And I'd bet my last dollar that the cow—Hannah—will be home by dark."

Sheba heeled her mule into a trot. "I might warm up some beans. Make fresh biscuits."

Frank slouched a bit in the saddle. *God protect the man. And his half-wit brother, too.*

The High Plains had not seen a winter this cold in a hundred years. Frank stayed around his ranch, mending harness and just trying to stay warm.

The second warm spring day, he traveled down to Long-sought. He passed the Mounds place, and Sheba was in the side yard hanging out wash. She no longer wore a man's shirt because it would have been too small. A baby takes up considerable space in a woman's belly.

Bill walked out to the road to greet Frank. "Made it through the winter all right, I see," he said. "First time we can get with a preacher, we're gonna get married."

Frank nodded. "Yeah. Reckon that would be a good thing to do. Tell me, how's your brother doin'?"

"Well, I'll let you see for yourself." Bill turned and shouted toward the barn. "Booger. Booger, get on up here. See who stopped by to see us?"

Booger came around the corner of the barn, and Frank noticed that he, too, had put on weight. Hannah, a red ribbon tied to her tail and her horns polished to sheen, followed him closely.

★ ★ ★ ★ ★

In less than five minutes, Frank was moving southward to Long-sought, his mule traveling at a bone-jarring trot.

Well, God, I asked you to help the Barksdales. I reckon in your own way, you did.

★ ★ ★ ★ ★

THE HANRAHAN

★ ★ ★ ★ ★

Geese and sandhill cranes in ever-changing V-formations peppered the blue sky and cautiously followed the warmth, stopping for days of rest along the Canadian River and the great *playas* that lay like huge saucers embedded in the flatness of the Llano Estacado. Spring was progressing northward, silently moving across the Great Plains as it had done for thousands of years—long before the Indian warriors ruled and massive herds of buffalo darkened the landscape. The blue grama and buffalo grasses were greening, and the sand shinnery oaks were developing leathery leaves. Mesquite was promising blooms, and advance honeybee scouts buzzed through the low-growing plants, reconnoitering for nectar to support their virgin queen.

Frank Rule survived the cold weather as he had in the past, mostly just trying to stay warm. He busied himself around his small ranch, feeding his meager herd of cattle, mending harness, and hunting buffalo chips. He neither sought nor made an effort to avoid the isolation of winter up here on these wind-driven plains.

Occasionally, he talked aloud to himself, his voice ragged from disuse, words poorly formed. Just when he surrendered to the futility of conjuring Ellen, his long-dead wife, and despaired that he would never hear her voice again, she would come to him in the predawn, her voice soft, her smell so real he could almost taste it. He would keep his eyes closed because he knew that light vanquished her. But, no matter how hard he tried, as

131

darkness ebbed and light became almost audible, she would fade, leaving him to cope with the loneliness and madness that gnawed at him.

Yesterday, he'd made a pot of coffee and sat before the shallow fireplace, staring at the dull-gray shotgun resting in the antelope-hoof rack above the mantle.

Hey, Frank, it's me, Old Scratch. Didn't want you to think I'd deserted you. I've been busy up to the north. Spreading smallpox among some of the Indians that live along the river. Figured I'd swing by and check on you. Saw you looking at that shotgun. If I was you, my wife and family dead and all, I believe I'd put the end of the barrel in my mouth and blow my brains out. Nobody would even know you were gone. Nobody would even miss you. 'Course, knowing you, you'll probably just hang around here and be miserable for the rest of your life.

As he'd been doing for years, Frank ignored the voice. But it was getting harder.

Weeks ago, Frank discarded February from the Longsought Feed and Seed calendar. It irritated him that he had not checked off the days, but he decided today was probably about the twentieth of March—it did not make any real difference—a week or day, one way or the other, just as long as daylight was lengthening.

This morning the rising sun was sullied by a high layer of slate-gray clouds, their ceiling hundreds of feet higher than the flight of northbound geese. Frank led Red, his best road mule, into the stock shed. She had a nice easy gait—almost a short lope—and covered the ground smoothly as a saddle horse. Last fall, he'd bought a Mother Hubbard saddle from a down-on-his-luck Kansas drover. Over the winter, he cut out and sewed a leather *mochila*—he had seen one on a Pony Express rigging. It fit snugly over his saddle, and its four *cantinas* could hold all the supplies he would buy in Longsought. After he jammed the L. C. Smith shotgun and the Sharps rifle down into their scabbards, he tied his bedroll behind the saddle and then, as an afterthought, put a pack frame on a second mule before setting out southward. Panhandle weather was always iffy—a man couldn't be too well prepared.

The Hanrahan lived at Longsought before anyone, except maybe the Comanche and the buffalo and whatever beast that came before them. Perchance he knew his own first name, but no one else did. So, over the years, as more settlers came to the Llano Estacado, more Indians left, and most of the buffs were killed by hide hunters, the old man became simply known as The Hanrahan—not Mr. Hanrahan, or Hanrahan, or Old Man Hanrahan—just The Hanrahan.

Legends are hard to come by up on the High Plains. Billy Dixon, who shot a man off a horse with a 50.90 Sharps at just slightly less than a mile, might be one. Or mayhaps the halfbreed Comanche war leader of the Quahadi, Quanah Parker, might qualify. But even if they had, they would have run a poor second to The Hanrahan.

He had rescued children stolen by the Comancheros; looked after the well-being of widows and orphans; doctored sick livestock and occasionally their owners; fought prairie fires; helped deliver babies; and, if it became necessary, righted wrongs with gunfire.

Now he was old. His eyesight was fading, and while he remembered these stark plains when white men were as scarce as an August snowstorm, he could not remember what happened yesterday or his best friend's name. Arthritis had twisted his fingers, and his left hip was twice broken—once when a horse fell on him and the second time when he was trampled by a buffalo. Only four of his teeth remained, but he boasted he

133

could eat anything except parched peanuts and pork rinds.

He lived in a south-facing sod house near the grove of cotton-wood trees that grew on the bank of Longsought Creek. Two years ago, an itinerant carpenter installed a single window in The Hanrahan's soddy in exchange for a milk cow. His floor was still packed dirt, and he burned buffalo chips in his small tin heater—but the natural light from the tiny window was a great improvement. During the cold months, days might pass without a sighting of The Hanrahan. Then a townsman or a cowboy with an extra slab of beef or side of salt pork would just *happen* to stop by and check on the welfare of the old man.

With spring and the increased activity of prairie dogs, there would be sightings of The Hanrahan along the creek, fishing in the spring runoff or walking Cob, his three-legged shepherd dog. As summer came and the wild grasses of the prairie danced with the unceasing wind, the old man would hobble into town and take up his station outside the Antelope Flag saloon. Mild days, he sat in the sun on the whittler's bench in front of the saloon; as the heat of the summer intensified with the longer days, he sat in the shade on the east side of the building. The dog apparently approved of the man's choice of seating areas, and he comfortably curled at The Hanrahan's feet.

Around noon on most summer days, Mable, the woman who owned the Good Eats café, sent the dishwasher with a plate of food to The Hanrahan. He always made a feeble effort to pay, but under strict orders from the proprietress, money was never accepted. Many years ago, a thin, shivering, pregnant girl of fifteen had taken refuge in his soddy on a cold, rainy night. Now, Mable was working off a debt of kindness that she could never fully repay.

Twenty years ago, The Hanrahan confessed to a preacher about killing a man over the disputed ownership of a bottle of whiskey. He had not bought a drink of alcohol since. He still drank; he didn't buy.

He often spoke of death—his own—and this made the men with creaseless faces, strong arms, and no trace of gray in their hair uncomfortable. However, he spoke of other things too: the innocence of children, the kindness of strangers, the loyalty of a good dog, and the joy of riding a smooth horse across the endless plains.

He would have been surprised and embarrassed at the love Longsought had for him.

The last hour of the trip into Longsought was miserable. The north wind that caused the mules' tails to whip against their bellies brought driving rains that quickly turned to sleet. After tying the cotton bandana over his head like a woman's scarf, Frank pulled his hat snugly down on his head and turned his coat collar up. He draped the bedroll around his body, but as the temperature dropped to just under freezing, there was no comfort for unsheltered man or beast.

The livery was deserted. Frank opened the gate and took his mules into the barn. Horizontal snow followed, penetrating the walls' finger-width cracks and sweeping down the long hallway through the open doors. The animals stood patiently, steam rising from their flanks, while Frank removed their saddles, then with his fingers raked ice from their manes and tails.

Frank dumped two scoops of grain into the feed trough and, satisfied the mules were cared for, walked down the ice-crusted street to the warmth of the Antelope Flag Saloon.

The Hanrahan knew a storm was on its way. He had seen three flocks of wild geese fly northward from the shelter of Longsought Creek, then return before sunset. They were sensing something in the air that man could not yet see. The prairie dogs had been sitting outside enjoying the spring sunshine, then yesterday morning disappeared down their burrows, giving their grassy town a sense of abandonment.

With Cob hobbling behind, The Hanrahan traipsed to town and made his first stop at Elijay's store. He purchased a pound of meal, a small sack of beans, and a bag of Arbuckle's coffee. After deliberating and counting his diminishing coin supply—odd jobs for a man his age were occasional at best—he decided to forego the purchase of a tin of apricots.

At the Antelope Flag, Oscar stood the old man one free drink and offered a second, which The Hanrahan declined. Long ago, he had learned the best guarantee of receiving the first free drink was never take a second.

Mable, the café owner, stood on her front porch and watched the old man walking along the street, the wind whipping his pants against his frail and bowed legs. He had traveled less than a block when the dishwasher from the Good Eats caught up with him and presented him with a metal lard bucket containing four boiled eggs, a steak sandwich, and half of a peach pie.

The old man continued to his dugout as marbled, silver-gray clouds raced southward. He and the dog stood outside the soddy, both sensing something foreboding. The Hanrahan remembered the time when he would have been scurrying around the pasture gathering cattle on days like this, but those days were far behind him, and now he had been reduced to taking care of a three-legged dog—or maybe it was the other way around, and the dog cared for the man.

East of Longsought at the Caprock Escarpment, the Llano Estacado gives way to land of shallow ravines, grama grass flats, and wooded areas of mesquite, sumac, and sand shinnery oaks. The Comanche considered the escarpment a land of friendly spirits and fought roving bands of Kiowa and harassed white settlers who ventured into the area.

Coyotes thrived here, living in small packs and eating anything they could find, from unwary jackrabbits to grasshoppers and berries.

The Comanche admired the ways of the coyote and considered him a trickster figure. They believed he was a clever creature and often helped humans but was flawed with dishonesty, recklessness, and impatience. They admired his ability to hide and hunt in the dark. Some Indians believed the coyotes' howls were conversations with the dead or with the spirits of those who would soon die. Others claimed they had seen the coyotes shift shapes, becoming men or buffalo or even red wolves. To kill a coyote with anything other than a lance was bad luck and frequently caused the guilty warrior's wife to give birth to a stillborn male child.

Of the Comanche bands who lived along the escarpment, almost every medicine man had seen Old Silver, a coyote of unusually large size. His coat was almost white, and he appeared as a smoky vapor in the moonlight. He was older than the oldest living man, yet he moved with the grace of a shadow.

As the storm clouds scurried across the plains, Old Silver tested the winds and experienced their surging energy. He sensed something else, something foreign, something that he could not immediately identify. He turned to the west and moved to meet the impending storm.

It snowed for three days. In the parts of the village of Longsought not victimized by howling winds, snow covered the ground to a depth of two feet. Where the town was unprotected from the full force of the blizzard, the violence of the tempest drove snow up to the eaves of many buildings. At the rear of the Good Eats café, the gusts had their way with the snow, massing a drift that almost reached the second-story gable.

Three hours after the blizzard started, Frank Rule left the

Antelope Flag and moved back to the livery where his mules were stabled. He fed them more grain and two forks of hay. In the loft, he spread his bedroll, pulled his hat over his face, and burrowed into the softness of the hay.

On the afternoon of the third day of the blizzard, The Hanrahan heated a pot of last night's coffee and ate two boiled eggs and the last of the peach pie.

Cob, his three-legged dog, stood at the soddy's single door and scratched the dirt floor. It had been only four hours since the dog had been outside and left irregular, yellow marks in the snow. The Hanrahan pulled on his boots and jacket. Probably be a good time to make his own yellow marks—no need in opening the door more than necessary and letting the soddy's warmth out into the cold. It might be days before he would be able to hunt buffalo chips to feed the hungry tin heater.

He opened the door, and the frantic dog squeezed past him. A jackrabbit, only slightly smaller than the dog, erupted from the downwind side of the dugout and, with powerful lunges, fought his way through the knee-deep snow toward the creek. Cob let out a startled yelp and bounded into the snow after the frightened hare.

The Hanrahan put two fingers in his mouth and whistled, the kind that usually stopped Cob in his tracks. But the excited dog kept plowing through the snow in pursuit. The man continued to stumble through the drifts and call the dog.

The drifts were deeper on the north side of Longsought Creek. The dog crossed the frozen stream, climbed the south bank, and continued the chase. The Hanrahan tumbled over the rotting corpse of a snow-covered cottonwood tree, fell, and lay still for a few minutes. Groggy and disoriented, he finally stood and found that the wind was howling again, and the driving snow had obliterated his tracks and any outline of the soddy.

The whiteness lay in smooth, undulating sheets, and he was as lost as a blind man in a strange world.

Miles to the east near the edge of the blizzard, the ancient coyote the Indians had named Old Silver stood on the edge of the escarpment and howled, breath briefly clouding the air before fading into the darkness. His image became obscure, lost its shape, and formed another comprised of slanted edges and sharp points that lifted upward into the leaden sky.

Around midnight, the blizzard lost its soul, and peacefulness settled over Longsought. At first light, Frank, so hungry that he was sure his backbone was rubbing against his belt buckle, climbed down from the hay loft and waded through waist-deep snow drifts to the Antelope Flag.

The saloon was packed. Passengers on the Denver-bound stagecoach had commandeered chairs and a round table and sat in one corner of the room, seeming glad to be separated from the assortment of cowboys, teamsters, sheepherders, drifters, and riffraff. Considering the mixture of people, things were almost calm inside the Antelope Flag. Twenty-four hours ago, the last drop of whiskey disappeared down Oscar's gullet—he owned the saloon and figured it was his privilege to have the final drink. Now he stood behind the bar, a three-foot section of a pick handle he'd named the Knot Maker within easy reach.

Frank waded through the crowd, stomping snow from his boots. "Don't reckon a man could get a drink in here on a cold day like this?" he said.

If Oscar had not been so sleep-deprived and tired, he would have found the question humorous. "No, not a damned thing to drink. And I can't serve you no chocolate cake either."

"Looks to me like you ought to complain to the owner. 'Specially about running outta whiskey."

"Hell, Frank, that ain't funny. I'm the owner, or might as well be. Could've sold two barrels of beer and 'bout that much whiskey if I'd had it. Everybody in here is either bellyachin' about no alcohol or no food. I'm 'bout to run their sorry asses out into the snow. See what they gripe about then."

Frank's guts growled and he held his hand over his stomach. "Reckon they got any taters and onions over at Elijay's store?"

Oscar laughed. "Don't see why not. They ain't had no customers in three days."

Frank's guts growled again. "You still got that big cast-iron kettle out in back? The one that Chinaman used to boil clothes in?"

"Yeah. Nobody round here would steal nothing that might cause 'em to have to work. What you gonna do? Make a big pot of vegetable snow cream?"

Frank buttoned his coat and turned the collar up. "Get one of the fellers to go over to the store and buy all the taters and onions they got. Scrub that kettle. Set it up out in back. Get enough wood together to fire the pot for a couple of hours. Cut up them vegetables. Then don't do anything else until I get back."

The Hanrahan grasped the front of his tattered jacket and tightened it across his thin chest. His hat loosened, lifted, and skittered across the shimmering snowbanks before becoming airborne and disappearing into a cane thicket. Cob, coat matted with ice, reappeared, running his back trail, still seeking the scent of the rabbit. The dog tumbled down the creek bank and slid across the ice into a clump of driftwood. Right by the frozen creek, the old man rolled over on his belly and, crablike, worked himself down the steep bank. He reached the ice, stood, his feet lost their purchase on the slick surface, and he fell. Stunned, he sat on the ice, his right arm at an unnatural angle, the jagged end of a bone protruding through the sleeve of his jacket.

Cob crossed the ice, nails slipping on the frozen surface. He stood whining and licking the old man's face. Blood gathered in the hollow of The Hanrahan's temple, and the dog raised his head and howled.

Frank retraced his steps to the livery. Earlier, he had seen two pronghorn bucks foraging on wind-blown straw near the back of the barn. The rancher retrieved his Sharps, braced it on the livery's gate, aimed, and fired. The younger buck flinched, front legs buckled, and fell head first to the ground. The other buck bolted in a shower of snow and shards of ice, leaped the corral fence, and raced away. Frank dragged the dead pronghorn into the barn, skinned it, and an hour later, with fifty pounds of fresh meat across his shoulders, traipsed through the snow toward the saloon.

Hey, Frank, Old Scratch don't know what to think about you. Walking around out here in this freezing weather. You ought to cook this meat and feed yourself. Let these other rascals look after their own hides.

At the back of the saloon, a clean iron kettle partially filled with vegetables and water awaited. Frank added chunks of antelope meat and started a fire under the pot. Two hours later the saloon was empty. People with every type of dish imaginable crowded around the bubbling kettle, stomping snow from their feet and whiffing the stew. They were awaiting their turn for what had to be the best stew ever cooked outside in a cast-iron wash pot and stirred with a branding iron behind a bar on a snowbound, Texas morning.

The great bird flew westward, the edge of the escarpment more distant with each movement of its powerful wings. Below, irregular shapes of the raptor's shadow shifted with the contours of the snow-covered plains.

The Hanrahan stood and tried to gather his bearings. Although the sky was clearing, the wind had increased and created a ground blizzard—a visually impenetrable wall of whiteness. The old man cradled his broken arm against his body and climbed the south bank of the creek. Ahead lay the great whiteness. He stumbled into it.

Behind him and across the creek, the soddy door closed silently.

"Got a foot of stew left in the bottom of the pot," Frank Rule said. "Anybody got any room left in their belly?"

Mable from the Good Eats café laughed. "Don't know when I've eat anybody's cooking 'cept my own. Frank, you ever decide to give up ranching, I just might take you on as a cook."

Oscar scurried around the black kettle gathering bowls and plates. "We got enough stew left to feed a dozen hungry folks. What say we take some down to The Hanrahan? Bet his old bones would benefit from something warm."

Frank was glad to get away from the stew pot. "I'll go get Red. Be a whole lot easier riding through the snow than walking. Time I get back, you can have me a bucket of stew ready to go. I'll ride down to the creek and cheer that old rascal up."

The whiteout was lifting. The Hanrahan could see his hand in front of him and the dog behind him. But he didn't know which way to travel, and if he went in the wrong direction, he would never see his dugout again.

Frank pounded on the dugout's door. There was no answer. He pushed his way inside and placed the bucket of warm stew on the floor. The fire in the tin heater was little more than a few smoldering buffalo chips; a dirty plate sat on the three-legged table; there were no other signs of life.

He shoved the door open again and studied the scrape mark it made as it pushed snow into a foot-high ledge. At some point toward the end of the blizzard, the door had been opened. Since there was warmth at the tin heater, Frank figured the old man had been gone from the soddy for less than half a day—hopefully, a lot less. A man frail as The Hanrahan would not last long in the cold and the driving snow: maybe hours, not a day.

Frank climbed back in the saddle and slowly rode away from the soddy, scanning the snow for tracks. Immediately, he picked up the first signs. The weight of the struggling man had packed the snow into footprints that turned to ice. Once the wind swept the loose snow away, the tracks were easily followed until they ended at the creek. The rancher dismounted and found weeds and brush broken where the old man had gone down the steep bank. He followed the path to the frozen creek and found drops of dried blood on the ice but no sign of The Hanrahan.

The cowboy stood and looked up and down the creek bed. Nothing. He walked to the south side of the creek and found more broken weeds and brush, but this time, the broken vegetation pointed up the bank. This was where the old man had climbed out of the frozen creek bed. He was moving south, away from his home and safety!

Frank trudged through the drifts and got Red. He found a place they could cross the creek, then walked along the stream bank until he found where The Hanrahan had climbed through the weeds. Before him, the direction the old man had certainly traveled, the snow was smooth. The wind would have deeply buried any tracks. The prairie lay in front of him—mile after mile of unchanging whiteness. It would take days to search it. The Hanrahan would be dead long before he could find him—if

143

he ever found him.

He took his binoculars and glassed the expanse before him. He did not notice the large bird flying in tight circles above, nor did he hear the high-pitched, piercing chirps.

Two miles from the soddy, before it saw them, the great bird had sensed the presence of the man and the dog struggling through the snow, their paths erratic.

Frank traveled a quarter mile downstream, the mule laboring through the drifts. Nothing. No human tracks. No dog tracks. Nothing.

He turned back upstream, retracing Red's tracks. At the point where he'd exited the creek bed, something large, perhaps a range bull or a buffalo, had come up from the creek after he had. The tracks were not there half an hour ago, and now they were—deep and wide, something powerful and broad plowing southward through the waist-high snowdrifts.

Frank pulled the Sharps from its scabbard, jacked a shell into the chamber, and turned his mule to follow the tracks. The broad path was as straight as if it followed a surveyed line, and he could see no end to it.

He was not a man easily frightened, yet he felt dryness in his mouth and a tightening of his throat. His heart rate increased, and his breathing turned shallow. He did not know what he was about to follow but knew one thing: he'd never encountered anything as powerful and big.

A mile from the creek, the path through the snow had narrowed from three feet in width to one no wider than what a weasel or a mink would make. But still, the path continued southward. Frank stood in the stirrups and shaded his eyes from the brightness. A hundred yards away, an eagle floated in a tight circle around a slender plume of gray smoke snaking upward from a clump of mesquite bushes.

Frank slid from the saddle and stood in the snow. He cradled the Sharps in the crook of his left arm and moved forward toward the smoke, following the narrow path, finger curled around the rifle's trigger.

The Hanrahan sat before a small fire on the downwind side of a cluster of mesquite. The force of the past days' wind had lifted the snow over the bushes, leaving a patch of grass free from the whiteness. The old man was naked except for a buffalo robe wrapped around his bony shoulders.

Only one lamp still burned inside the saloon, stretching the shadows of the two men abnormally long and wide. Earlier, Oscar had added a dozen lumps of coal to the stove, but now they were gone, and the room was chilled.

". . . naked?"

Frank nodded. "Yep. Naked as the day he was born."

"Except for the buffalo robe."

Frank stood and backed toward the stove, pulling his trousers tight across his butt cheeks, seeking a final bit of warmth. "Yeah. The robe looked soft as a bed quilt."

"And he had a fire?" Oscar asked.

"Yeah. Little one. The kind Indians make when they don't mean to stay a long time—just enough to warm up a bit. The Hanrahan held a strip of dried buffalo meat that he'd been gumming on. Had a little tin pot of some kind of mush. He was a whole lot better off with food than I was. And a damned sight warmer, too."

"But he's going to be all right?" Oscar said, his words midway between a statement and a question.

"Yeah. Doc said he was one tough sumbitch. Gonna lose the

tips off some fingers. Part of an ear. Maybe a toe. I don't know how in the hell he's alive."

Oscar nodded and held his hands near the fading warmth of the stove. "Last count, there was nine men and one woman what died in the blizzard. Feller came by yesterday and told that McGregor up in Ochiltree County lost better than fifty head of cows and about half that many calves. Said there was dead cows all over the Panhandle, drifted in against fence corners, some of them stacked up in sinkholes, some mired down in playas."

Frank's face soured up. "Damn."

"Tell me about The Hanrahan's dog?"

"Never saw him. Mayhaps the wolf got him."

"Wolf," Oscar exclaimed. "Hell, you never said anything about a wolf."

Frank looked at the floor and shook his head. "Hadn't seen any wolf tracks. Hadn't heard one howl. Then all at once, that big bird that I'd seen circling started making this loud whistling noise. Did a dive at something that was hiding in a low place. Big explosion of snow. Old wolf reared up on his hind legs and started slashing at the bird. I missed the wolf with my first shot. Got him with the second. I figured the bird might tear into him, with him dead and all. But he didn't, just kinda rose up and turned east. Acting like his job was done. Big strong wings beatin' against the cold air." Frank shook his head. "I ain't never seen a bird near that big or one fly that fast. One minute he was there; next minute he wadn't much more than a speck in the sky."

Oscar sat on a battered chair, leaning forward, hands cupped over his knees. "Never heard nothing like it," he said. "So, you just loaded The Hanrahan on the mule and come back here."

"Well, wadn't quite that easy. I walked back and got Red, come back and wrapped the old man up in the buffalo robe, and put him in the saddle."

146

"Then just followed the trail back to the creek and . . ."

"No. You see, there wadn't no trail."

"But you'd followed one down there. You said yourself that it looked like one a buffalo or a big range bull had plowed."

"It did. That's the way it looked going down there, but there wadn't no tracks when I started back. The wind had laid earlier; wadn't no blowing snow to cover the tracks—just wadn't no tracks. Don't ask me. I can't explain it. Couldn't see any of my tracks. Couldn't see any of Red's. Snow was just as smooth as a baby's hind end. If I hadn't been able to see that stand of cottonwood beside The Hanrahan's house to get a line on which way to go, I might still be wandering around out there myself."

The lamp was running out of kerosene, the flame fading and sputtering. For a minute, the two men sat silent in the cold room.

"What do you make out of all this?" Frank asked.

"Well, I'd say you'd been dreaming or drinking somebody else's whiskey, if I didn't know better."

"I got a question for you, Oscar." Frank paused like a man will do when he is going to ask a question he'd rather not ask. "You believe that things can change shapes? I mean like from a bird to a buffalo, or maybe a woman. Ever seen or heard tell of anything like that?"

Oscar rubbed his thumb against the stubble on his chin and frowned. "Can't say as I ever saw it. Indians, 'specially those old medicine men, say they seen such things happen. Maybe you've got to be an Indian to see it. What do you think?"

"Oscar, you think that bird guided me to the old man? Think he might have turned into something big and plowed the trail so I could find him? Then when I got close enough, turned into a weasel so he could make better time? Then turned back into a bird so I would find The Hanrahan and then see the wolf?"

Oscar stared at Frank and shook his head. "Bigger mystery

than that. You said the old man was naked 'cept for a buffalo robe, and there was food in front of him."

"Yeah. All true. I got The Hanrahan back to his soddy and got a fire going. Old man kinda roused up some and asked me about the Indian women. I figured he was fixin' to die from the cold and was outta his head.

"He kept mumbling about how they had took their clothes off and put him between them. Hugged him. Put their titties against his face. Got him warm. Then fixed him that porridge. Said he needed to thank them."

"Hell, that was just an old man took with fever, rambling on."

"No, that ain't true." Frank looked around to make sure that he and Oscar were still the only two people the room. "I got that little tin pot and that robe down at the livery. Got them hid under my bedroll."

Oscar stood and walked to the window. A sickly gray dawn was progressing from the east. He turned, looked at Frank, and shook his head. "The hell you say." He shook his head again. "Don't want to see that robe or that tin pot. Don't want you bringing them in here. And I'm damn shore not gonna tell anybody what you just told me. And if I was giving advice, I'd tell you to keep this stuff about the naked Indian women out there in the snow feeding The Hanrahan porridge . . . and buffalo changing into a bird—well—under your hat."

The Hanrahan was staying at Weatherford's boardinghouse a few days—just until he got back on his feet and his arm started healing, he insisted. Before Frank left to go back north, he stopped by to see the old man, who was sitting at the dining room table soaking crusts of bread in a cup of tepid coffee.

"Frank, I owe you," he said, struggling to stand and then giving way to his weakness. "Saved my damn life. I'd have froze out there, and wouldn't nobody have found me 'til spring. Wouldn't have been nothing but a pile of old, bleached-out bones."

The rancher watched the old man's eyes, looking for some signal that they were sharing a secret. He wanted The Hanrahan to make some offhand remark—something about the porridge or the Indian women's warm breasts or the buffalo robe.

"Aw, you'd have been all right."

The Hanrahan adjusted the cloth sling that supported his broken arm. "No. No, I wouldn't. I'd done started seeing things. Indian women. Smelling food. I'd done give up. I was a goner. Can't tell you how glad I was to see you."

Frank took his hat from the table and stood. "I'll look in on you from time to time. See that you're still kicking."

The Hanrahan gummed on a crust of soppy bread, swallowed, and said, "You know I lost my dog, don't you? I'd shore like to have a pup. Any chance you might come across . . ."

"I'll try to have a pup for you next time I see you."

Satisfied, The Hanrahan reached for another crust.

Astride Red and trailed by the pack mule, Frank Rule traveled north away from Longsought. On his stop at the livery, he'd stuffed the buffalo robe and the tin pot under a loose floorboard in the harness room, then pulled a feed box over it.

He would deal with all that later. Sometime when his head was clear.

But he couldn't help thinking about the bird and how it had guided him. And the Indian medicine men. If they had seen things change shape, and if they had some kind of mystical power, could one of them help him find his Ellen, help bring her back from the dead?

Outside of Mobeetie, an old blind Indian called Gray Spot lived in a long-abandoned buffalo hunter's camp. Folks said that he was once the most powerful medicine man of all the Comanche, and he could conjure rain to put out prairie fires. Once he had even brought a long-dead war chief back to give counsel before a great raid against the white man.

The wind had picked up and was shredding the fog rising from the scattered snowbanks. Perchance, Gray Spot could raise Frank's wife from her grave. Or, mayhaps the old Indian could show him the way to Ellen. That might be the easiest way. Just take his shotgun, blow his brains out, and put his trust in the power of Gray Spot.

★ ★ ★ ★ ★

THE HIGHLANDER

★ ★ ★ ★ ★

Frank emptied the Arbuckle sack. He could manage without many things, but coffee was not one of them. Also, he was down to two cans of peaches and one of apricots. He did not relish a trip over to Longsought, but mayhaps a café-cooked meal and a shot of whiskey might brighten his spirits.

Shortly after daylight, Frank saddled Red, his favorite road mule. She had a nice easy gait—almost a short lope—and covered the ground as effortlessly as a saddle horse.

Uh-huh. Gonna go down to Longsought. Perchance have a drink. Might snuggle up against that red-haired woman that works the upstairs room at the bar. 'Bout time we looked at some female other than a chicken or a cow. Old Scratch needs to feel the soft touch of a woman. Yes, sir!

At the old Mallory place, young men full of piss and vinegar practicing their alcohol-diminished marksmanship had shattered most of the house's windows. The collapsed well-shed, a heap of mismatched planks and rusted tin, crouched in the weeds as if ashamed of its disarray. A coyote peered from beneath the outhouse, then quickly withdrew as Frank came closer.

Farther down the road, Beersheba Mounds stood at the woodpile hacking on twisted mesquite branches with a dull hatchet. A little boy wearing a faded cotton dress stood by her side, waving timidly. "Well, I guess you've heard by now. That no-good husband of mine and his stinking brother took off.

153

Left right in the middle of the night. I'd give him the best couple years of my life. Look at me now. I'm telling you, Frank, I'm done with men. Plumb done."

Frank nodded and said he was sorry, then put the spurs to the red mule.

Way to go, Frank. A little of my smarts musta rubbed off on you. I'd druther not get tangled up with that 'un. My old daddy used to say a woman that looked like that had been whipped with an ugly stick. Woman is so damned ugly, I ain't sure she qualifies as a female. Another thing, I bet she ain't had a bath in a month. Musty smelling from ten feet away. Reckon what it would have been up close.

Frank tied Red at the hitching rail in front of Elijay's store and loosened the saddle girth. He was a disciplined man and knew it was best to buy groceries before visiting the Antelope Flag Saloon. He'd decided he could live a lot longer without alcohol than without coffee. In ten minutes, he'd completed his purchases, stuffed them into his saddlebags, and crossed the dusty street to the saloon.

"Good afternoon, sir," Oscar Parks, the barkeep, greeted the rancher.

Oscar and Frank had worked together on a cattle drive years ago. Young Oscar—a product of an on-again-off-again, fiery relationship between a gypsy horse trader and a riverboat waitress—had been the chuck wagon cook's helper, and many of the cowboys called him a mongrel and made him the butt of practical jokes. Frank was a seasoned drover and kind to the swarthy young helper; Oscar never forgot.

Frank nodded and placed a cartridge on the bar.

Oscar smiled, palmed the bullet, and replaced it with a shot glass. "Guess you want the usual?"

It had been four months since Frank was in the bar, and Oscar acted as if it were only yesterday. "Reckon things are go-

154

ing good for you?" he asked.

Frank grunted, downed the shot, and put another cartridge beside the glass. "Seen worse days, I reckon." This time he sipped the whiskey. When the glass was empty, he turned it upside down and slid it toward Oscar. "That'll do me."

Oscar glanced at a corner table where the bar's nominal owner, Old Grumpy Pendleton, sat engrossed in a game of double-deck solitaire. The bartender had wanted the day off, but Pendleton refused, saying Oscar owed him too much money to be taking off. The barkeep righted the glass and refilled it. "On the house," he said and grinned.

Frank nodded. " 'Preciate it. You just doing this 'cause I'm such a good customer, ain't you?"

"And cheerful. And outgoing. And handsome. And rich."

Frank shoved his hat back on his head with his thumb. " 'Specially rich. Lost two cows and a calf before the grass got long enough for even a sheep to graze. I'm kinda thinking about pulling up stakes, going back to the Mexico Territory. Least cows don't freeze to death there in the border country."

Oscar checked the bar owner—still engrossed in his solitaire game—then poured another free one. "There's a Scottish man named McGregor staying over at the hotel. He's got this big spread in Palo Duro Canyon just east of Charlie Goodnight's holdings. Last week, he finished putting together three of the biggest ranches up in Ochiltree County, right up there next to the Indian Territory."

"I ain't that hard up. I'm not going to work as a ranch hand for some foreigner. Be paid 'thirty and found' ain't for me."

"No, he ain't looking for no hands. But he had a bull shipped to Oneida. Wants somebody to go get it and take it up to his Ochiltree County ranch."

"Well, he's got a ranch at the canyon. Why don't he get one of his hands down there go get the bull? Ain't they got horses?"

"Don't think this is a regular bull. Come over on a ship from Scotland. One of his ranch hands was in here the other day, said the bull would go eighteen hundred if he'd go an ounce. Ornery critter. Busting up the holding pens at the cattle yard. Pen boss told McGregor that he's got a week to get the rascal out, or he's gonna put a bullet in him. The bull, I mean!"

Frank raised his eyebrows and looked at the bartender. "Why you tellin' me all this?"

Across the room, Old Grumpy shuffled the double deck and laid six cards face up on the table. Oscar poured Frank another free drink. When the rancher finished it, the barkeeper took the glass, polished it with a rag, and put it on a shelf. "Old Man McGregor is a good customer. Always leaves four bits on the bar for me. I told him I knew a man that perchance could help him with his problem."

The boardinghouse dining room was empty except for a ruddy-skinned man with a curly, gray beard sitting at the long table, reading a month-old newspaper.

The rancher crossed the room and stood before the table. "I'm Frank Rule."

"Guid evenin'. Ye the man Oscar telt me aboot?"

"Yes, sir, I reckon."

"Barkeep told you whit I needit?"

The rancher rolled the Scot's words around in his head; he knew he was hearing English, but he had never heard it sound like this. "Understand you got a bull you wanted brought up from Oneida."

McGregor pushed away from the table, lit his pipe, and chuckled. "Not juist any bull. He's a Highland. Must have the blood of cattle that roamed the islands centuries ago. Scary big. Never saw any other one near his size. Stubborn. Always lookin' for a ficht."

156

"Oh, he's always looking for a fight. Is that the reason none of your men won't do the job?"

Old Scratch thinks you are right; old man's cowhands ain't worth a damn.

McGregor smiled. "Noo. Noo. They are more accustomed to cows an' calves. Docile livestock. They've had as much experience with a mighty animal like this as they have roping buffalo. Understand you are a hardy chap. Willing to help with difficult problems. And at a reasonable cost."

Frank eyed McGregor's coffee and wondered if it was a special brew that only men from Scotland drank. Wondered how it tasted. "I can help you. Don't sound like an easy job, though. What are you paying?"

"Hoo does fifty dollars sound tae ye?"

Old red-faced fart! Owns all that land. Now he's got a bunch of sissy cowboys working for him, and he's looking for somebody to do the tough work. 'Sides that, Old Scratch don't know what to think about a man who won't offer another man a cup of coffee. Why don't we just walk right out the door? Go back and spend more time with Oscar. Old Grumpy Pendleton is most likely passed out by now.

Frank studied the man in front of him: wool clothes, white shirt, polished boots, a heavy gold watch chain draped across his belly. "How does a hundred dollars sound to you?"

"Hoo aboot sixty?"

Frank turned his head to the side and made a dismissive gesture with his hand. "A hundred and you'll have your bull in ten days."

"Ye won't come doon oan yer price?"

"No, I won't come down on my price unless you come down on the size of your bull."

McGregor smiled and swallowed the last of the coffee. He stood, took a leather wallet from his jacket pocket, and spread a half-dozen tens and two fives on the table.

Frank stepped away from the table, buttoned his coat, and turned the collar up. "Be seeing you, Mr. McGregor. But I won't ever see your bull."

The Scot added two tens to the money on the table, then gapped his wallet open and displayed its emptiness.

Expressionless, Frank Rule shook his head.

McGregor pulled a three-inch-thick packet of money from his pocket and peeled off two fives. He gathered the money from the table, joined it with the fives, then spread the bills across the table like a professional gambler. His index and middle finger marched across the bills, his lips whispering the count, then he raised his eyes to meet Frank's. "A hundred. My big bull is named Maon."

Did you see that wad of money? Bet the bank ain't got that much in it. Believe, Frank, that you could have squeezed more money outta that feller. But, you know that stuff about a bird in the hand is . . . well, this time it's cash in the hand. Maybe you can hold him up on the back end when you give him his bull. Won't hurt to try.

After he completed negotiations with the Scotsman, Frank returned to his ranch and sacked a few provisions—a slab of jerky, can of beans, packet of coffee, a skillet, and a coffee pot. He harnessed a pack mule, saddled Red, shoved the L. C. Smith shotgun and the Henry rifle down into their leather scabbards, and set out southward toward Oneida.

Frank traveled through most of the night, sitting in the saddle dozing, the mules plodding the freighter's road without guidance. Ten miles north of Oneida, he stopped at a playa, watered the mules, and made a pot of coffee. The town rose in the paleness of the false dawn, breaking the plane of the southern horizon in small, irregular-shaped squares.

The stockyards, a conglomeration of metal-topped sheds and

wooden livestock pens pierced through the center by the east-west railroad, lay north of the town. Small clouds of dust and flies hovered over the conglomeration as riders moved livestock from pen to pen and to and from rail cars.

Old Scratch is gonna let you in on a secret, Frank, stockyards all smell the same—bad.

Frank tied his mules to a hitching rail in front of a ramshackle building identified by a weather-beaten sign as OFFICE. Inside, a grizzled man sat at a rolltop desk entering figures in a tattered ledger. "Ain't gonna be shipping nothing else today," the man mumbled, without looking up from his calculations.

"You the pen boss," Frank asked, "or you just the man that does the figuring and the bitching?"

The man raised his head and launched an amber stream of tobacco juice at an overflowing spittoon nestled beside an empty coat tree. "I'm L. V. Perkins. I run the whole damn shebang here. Do the buying and the selling and the shipping and the receiving and the hiring and the firing. You got any of them needs, I'm your man. Otherwise, you best go somewhere else and find another man to aggravate."

Whoa, Old Scratch is seeing a real smart aleck. Probably scratches his balls when he thinks and scratches his head when he takes a leak.

"Well, Mr. Perkins, my name is Frank Rule. I come down here from Longsought to fetch Mr. McGregor's bull. Been hired to take the critter up to Ochiltree County. I'm not accustomed to bein' talked ill to. If it's gonna put you in a snit, I'll ride outta here on the same mule I rode in on. You got any problems with that, you can take it up with the Scotsman."

"Oh no, wait, wait. You've come for McGregor's bull. You're just in time to stop me from making a steer outta 'im. Ornery cuss has 'bout wrecked all my pens. Acts like he owns the whole damn lot. And another thing, he's tried to romance ever' cow in Oneida."

Old Perkins runs backwards when he needs to, don't he? Maybe you ought to gig him a bit more, see if he runs sideways, too.

"Show me where this fire-breathing animal is, and I'll be on my way."

Perkins crossed the office and looked out a window decorated with several years of flyspecks. "Where's the other hands what's gonna help you?"

Frank folded his arms across his chest. "I don't need no help."

Perkins turned away from the window. "No help! Brother, you're either crazy or you ain't got no idea what you are dealin' with."

"Look, just show me. Got one bull, got one man. We're wasting daylight."

McGregor's Highland bull, Maon, stood at the back of the pens, ripping immature leaves from a mesquite bush.

"See there," Perkins said. "Ain't no normal animal'll try eatin' a mesquite leaf 'cept maybe a starving goat. Now, you see what you are gettin' into."

Frank judged Maon would go to just under two thousand pounds and stand near five feet at the top of his shoulders, just smaller than the average buffalo bull. The animal's shaggy coat was a rich red, denser and longer around his shoulders and head. The bull shook his head as if trying to shake the hair from his vision and get a better look at the short, stubby cowboy standing before him, lasso dangling from his right hand.

Perkins, clinging to a hayrack two pens away from Maon and Frank, shouted, "Watch them horns. They ain't near as long as that stuff that comes up from the border country, but they are sturdy, and he can rip a plank outta a barn door. Or bust a rib loose from a horse."

Almost as if taking Perkins's words as a signal for action,

Maon charged. Frank scrambled over the wooden fence with agility that would have caused envy in a ground squirrel. The bull slid to a stop just before crashing into the fence, glared at Frank, and then stuck his horns into the wooden fence and wrenched his massive head side to side. As the planks gave way, Frank climbed into the next pen.

"You gotta get outta the pens so the bull can't see you. 'Cause he'll bust every gate down tryin' to get to you," Perkins shouted as another gate splintered from Maon's onslaught.

Frank and Perkins retreated to the safety of the pen master's office.

Frank scraped the manure off his boots and inspected his torn shirt. "Gonna need a cow doctor."

Perkins recovered from a spasm of laughter and said, "Ain't but one vet in town, old Doc Hickerson. I can guarantee that he ain't gonna get within fifty feet of that critter. Told me the other night that he'd about give up being stomped by livestock. Considerin' becoming a professional ladies' man."

"Don't need him to help me," Frank said. "I want to buy a nose ring and a sheep bell from him."

Three cowboys leaned back against the bar at the Trail's End saloon. Each had one boot heel hooked behind the brass rail and both elbows propped atop the polished wooden bar. Nobody was drinking; nobody had any money. This was Friday; payday was Saturday. Their monthly wage of thirty dollars and found—and they hadn't found a damn thing in the past six months—came up a bit short, as it always did. When the cowboys walked into the saloon, Bad Bob, the bartender, hid the bowls of peanuts that customarily sat on the bar. The three men had been here for two hours, and while they had not worn out their welcome, they were working on it.

Frank Rule came through the saloon's batwing doors and

crossed to the bar. The cowboys stared at him. The short, fat man wearing glasses and a parson's hat looked out of place among these lanky men with their flat-crowned Stetsons, leather chaps, and low-slung holsters. But the sawed-off, double barrel L. C. Smith in his right hand gave the fat man credence—and respect.

"I'm looking for hard-asses who'd like to earn a dollar for five minutes' work," Frank said. "Wouldn't even have to get off their horse."

"You figuring on robbing a bank?" the only smooth-shaven cowboy in the trio asked.

"No. If I had that in mind, I'd have done it by myself," Frank said.

"You be willin' to throw in a shot of whiskey?" another cowboy asked, grooming his preposterous-sized handlebar mustache.

Frank looked at the men and nodded. "Yeah. After we get done."

"Done with what?" Smooth Face asked.

"Need a couple of you fellows to drop a rope around a bull so I can run this through his nose." Frank spun a five-inch ring on the bar. Even in the dull light, the brass gleamed wickedly.

"Must be a big bull," a cowboy wearing a soiled red kerchief said.

Frank nodded. "Big enough, I reckon. Right now, he is a guest over at the stockyards."

Mustache Man laughed. "Tarnation, you talkin' 'bout that monster McGregor bull, ain't you?"

Frank nodded. "That'd be about right. You boys ain't scared of no overgrown calf, are you?"

The cowboys turned and stomached against the bar. In low voices, while occasionally looking over their shoulders, they discussed Frank's proposition.

As one, the trio turned toward Frank. Kerchief Man said, "We'll do it. The three of us. Might say, we're a team. You can pay us when we get done. But we got to have two shots of whiskey. Each. 'Fore we leave the bar."

Frank considered their request, nodded to Bad Bob and held up six fingers.

Old Scratch ain't sure about cowpokes that's got to get likkered up for five minutes' work. Sounds like they are scared. Ain't right sure 'bout their backbone.

Perkins opened the gate. Maon slung the hair from the front of his face and snorted as Frank and the three cowboys rode into the main holding pen. The bull grumbled, his voice the low rumble of distant July thunder on a sultry night. He lowered his head and pawed the ground, throwing sheets of sand and clumps of dried cow dung into the air and onto his massive shoulders.

"I'll get a rope over his head," Frank said. "He'll come after me. One of you fellers get another rope on his head and the other two try to get a loop around his heels. We'll get him on the ground, stretch that old mister out. I'll give him a little nose jewelry. Help him with his manners."

It was an outstanding plan, a magnificent plan; except Maon, certainly one of the major participants, was not consulted nor had any input into what was about to transpire.

Business at the Trail's End saloon was never better. On what had been a slow week, every cowpoke in Oneida gathered at the bar to hear about the bull wreck down at the stockyards. L.V. Perkins was considered an authority in this disaster. After all, he had spent twenty years at the loading pens and been involved in or seen about everything that could go wrong with cattle turn into bone-breaking, horse-crippling disasters. "Never saw so many cowhands get stomped by one animal in my life. And this feller here," Perkins said pointing to a heavily mustached cowboy, "was slam-damn in the middle of it."

Milfred, heretofore referred to as Mustache, sat in a wooden chair in the middle of the saloon, his left leg encased in a wooden splint constructed of two planks wrapped in a plow line and with his heel resting on a second chair. "Hell, you make it sound like it was all my fault."

"Well," Perkins said, shrugging his shoulders and extending his hands out like a speaker making a point to his entire audience, "you was a big part of it."

Frank's lariat whistled through the air and settled around Maon's horns like a light-brown halo. The bull stood, calmly contemplating this outrageous act: this man wearing the funny-looking hat and sitting on the red mule had not only ventured into his pen but had the audacity to fling a rope around his head.

Mustache, heartened by the bull's complacency, sent his lariat in a near flat arc, and it, too, dropped around Maon's head. Quicker than you could snap your fingers, Mustache wrapped the rope around his saddle horn, and his horse sat back on its haunches, tightening the lasso uncomfortably around the bull's head. Had Maon been a camel, this would have been the last straw.

Before Frank could tighten his rope, Maon charged Mustache's horse and slammed it against the fence. That accomplished, the bull turned his attention to Frank and Red. The mule was agile as a cat. Frank desperately hung on as the mule darted around the lot, hotly pursued by the bull.

Maon would have caught and gored Frank's mule except the bull's pursuit was slowed by the effort of dragging Mustache's horse. The off-balanced horse had been jerked down by the bull's lunge at the red mule and was being dragged across the ground on its side. Adding to the confusion were the curses and screams of Mustache, who was partially pinned under the horse and making his own gouge marks through the sand and cow manure.

As good cowboys are prone to do, both Smooth Face and Kerchief were doing their damnedest, attempting to rope Maon's back legs.

However, Smooth Face's horse, unaccustomed to seeing a runaway mule and a horse dragged by a bull, apparently decided to jump the pen fence and escape this madness. Unencumbered by the rider's weight, the horse might have been successful, but Smooth Face clung to the saddle just long enough to disrupt his horse's footing and bid for freedom. Now, the horse was almost balanced on the wooden fence, squealing, front feet flailing on one side and rear feet dancing wildly on the ground on the other. The dislodged Smooth Face was rolling on the ground trying to evade his horse's thrashing hooves, dodge the panicked red mule, and stay away from the enraged Maon.

Even though Kerchief's horse was seasoned, mild-mannered, and dependable, this was too much. The animal went crow hopping around the pen, its rider seldom seated in the saddle while hanging onto the horn with a death grip.

Amidst all this, the cowboys' lariats lashed through the air and danced across the ground like tall-grass snakes in a Texas tornado.

Perkins and a half-dozen cowboys watching the melee were doing a lot of "hot-damning" and beating each other across the shoulders with their hats. They would have paid good money for this entertainment, and now here it was, free.

Smooth Face fought his horse off the fence, and Kerchief got his horse under control. Mustache's horse regained its footing, and as a testament to the rider's grit, he pulled himself back into the saddle.

Smooth Face and Kerchief roped the bull's hind legs. Frank and Mustache's ropes were still looped around Maon's head. The riders sat their horses back and somehow, in all the tangle of ropes and after sixty chaotic seconds, the massive bull stood in the center of the pen undaunted but temporarily defeated.

Frank stepped down from the saddle. Clutching his pocket-knife in one hand and brass ring in the other, he walked toward the bull. With nostrils flaring and slobber streaming from his mouth, Maon waited, wet with sweat and little but the whites of his eyes showing.

At the Trail's End, Milfred shifted in his chair, took a drink of beer, and then wiped the suds from his mustache. "Tell you, fellers, if that old bull had knowed what was comin', I do believe he would have kept fightin'. That Frank Rule feller walked right up to the bull like he wadn't no more dangerous than a ten-year-old milk cow."

Perkins became worried Milfred was about to take over his story and interrupted. "I had no more idea than a goat what he was about to do. But the bull had give a little slack in the rope. Quick as a hiccup, Frank wrapped his lariat around a snubbing post that musta' been buried ten feet in the ground—bet that post was stronger than any tree here in the Panhandle. He made a little motion with his hand toward his mule and danged if that red mule didn't commence to pullin' backwards, drawing that bull's head right snug against that post. The other fellers kept the heeling ropes tight so the bull couldn't run sideways or kick."

"Wait a minute, Perkins, you was two pens away from what was going on," Mustache said. "I was fifteen feet away and had a clear look. Frank took his knife and bored a hole in the bull's nose right there where the cartilage is the thickest 'tween the air holes. Old bull was a-bellerin', tryin' to paw with his front feet. Switching his tail like he was fighting a army of flies and shittin' with every other breath. Frank opened the ring up and run one end through the hole, come out the other side, and he bolted the two ends together. Blood and snot was going everywhere. He took a piggin' string from under his belt, tied it to the ring, and looped it through the lariat that was holding Maon's head to the snubbing post. When he got done, he motioned for us to let our ropes loose."

Frank wiped the bloody knife blade on his pants, folded it, and dropped it in his hip pocket.

"Old son," he said, "it's about time you learned some manners. I'm gonna explain something to you. Gonna do it just once. Gonna leave that lariat 'round your head—more you fight it, tighter it's gonna get. You keep fighting it, pretty soon it's gonna feel like your horns are 'bout to get squeezed off your head. Don't know if you know what a headache is, but come morning, you'll know."

Tell him about his nose. Tell him he is going to learn what real pain is if he don't pay attention to what you're telling him. Dang, but Old Scratch really likes to see a bad bull get what's coming to him. Fact is, I'm studying about a couple of smart asses that I just might ring their noses.

"And your nose is gonna be sore. Damn sore. You gonna find out that when I pull that little pigging string to the left, you are gonna need to walk that way. To the right, you walk to the right. If I pull it straight back, that means you gonna stop."

Yeah, you are going to get along with Frank. I guaran-damn-tee it.

A telegraph operator who was a little late into the story asked,

"Where are they? What is the big, bad bull and the cowboy doing now?"

Perkins dropped two bits on the bar, tilted his head, and threw the shot of liquor down in one gulp. "We left 'em both right there in the shippin' pen. Bull with his head pulled against that snubbing post like he was loving it to death."

The telegraph operator again: "What was the cowboy doing?"

Milfred stirred, looking for a position that would ease the pain in his leg. "That Frank Rule feller got him a three-legged milk stool. He's sittin' on it 'bout five feet from the bull's face. Said he was gonna spend the night right there. Said he was teaching the bull 'bout what a master looked like."

Somebody asked, "Reckon y'all gonna take him something to eat?"

Milfred shook his head. "No, reckon not. He did ask me to have somebody bring him a cup of coffee in the mornin'. And he wanted a needle—the kind you sew feed sacks up with—and a couple feet of strong, black thread."

It was a long night, probably longer for Maon than for Frank.

Sometime around midnight, the bull stopped pulling against the lasso and decided the pain beneath his horns was tolerable if he stood still, extremely still, and leaned his head into the snubbing post.

One of the pen riders brought Frank a kerosene lantern. He placed it on the ground at his feet and regulated the flame to the maximum brightness without smudging the chimney. In the dimness, Maon's seldom-blinking eyes glowed an eerie blue-green. Ten feet from the bull, Frank sat motionless on the milk stool, arms folded across his chest, legs in front of him and crossed at the ankles.

Near daybreak, a pale fog drifted through the pen shrouding

the man and the animal. Neither had changed position throughout the night.

Two cowboys, both last-night casualties of an awful stretch of cards and a worse run of whiskey, sat on the Trail's End porch leaning back against the bench where the habitual loafers sat and whittled. An old man with a stiff leg, victim of a runaway freighter's wagon, shuffled back from the stockyard and adjusted his stride so he could step up on the narrow porch.

"Well?" one of the cowboys said.

The crippled man hesitated, one foot on the porch, the other on the ground. "That Rule feller is still down there. I carried him a pot of coffee and a cup. Asked if he needed anything else. Said he was okay. Just needed more time."

"Time for what?" the other cowboy asked.

"Teachin' the bull. Man said he figured that by dark the bull would have learned most of what he needs to know before they headed north toward Longsought."

The first cowboy asked, "Both of 'em still looking at the other 'un?"

"Yeah. Bull still got his head pulled right tight against the snubbing post. Did see that Rule feller get up off his stool and take a bucket of water to the bull. Old bull snorted, switched his tail right vigorous, but he never drunk nothing. Man poured the water on the ground and told the bull, 'Old son, I'll see what you think about water a little later.' "

Like Israelites crowding around to watch the Red Sea part, cowhands moved down to the stockyard, first one by one, then in small groups. Some sat on the fence, while the more adventuresome went inside the pen, sat, and leaned back against the sturdy boards.

Frank had moved from his three-legged stool and now squatted less than two feet from the bull's sharp horns.

"Been there more'n a hour," somebody told the new arrivals. "Just lookin' that ole bull right square in the eye. Bull blinking ever' once in a while, but I don't believe Frank has blinked in the last five minutes. 'Bout the only change I've seen is, the bull has started to sweat. Don't know if he's just tired of standing there or tired of Frank lookin' at him. But whatever it is, I believe the bull is startin' to give way."

Feeling his importance, Perkins strutted into the pen carrying a pail of water and a packet containing a yard of heavy, black thread attached to a long, curved needle.

Frank took the sheep bell from his jacket pocket, shook it gently, and the faint tinkling crept through the pen. Then he took a step and held the bucket of water under the bull's muzzle. Maon snorted and sucked in a couple of deep drinks. Without taking his eyes from the bull, Frank removed the bucket and stretched his hand out behind his back. Perkins stepped forward and laid the threaded needle in his palm.

Bad Bob lit the last of four lamps, and the Trail's End saloon came alive with muted-orange light.

Doc Hickerson took a drink of beer and wiped the foam from his lips. "Tell you, fellers, that man is a slick hand with a needle. 'Fore that bull knew what was happening, Frank had stitched one of his eyelids plumb shut. Soon as the bull quit bellowing, Frank rang the bell and gave him another drink from the bucket. Then quicker'n a wink, sewed the other eye shut. Old bull just stood there, sweat running off him like a whore in church. Frank rang the bell again and gave Maon another drink and said, 'Boys, go on home; show's over.' "

Milfred the Mustache shifted in his chair. "Where is he now?"

Hickerson took another drink of beer. "Man or bull? Rule is over at the café eatin' a chicken-fried steak. Bull is still standin' up there at the shipping pens, head tied to the snubbing post, shiverin' like a dog what has been shittin' peach pits."

At first light the next morning, Perkins and Doc Hickerson walked across the dusty street to the shipping pens. Maon, Rule, and the red mules were gone.

"Hey, Perkins, come over here. You gotta hear this." Bad Bob wiggled his crooked finger at the stockyard manager.

A toothless man, skin wrinkled as a ten-day-old prune and the color of a burnt biscuit, wearing baggy pants, leaned against the bar. Ten years of living out in the harshness of the Llano Estacado gathering buffalo bones ruins a man—inside and out.

Bad Bob refilled the diminishing supply of peanuts in the bowl and scooted it toward the center of the bar. "This here is Gus," he said as introduction. "He's brought a wagon load of buffalo bones to the rail siding. Got in this morning."

Gus hadn't scraped the hair off his face in three weeks and had taken his last bath a couple of weeks before that. Perkins nodded and kept his distance. He knew what a bone picker smelled like and did not want any extra reminding.

Gus eyed Perkins's half-full mug. "I'm a bit short," he said. "Don't reckon you'd be opposed to buyin' a man a beer, would you?"

Bad Bob waited until Perkins nodded, then poured a beer and flicked the foam off with a grubby finger. He slid the mug along the bar, and the bone hunter's hand intercepted it with the speed of a rattler picking off a scampering field mouse.

"Go ahead. Tell him," the bartender said.

"It was night 'fore last," Gus said. "I was camped out up there at that big playa on this side of the Canadian. Got my mules took care of and was settlin' down to cook me a bite. Heard something comin' along the freighter's road. Got my gun and laid behind the wagon, figurin' it might be a Comanchero or somebody out to steal my mules. They got in close enough, and I could see it was a man and two mules. And right there in the middle was the biggest gol-damn bull I ever saw. Why, I've seen buffalo bulls that wadn't that big."

"Dang. It's that Rule feller, ain't it?" Perkins said.

Gus took a couple of swallows of beer and belched. "Yep. Said his name was Frank. 'Bout all he said. Never was 'round a man talk as little as that feller."

"They spent the night with you?"

"Yep," Gus said and gummed a handful of peanuts. He drained the beer and looked forlornly at the wooden beer keg behind the bar.

Bad Bob looked at Perkins, and the stockman nodded. Gus, gums spotted with red peanut skins, grinned when the barkeeper drew him another beer.

"Yes-sir-ree. That old bull had a ring through his nose. Had a piggin' string run through that ring and up around his horns somehow. Acted like he was blind as a bat. 'Bout that time, I seed that his eyelids was sewed shut. That Rule feller had a little ol' sheep bell. He'd ring it, and that bull would follow him like a puppy dog. He knew he was safe followin' the bell. Tell you another thing, he was a big sumbitch, but Rule had him tamed down like a baby. Never saw nothing like it, and I've been around nasty bulls and wild horses all my life."

Oscar Parks stood outside the Antelope Flag Saloon in Longsought, looking westward down the dusty street and shading his eyes from the late afternoon sun. "Good Gawd! Would you look at that."

Three cowboys heard Oscar's shouts, left the domino table, and came out onto the saloon's front porch. Two whittlers rose from their bench and stepped into the street for a better view.

An Indian, his wife, and three children joined the crowd of onlookers. The village's brindle cur crawled from under the porch and stood staring, his head cocked quizzically as if he could not believe what he was seeing.

Followed by Red and the pack mule, the massive Maon approached. His long, curved horns and reddish hair glowing in the setting sun gave him the appearance of some hellish specter from another world. Sitting on the bull's broad back, Frank Rule looked as much at home as if he were sitting on the back porch steps.

The conglomeration swung to the right and stopped in front of the saloon. Frank slung his leg across the bull's shoulder, dislodging a cloud of red dust, and stepped down onto the packed dirt. He secured the small rope attached to the bull's nose ring to the hitching rail with a half-hitch, then ground hitched the mules.

Frank removed his dusty parson's hat and slapped it against his leg. A thin veil of crimson drifted up and clouded his glasses, causing him to pull his shirttail out of his sweat-stained pants and polish the lenses. Under his left arm, the rancher carried a six-foot river cane with a sheep's bell attached to the little end with a strip of faded rag. He wound the rag around the cane, muting the bell, and stuck the contraption under the saloon's porch.

Oscar shook Frank's hand. "Old son, that's the damnedest thing I ever saw. I do believe that if Old Grumpy was here, he'd stand you to a drink. Since he ain't, I'll take it on myself to do it."

Oscar worked up a sweat filling beer glasses and pouring shots of evil-smelling whiskey. The till was overflowing, and the saloon owner would never miss the free drinks Frank consumed.

"Looks like that bull is blind as a bat," one of the whittlers said.

"Temporary," Frank replied. "Soon as I get him up to McGregor's place in Ochiltree County, I'll cut them stitches out. Ought to make that old bull mighty happy. Seeing again and everything."

"How do you guide him?"

"It's a secret," Frank said, little crow's feet growing at the outer corners of his eyes.

Oscar might have been just a bartender, but he didn't miss much. "Hell, Frank, it's the damn bell, ain't it?"

The rancher grinned again. "Yeah. I get ready to give him a drink, I'll ring that little sheep bell and shove a bucket of water under his nose. Want him to go left, ring the bell on the left side of his head. Same thing is true for going to the right."

"And if you want him to stop?"

"Pull back on that piggin' string that's tied to his nose ring. He ain't dumb. Hurt his nose so bad, he don't even think of taking another step. I give him some slack, and he'll ease on down the road. Three hours after we left Oneida, we'd reached a pretty good understandin' about who's giving orders and who's taking orders."

One of the domino players—a practical joker with a beer-engorged bladder—left the saloon and made a trip to the toilet that straddled the ditch out back. On his return, he came by the hitching rail where the bull was tied. He'd seen the river cane and the sheep's bell when Frank shoved it under the porch. Now with the bell hidden under his coat, he crossed the saloon floor to the bar just in time to hear the last of Frank's remarks.

"You mean to tell me," the joker said as he removed the river cane from his coat, "that if I rang this little bell, that big old bull would come to the sound?"

"Don't do that!" Frank yelled.

Left arm pulled against his chest by a bar-rag sling, Oscar sat across a three-legged, teetering table from the saloon owner, Old Grumpy Pendleton. "Yes, sir. That's how it commenced, and there wadn't a damn thing I could have done about it. If you'd been here, wadn't nothin' you'd have done about it either. Hell, if there had been a platoon of them troopers from Fort Elliott and two second lieutenants, same thing would've happened."

Old Grumpy glared at Oscar, folded a chaw of tobacco into the back of his jaw, and searched for a spittoon. The saloon had three, one at either end of the bar and one by his chair—all three upended, their cloudy, amber contents emptied on the coarse wooden floor. The man puckered his lips and spat into a dozen dominoes that appeared to have sought refuge beneath an overturned chair.

"Once that damned feller rung that little old bell, it was Katie-bar-the-door. First thing I heard was the hitchin' rail bustin' loose, then the planks popping as the bull come 'cross the porch toward the bell. If his horns hadn't stretched out so wide, he'd have got in here quicker. He couldn't get through the door. Turned his head sideways and with one horn took out the door framing. And then he was inside. You see what went on?"

Old Grumpy stood. "Yeah. Broke three cases of whiskey, split four kegs of beer. Turned the bar over. Tore the whole damn front outta the piano. Ain't a table in here that's got four good legs. And I counted four chairs that's fittin' to set in. There was fourteen men in here when the bull come through them swingin' doors. Outta them men, there's eight broke legs, nine broke arms. Smartass domino player that started all this, don't know how you count him. But having a bull step smack-dab in the middle of your face whiles you're flat on the floor is a whole lot worse than a broke arm or leg."

Oscar crossed the room and stared through a smashed window at the prairie-dog town that spread eastward toward the creek. "I don't know what to say. It weren't my fault."

Old Grumpy had moved to the middle of the room and looked over the damage as if he'd never seen it before. "And the worse damn thing is the busted mirror. Right there, on top of everything else, is seven years of bad luck. Well, it ain't gonna be my bad luck. It's yours. I'm moving to Abilene. Tomorrow! And I ain't payin' you another damn dime."

"You can't do that." Oscar turned his head away from his boss and snapped the bar rag at a fly that was grooming itself on the crown of a squashed hat nestled under the coal stove. "You owe me for a week's work. And probably that much more for makin' me water down whiskey for the past three years. I know some mighty mean husbands that would be damned upset if they found out that their wives had been—"

Old Grumpy held up both hands like a victim in a bank holdup. "Don't see any need to go into all that. Some of it would get you in as much trouble as—"

"I ain't done nothin' but watered whiskey. But that stuff with them women . . ."

Old Grumpy moved to Oscar and laid a hand on his shoulder. "Tell you what. Say I deed this mess to you—lock, stock, and barrel. We'll call it even on the back wages, won't never talk to nobody about waterin' the whiskey. And you damn sure won't talk about me and them women."

Within an hour, and gripping a small, hastily packed valise, Old Grumpy Pendleton climbed into a southbound stagecoach.

Remembering his gypsy father's instant remedy for bad luck brought on by breaking a mirror, Oscar took three of the larger shards of glass out to Boot Hill and touched them to a tombstone.

That's how Oscar became the happy proprietor of a watering hole in the High Plains town of Longsought. On the day he reopened the saloon, he painted over the Antelope Flag name and repainted: The Red Bull.

Well, ain't that just like a no-good domino player. Poking his nose in something he ain't got the foggiest notion of what he's doing. Old Scratch thinks it serves him right, the bull steppin' in his face and all. I think he got off pretty light, if you ask me. Which you never do.

Frank rode northward toward Ochiltree County, progress slowed by the slow-paced red bull.

The saloon incident in Longsought had put off his journey by at least a day. It didn't take Maon more than a couple of minutes to demolish the interior of the Antelope Flag, but it took Frank more than an hour to extract the beast from the shambles. He took the bull and the two mules to the creek, tied them in the shade of a cottonwood tree. Another half day was spent helping Oscar throw debris out of the saloon and into the street.

If you hadn't taken time to help Oscar clean up that mess, we'd have been at McGregor's ranch by now. Been rid of this damn bull. Gone over to Mobeetie. Perchance had a touch of alcohol. Might even had a chance to rub up against some woman flesh.

Frank ignored Old Scratch's gibes.

They camped that night in a shallow, rocky ravine three miles south of McGregor's ranch. After having coffee and two biscuits the next morning, Frank saddled Red. Maon lay on his stomach, chewing his cud, listening to the movements in the camp. When Frank rang the sheep's bell, Maon stood and stretched his neck, then curled his upper lip, testing the morning breeze with his tongue.

Frank rode alongside, dropped a lariat around the bull's horns, and hurriedly wrapped it around a rock outcrop. Once again, Maon found his face snug against something he could not move. The rancher dismounted and moved to the bull's head. Last night he'd sharpened the blade of his nine-inch knife against his boot sole. With the point of the blade, he delicately removed the stitches from Maon's eyelids. The bull stood blinking, eyes unaccustomed to the brightness. Frank maneuvered the nose ring until he reached the bolt and unfastened it. He extracted the ring and replaced it with a cord smaller than a wooden pencil. The bull didn't know the difference between the ring and the cord, and when Frank and the red mule moved out, Maon was glad to ease the pain in his nose by walking peacefully behind the rider.

A boy less than ten years old, the ranch cook's son, was walking from the well with a half-filled bucket of water when Frank and company rounded the corral. Stunned by the size of the bull, the boy, eyes widening, stood for a second before abandoning the bucket and sprinting for the ranch house, shouting, "Hit's here, hit's here. Mama, tell Mr. McGregor, hit's here."

Frank leaned from his mule and opened the corral gate. Maon followed him inside and stood without flinching as Frank removed the cord. Not realizing his freedom and without moving, the bull watched as Frank rode out of the corral and closed the gate.

McGregor, still cleaning shaving soap from his face, came from the house and stood by the fence, admiring the bull. "Weel, by damn. Ye did it."

Frank stepped off the red mule. "Yes, sir. Just like I promised. A day sooner than I promised, and I apologize about that. I was kinda surprised that old boy is pretty good on the trail."

McGregor squatted and stared at the bull between the corral

poles. "Ye hud na trouble wi' th' animal?"

"No, sir. Took a day or two in Oneida for us to get acquainted to each other. After that, might say our trip was right pleasant."

The Scot climbed up on the gate and looked at the bull. A single drop of blood dripped from Maon's nose. "Looks like he might have hurt his hooter."

"Well, sir. Believe he might have got hung up in a mesquite bush coming up the bank outta the Canadian. Week or two, he'll be good as new, I'm betting."

McGregor shaded his eyes and leaned forward. "Seems he's weeping."

"Grazing last week, he got grass seeds in his eyes. I've been washing 'em out every day. They are a whole lot better. You gonna be surprised at how good he sees tomorrow."

"Yer a hell o' a man, Frank Rule, a hell o' a man."

The rancher shook the Scotsman's hand. "Guess we better be getting on down the road toward home."

McGregor seemed reluctant to loosen his grasp. "Cuid ah convince ye tae wirk fur me? Top wages."

Now. Right now is the time to hit him up for a little extra money. Old Scratch thinks you can get another ten dollars from the old man. Looks like you've got him hooked pretty good. Might even get twenty.

Frank stepped up into the saddle. "No. Got this little place of my own south and west of here. Gotta be getting back. Wife will be expecting me."

Maon grumbled, a deep and rumbling sound from the bottom of his huge chest.

Frank kneed Red and turned back along the road away from the corral.

Maon stood in the center of the enclosure, snorting, massive head lowered, pawing at the dirt and flinging clouds of dust and clumps of dried cow manure over his shoulders.

Frank turned and tipped his hat to the Scotsman.

Maon charged across the corral but slid to a stop at the edge of the enclosure, glared toward the diminishing image of the cowboy, and snorted. The Scotsman and the cook's son retreated toward the ranch house as the bull wrenched his huge head side to side in the gate, splintering planks and loosening nails.

★ ★ ★ ★ ★

THE SHAMAN

★ ★ ★ ★ ★

No one walks behind a Comanche medicine man. Frank Rule would learn this on a moonless August night when the wind hovered motionless over the Llano Estacado, and the coyotes hauntingly cried somewhere out in the darkness.

Summer appeared almost as soon as the remains of the snowstorm faded from the Llano Estacado. In the past, summer brightened Frank, but his moroseness lingered this year. Ellen had never seen Frank's ranch—the Indian killers had taken her life before she had the opportunity to see her new home—but still he heard her voice in the stirring of the buffalo grass and the slightest tremble of the oak leaves along the creek.

The nights were the worst. The stillness of the house was maddening. Ellen seemed to whisper his name in the darkness. Always from another room. As he moved, the voice moved. Never in the same place where he stood. He lay on the hard floor in what was to have been their bedroom, hands cupped around his ears, peering into the darkness.

He heard other voices, too. His sons, Billy and Joseph, called him, wanting help to saddle a horse. His daughter, Shirl, begged him to come out into the yard to see the mud pie she'd baked.

But, other than Ellen, the most frequent voice he heard was one that he hated most.

Old Scratch has been thinking. I believe that if you ain't gonna kill yourself, you're gonna wind up crazy like The Hanrahan. Seeing circling birds, red wolves, little pots of bubbling mush. Buffalo robes and naked Indian women. Wait! Them naked Indian women. Now that's got some potential.

Bleary eyed from lack of sleep, Frank stood at the edge of his corral watching a dust-devil toy with a bird feather, moving it in a narrow circle across the packed dirt. The wind increased, and the feather lifted over the corral fence and set out on an irregular path toward the northeast. Mobeetie lay to the northeast. And the Indian, Gray Spot.

"Ma sent me up to get you." The Widow Holley's son stood at the edge of the corral. His pants were too short and so threadbare his drawers would have shown—if he had worn any. "You probably don't remember me. I'm Maris. June Holley is my ma. Jo Nell throwed the dog over in the old cistern. It's dry down there so she ain't drowned. But she's had pups. We been dropping table scraps down to her. She's still alive, but we think all but one of the pups is dead."

Frank studied the boy: shaggy-haired, dirty, barefoot, could not have been more than ten or eleven. "Who is Jo Nell?"

"My sister. I'm right smart bigger than she is. 'Course, I'm a year older. Ma says sometimes she don't act just right. I think she is still tryin' to get over Pa dying."

"Maris, how you know the dog's only got one pup still living?"

"We let a lantern down in the cistern. Just saw one pup still moving. Some over at the side was still. Ma said they's probably done gone." The boy looked up at Frank and wrinkled his nose up as if he were recalling the odor. "And it stinks pretty bad."

Frank lost the battle of keeping a straight face and wrinkles grew at the corners of his eyes. "Why you tellin' me all this? Ain't my dog; ain't my cistern."

" 'Cause Ma says you're a good man. Will help us out. I'd go down in there and get the dog, 'cept Ma ain't stout enough to pull me out. I believe I could pull her up, but she's afraid I can't. Mr. Frank, can we count on you? Ma says I can work in your garden to pay you back. I'm pretty strong and can tell the difference 'tween taters and weeds." Maris hitched his ragged pants up over his skinny hipbones. "I 'spect I might even be able to help you break horses. I've been riding the milk cow around in the barn lot when Ma wasn't looking."

Frank pulled Red to a stop in June Holley's yard. Things had deteriorated after Everett's death. The wind was stripping boards off the corner of the house, two windowpanes were broken, and the fences sagged enough that a long-teat cow could step over it without fear.

Maris slid off the mule's rump to the ground as if he were accustomed to riding double behind a real cowboy every day. "Ma, Mr. Frank has come to help us just like you said he would. And I got to ride behind him on his mule."

June Holley was in about the same shape as the ranch. The trauma of losing her husband to pneumonia pulled at her face and dulled her eyes. Up here on the High Plains, loneliness probably killed as many women as disease and old age combined. And the ones who did not succumb physically fought a losing mental battle.

"Frank, 'preciate you coming by. Most things, me and Maris can take care of. I was skittish about this, though, scared the cistern wall might give way and whichever one of us was down in there might be killed or hurt bad."

Maris tugged at Frank's sleeve. "Over here by the edge of the house."

The cowboy turned toward June Holley and looked past her, careful not to meet her gaze. "Glad to help." He cleared his throat. "Bet it won't take us two minutes . . . then, uh . . . I'll get outta your hair."

June looked toward the house and extended her hand in a gesture that had no defined meaning. "I've fixed dinner. Maris killed a rabbit. So, it's rabbit stew and corncakes. We eat pretty light around here. Ever since Everett been gone, we . . ." her voice faded away as if Frank already knew the ending of the sentence.

Hey, Frank. Old Scratch thinks this widow woman sounds right lonesome. I've been looking at her. She'd be a purty handsome gal if she was fattened up some. You've not got nothing to do. Stay for dinner. I dare you.

"That's nice of you," Frank mumbled as he followed Maris toward the cistern.

Whatever kind of building that was supposed to funnel water off into the cistern was long gone. Probably a board had come loose, and the relentless wind had worried at the opening until one day a nail gave way, the next day another. The end was inevitable. Now the gusts were able to get a good toehold; soon the remaining boards went skittering across the prairie or lay in the short grass fading to the color of bleached buffalo bones.

The lip of the cistern was no more than a couple of feet high. Frank and Maris dropped to their knees and peered down into the darkness. The dog sensed their presence, looked up, and whined.

Maris looked at Frank. "See, told you she was alive. Her name is Susie. Over to the side there, see the pup that's still movin'? Don't know if it is a boy or a girl, so we ain't named it yet. We gonna get 'em out, ain't we?"

Frank walked to the corner of the yard and brought his mule to the cistern's edge. He uncoiled his rope and tied one end around the saddle horn. "Now, Maris, I want you to hold Red's bridle reins. She's not likely to run off, but I'd feel better if you held her."

186

Frank tossed the other end of the rope into the cistern. He tugged a pair of worn leather gloves from beneath his belt, pulled them on, and flexed his fingers. "All right, Maris. If you'll get me a croaker sack from my saddlebag, I'll be ready. Gonna slip down this rope and get the dogs. You hold on to Red when I start comin' back up the rope. I'm counting on you, now. You hear?"

Maris brought the sack to Frank, then stood by the mule's head with his feet spread apart as if he were preparing to hold a wild cow.

June stood under a mesquite at the edge of yard, a thin smile on her face, one hand rubbing the knuckles of the other.

Frank slid down the rope into the dimly lit cistern. A minute passed.

"You okay in there, Mr. Frank?" Maris called out, his voice thin and reedy with concern.

Frank's words half echoed from the cistern. "I'm comin' out. Hold Red."

The rope slapped against the lip of the cistern twice and tightened. Frank's head and then his body surfaced, the wiggling croaker sack attached to his belt with a tie-down rope.

Both the mama dog and the pup, gaunt from hunger, scrambled from the sack when Frank placed it on the ground.

Maris dropped to his knees and cuddled both dogs, then looked over his shoulder toward his mother. "We done it, Ma. Me and Mr. Frank, we done it. We got 'em out."

Frank Rule sat at the kitchen table with June Holley. Through the open window, they could hear Maris and Jo Nell talking to Susie and her pup.

June stood and asked, "Could I get you some more coffee?"

"No, had enough," Frank said and spread his hand over the top of his cup.

"I don't blame you for not wanting any more. It's the third time I used the grounds, and they're getting pretty weak. Really, more like colored water." She looked down into the bowl containing the remains of the thin rabbit stew. "Guess you could pretty much say the same for the stew."

"Best stew I've had in a long time. Tasted kinda like the stew my . . . stew I use to eat when I lived in the New Mexico Territory."

June knew some of Frank Rule's history: the murder of his wife and daughter by Indians, the kidnapping of his oldest son, and the tragic death of his youngest son in Rose Cotton's boardinghouse fire. At least after Everett's death, she still had her children.

"I'm sorry, Frank," she said. "I didn't mean to stir up hurtful memories." She moved her hand across the table toward his, saw his fingers constrict, then withdrew her hand and placed it in her lap.

Frank stood, rolled down and buttoned his shirt cuffs, and took a deep breath. Without looking at June, he said, "A man told me that we weren't promised an easy life. Reckon we're both witnesses to that."

June tried to blink away the tears that were gathering in her eyes. "Yes, I guess we are."

Frank crossed the shaky floor of the kitchen and stood in the doorway leading to the porch watching Jo Nell cuddle the pup like a baby. "I'm gonna go down to Oneida in a couple of days. Get some horseshoe nails, cartridges, meal, stuff like that. I'll get you some coffee, a few groceries, maybe a bag of sugar. You think of anything else you need?"

June had not moved from the table, and she stared at the back of Frank's head. "That would be kind of you. But we are pretty low on cash right now. Can't pay nothing. Come fall, when we sell the calf, things will brighten up some. 'Til then, we'll get by best we can. But thank you anyway."

"Maris, bring Red over here," the rancher said as he looked through the open door and out across the prairie to where the sky touched the horizon. He turned slightly and briefly glanced over his shoulder toward the seated woman. "Never said anything about you paying. Neighbors are supposed to help out. Anyway, things will get better."

"Frank, you know things are not goin' to get any better. If I could sell this little piece of dirt for enough to get me and the kids a train ticket back to Illinois, we'd be gone before the end of the week. I loved Everett dearly, he was a fine man, and don't get me wrong, but he made a mistake when he brought us out here. He . . . we were not cut out for this part of the country."

Maris brought Red across the yard, and Frank swung up into the saddle.

June stood on the edge of the porch, arms crossed protectively over her bosom. "You'll stop by again, won't you? We . . . Maris needs to be around a man every once in a while."

Frank touched his hat brim, nodded, and turned out into the road toward his ranch.

Maris trotted along behind the mule until they reached the dry wash that cut across the barn lot. "Mr. Frank," he shouted, "you ever need any help, just come get me."

Frank did not look back.

The Hanrahan sat on the front porch of Weatherford's boarding-house, the mid-afternoon sun slanting enough to allow a shaft of warmth to wash across him. The broken bone in his arm was slow to heal, and the old man knew it had to do with his age.

"Dang," he'd said to the young woman clearing dishes from the table this morning, "it ain't like I'm racing with nobody, but I'd shore like to get back down to my own place 'fore I get so fat I can't button my britches."

"You'll know when the time comes," the young woman said as she ran a damp cloth across the table and swept the breakfast crumbs to the floor. "But, if it helps any, I do believe that you're getting a little stronger every day."

The sun comforted The Hanrahan, and his head tilted forward until his bony chin almost rested on his Adam's apple. His face collapsed into wrinkles and folds of skin, and his mouth slackened, allowing his lips to flutter as his lungs emptied.

"You need any help sleepin'?" Frank Rule stood at the edge of the street, Red and the pack mule behind him. "I was kinda afraid you might fall out of the chair and break the other arm."

The Hanrahan grinned. "No, I kinda got this sleepin' thing down pretty good." He shaded his eyes with his hand and peered out into the street. "That you, Frank Rule?"

Frank tied the mules to the hitching rail and stepped onto the porch. "Thought I'd stop by and see how you're doing."

"Doin'? Why, I'm spry as a spring jackrabbit. Want to see me hop?"

"No. I'll take your word for it."

"Frank, you know, I still owe you. Ain't right sure I'd have ever got out of that blizzard alive if it hadn't been for you."

The rancher sat on the porch and leaned back against a post supporting the roof. "Aw, you're a pretty tough old boy. You'd have done all right by yourself. 'Specially with them Indian women around. Keep your face warm 'tween their titties and all."

The old man's face wrinkled as he concentrated on Frank's words, searching for some link between what Frank was saying and what he himself remembered. "I don't know about all that. You reckon I might have been dreamin', trying to die, or something? I want you to know that I study on it some every day."

"Perchance something like a dream?" Frank said.

"Yeah, something like that. A dream. Yeah, a dream."

"But your dog's gone."

"Yeah, that wadn't no dream, for sure. He's gone. Wolf got him." The old man lost his focus, then returned to thoughts of the dog. "You promised me another one. Remember?"

Frank moved from the porch to the edge of the street and untied the piece of tarp covering a large mound on the pack mule's back. "Yep, I've got my eye on a pup. Might be six weeks or so. You wait that long?"

"Yeah, I've learned to be pretty good at waitin'."

"Hanrahan, I've got something to show you. You may not remember it, and you don't have to say anything if you don't." He unrolled a finely worked buffalo robe across the old man's lap and took a small tin pot from one of the folds. "Remember this?"

The old man ran his hand across the softness of the robe and then examined the pot. "It's true, ain't it, Frank? I never went crazy, did I? Them Indian women was real, wadn't they?"

Franked nodded. "I believe so. There was something. Something I can't understand."

The Hanrahan ran his fingers across the edge of the tin pot. "Frank, you reckon that old Indian had anything to do with it? Gray Spot. Or whatever his name is. The one up at Mobeetie. You think he coulda had a hand in all this?"

It took Frank a minute to wrap the robe around the tin pot and tie the bundle back on the pack mule. "I don't know, but I aim to find out."

Three hours into darkness, Frank reached June Holley's place. A pale-yellow light in the kitchen struggled to penetrate the windowpane before quickly dissolving in the heavy blackness. Frank slid from the saddle and untied two croaker sacks from the pack mule's wooden frame. He moved through the pitch

191

darkness and quietly deposited the sacks on the narrow front porch. Without looking back at the house, he crossed the yard silently as a shadow. Even Susie, the dog, never knew the man had been there.

Inside, June sat in a battered rocking chair before a shallow fireplace and the fading glow of seasoned mesquite coals. Her son's partially mended overalls lay in her lap, and early sleep was smoothing the wrinkles from her face. Her brain was changing from wakefulness to sleep; visions of a healthy Everett standing in a lush cornfield were materializing.

Asleep, Maris and Jo Nell lay on a tattered quilt at June's feet. Susie and the pup curled between the children.

In 1875, Colonel Nelson Miles chose a low plateau overlooking Sweetwater Creek as the site of a fort. The post was named Fort Elliott in honor of Major Joel Elliott, who had died at the battle against the Southern Cheyenne, Sioux, and Arapaho on the Washita River in the winter of '68.

Two miles southwest of the fort, the village of Mobeetie had existed before the founding of the outpost. The legendary Charles Goodnight, who knew about such things firsthand, described the town as, "patronized by outlaws, thieves, cutthroats, and buffalo hunters, with a large percent of prostitutes. Taking it all, I think it was the hardest place I ever saw on the frontier except Cheyenne, Wyoming."

Lou's Livery sat on the south edge of Mobeetie, its corral post and barns blasted a nondescript gray by the High Plains wind. Two spavined horses and a mangy burro stood in the dwindling shade of a mesquite tree waiting for darkness and the slackening of the west wind.

"Why the hell you lookin' fer a one-eyed Injun?" Lou sat on the edge of a dry watering trough and looked at Frank Rule through red eyes that proclaimed a night filled with too little sleep and too much alcohol. "You know we don't take too kindly to Injuns around here. Army pens them up like goats, and first thing you know they are out stealin' cows and raisin' hell in general."

Frank studied the man and decided he might be wasting his time. "Fellow I'm huntin' for is too old for any shenanigans. 'Spect he spends most of his days just waitin' for sundown."

"Yeah, that describes most of 'em, if you ask me."

Frank stepped in the stirrup and swung his right leg over the saddle.

Lou glanced up at Frank. "If I was lookin' for such a man as you are talking about, I'd go over to the fort, talk with some of them buffalo soldiers. 'Course, they ain't worth much more than that Injun you're lookin' for. Most of 'em was slaved 'fore the war, you know. But they usually keep a eye out for Injuns that ain't penned up."

Frank touched the brim of his hat and turned Red out into the dusty road. "Thank you kindly for your help."

The liveryman had not moved from his seat. "Don't reckon you got a drink of whiskey on you?" he asked.

"Ain't a drinkin' man," Frank said and heeled Red into a trot.

"Just my luck," Lou said.

To Frank's question, the sentry at the fort gate said, "Sur, that'll be Lieutenant Flipper you'll be needin' to see. First buildin' on the right, sur."

Lieutenant Flipper, lean as a racehorse and darker than any Indian, raised his head at Frank's knock. "Come in," he said and stood as the rancher entered the dirt-floored, cramped office. The office walls were covered with crude maps depicting trails, streams, and Indian tribal territories. The officer came from behind the battered wooden desk and extended his hand.

"I'm Lieutenant Henry Ossian Flipper. How may I be of service to you?" His deep voice was intensified by his Southern drawl.

"I'm Frank Rule. Got a little ranch down south of here. I've come up here huntin' a one-eyed Indian. You might've run across him. His name is Gray Spot. I hear he's pretty old."

Lieutenant Flipper crossed his arms across his thick chest. "This Indian, this Gray Spot. He's wronged you in some way? Stolen something? Cattle? Horses?"

"No, sir. Somethin' else."

"Mr. Rule, you are not very forthcoming. I don't have time to beat around the bush. We are a small outpost and quite busy. I'm preparing to take the Twenty-fifth out on a maneuver. We are scheduled to leave in"—he consulted a heavy pocket watch—"in twelve minutes. You are wasting my time and starting to vex me."

Frank smiled weakly and looked at the dirt floor. "I'm . . . I'm kinda . . . kinda ashamed to admit it. But it has to do with spirits. I hear tell that he . . . sometimes . . . sometimes is able to connect with the dead. And that he might have . . . other powers . . . maybe connected with other spirits. I know it sounds kinda far-fetched and you probably think that—"

"Mr. Rule, for the first fifteen years of my life, I was a slave in Georgia. My people had beliefs much stranger than that."

"You? You were raised as a slave?"

The outer edges of Flipper's eyelids narrowed as his cheeks rounded upward. His lips parted slightly, revealing square, white teeth. "Yes. And I graduated from West Point. You surprised at that?"

"No; nothing much surprises me anymore. Where is this West Point you're talking about? Back East somewhere?"

Lieutenant Flipper admired the stocky rancher's honesty and his straightforward manner. "Yes, it is back East. I think I might be able to help you with the Indian. There's a good chance one of our patrols has encountered him on more than one occasion. There's a buffalo skinner's trail leading south from the fort. Less than five miles and you'll come to a dry wash. Go up the wash about a mile until you come to an oak thicket. There's a partially caved-in soddy at the back of that thicket. Bet you'll find your man somewhere around there."

Frank nodded, touched the brim of his hat, and turned toward the door. "I appreciate your help."

Lieutenant Flipper followed the rancher outside and watched him step up into the saddle. "Good luck, Mr. Rule. I understand that spirits are more difficult to find than Indians."

It was dark when Frank reached the dry wash. He made a small fire, heated a can of beans, and boiled a pot of coffee. The hobbled mules were left to graze on the sparse vegetation. A safe distance away from the fire, Frank spread his bedroll and waited for sleep.

But the mules were restless and moved in the darkness. Somewhere farther down the wash, a den of coyote pups whined and cried with the sounds of distressed children. A deep cough off to the right, probably a buffalo straggler too old to stay up with the herd, Frank thought. An errant night wind rose, making the scrub oak leaves shift almost imperceptibly but enough to cause a slight whisper.

Frank lay in the darkness and wondered if the night movements might be a sign that Ellen's spirit was near. Mayhaps it was gathering from wherever souls went after their bodies died and turned to dust. Could she know that he was going to ask Gray Spot to return her to him or, if not her body, her spirit? Perchance if he concentrated strongly enough, she might come and visit him, place her cool hand on his forehead, lie here in the nighttime beside him and talk.

A sunrise bullied by thick clouds, instead of rising over the horizon, slowly materialized an hour later in the eastern sky. Eyes rimmed with redness from lack of sleep, Frank sat before the cold ashes of last night's campfire, a sense of dread heavy as a stone in his stomach.

He fed the mules a handful of grain and watered them at a seep, then drank a cup of cold, acidic, stomach-churning coffee. To the west, up the dry wash, he heard the yip of a dog. The Indian's camp could not be far away.

Frank smelled the camp before he saw it, smelled meat cooking, and also the excrement and urine odor found around camps where women are not present.

He had tied the pack mule at last night's camp and now walked in front of Red, whistling a scrap of a tune he no longer fully remembered, leading the mule around boulder outcrops and clusters of scrub oak. Frank believed that a man walking uninvited into a strange camp was less threatening than if he were horseback. He hoped the Indian would see things the same way.

He found the dugout and saw the dirt around the opening was packed and smooth from use—a sure sign that someone or something was sheltering in the dilapidated sod house. Other than the carcass of a jackrabbit skewered on a metal rod and roasting over a meager fire, there was no sign of life.

A whispery, swooshing sound, a thump, and Red shied away from Frank, almost jerking the reins from his hand. He stumbled before regaining control of the mule and then saw the shaft of a small arrow protruding from the weathered fender of his saddle. "What the hell—"

"Leave us alone! The next arrow will be in your stomach." The voice was high, reedy, uncertain.

Frank pulled his shotgun from its scabbard and dropped to one knee, scanning the bushes, waiting for a target.

The thin voice again. "I mean it, there's hundreds of us."

"Hundreds?" Frank questioned.

The same thin voice came from a different direction, "Maybe more. Maybe thousands."

An old man, nearly nude save for a wolf pelt, stood in the dark door of the soddy. He shaded his brow and in a phlegmy voice said, *"¿Quien esta afuera?"*

Frank moved the shotgun to the crook of his arm. "Just me. Frank Rule. Ain't nobody else. Not aiming to hurt anybody."

The old man changed to English. "Why is your mule actin' like that?"

"Somebody shot him with an arrow."

"With an arrow? When?"

Frank stopped looking at the old man and again scanned the brush for the owner of the thin voice. "Just now. Damn his hide. Near hit me."

"¡Mierda!" The old man lapsed back into Spanish.

Frank studied the Indian, his sparse hair, washboard ribs, leathery skin. "He said there was a hundred of them. Maybe a thousand."

The Indian smiled, picket-fence teeth blighted from age. "He is fifteen. He hasn't seen a hundred anything."

"He shoots my mule again, or me, I'm gonna fill his hide with buckshot."

The Indian walked from the soddy, squatted with heels flat against the ground, and examined the roasting rabbit. "You would shoot a boy?"

"He shot my mule."

"I believe your mule will live. The arrow has fallen away."

"Well, what if he'd shot my mule in the eye? Might have blinded him."

The Indian's face wrinkled, and his lips tightened in what was probably a smile. "Then I guess you could shoot him. Teach him a lesson. Become a legend, a killer of young boys!"

Frank was beginning to like the old Indian. "I really wouldn't want to shoot a boy."

"Most men of any character rather not shoot a boy, I suppose." The Indian turned and faced Frank. "Anyway, havin' one eye is not too bad. I have only one eye. Been that way for twenty years."

"You may be the man I'm searchin' for. What's your name?"

The Indian pulled a strip of cooked meat away from the rabbit's flank and tasted it. "Gray Spot. My name is Gray Spot."

Frank shoved the shotgun back into the scabbard and turned toward the Indian. "My name is Rule, Frank Rule. I'm from down south of here."

"Yes, We know."

"No," Frank said. "We've never met. Never saw you 'fore five minutes ago."

Gray Spot gave the rabbit a half turn over the fire, then inspected his work. He pulled another strip of meat off the carcass and extended it to Frank. "We know you've never met me. But We know you. You hunt men. Sometimes you carry evil in your heart. Sometimes you can fight it off; sometimes you can't."

"How you know such a thing about me?"

The Indian adjusted his wolf-skin robe just before his privates became exposed. "We know things."

"We? You mean you and the boy that's still hidin' out there in the bushes?"

"Don't mock me. We may be old, but We are not a fool. Old and fool are not brothers."

"Then who is that boy that shot my mule with that puny arrow?"

"We call him Wing. He claims his name is Wingford. He calls me GrPa."

"Okay, then who is this We you're talking about?"

"Sometimes, We are a bird; sometimes We are a wolf. We can be a prairie dog; We can be a buffalo. Sometimes, you can see Us. Sometimes not. Sometimes We ride the north wind." Gray Spot dabbed the moisture from his blind eye with an index finger. "Now, are you satisfied?"

Frank ate the strip of meat and licked the grease from his fingers. "When is the last time you . . . We saw me? Before today, I mean?"

"If you were a child, Mr. Rule, We would send you out onto the prairie with a basket to gather buffalo dung. Tell you not return until dark. A day spent answerin' your questions would seem like a week."

"But I'm not a child. And you are playin' games with me."

"We last saw you when you were searchin' for the man you call The Hanrahan. During the great snowstorm. We think he is a good man and worth saving. We led you to him."

"You were the bird?"

"Yes and no. We were everything."

Frank considered this information. "Nothin' can be everything. A dog's a dog. Fish is a fish."

"We can shift Our shape into whatever is needed."

"A wolf? Could you be a wolf?"

"Yes. We have told you that!"

"The old man, The Hanrahan. Did you take his dog?"

"Yes, that is part of the bargain. We take something; We leave something."

Frank shoved his hat back on his head. It was nearing noon, but the day felt heavy as if it had gone on for forever. "So, you . . . the wolf . . . took the old man's dog. What did you leave?"

199

Gray Spot hunkered down and gazed into the dying fire. "Did you not see what We left him?"

Wing had not been what Frank expected, nor had he ever seen anyone who looked like him. The boy's skin was white—not pale, but light as the finest flour. His white hair was straight and hung to his shoulders. The only color about his being was his pinkish-blue eyes, and they danced sluggishly as if his brain could not decide where they needed to focus. Frank thought he could count every rib on the boy's sinewy body.

"He don't do well in the sun," Gray Spot said. "Skin turns redder than a hot pepper and will peel off something awful. But he's a good night hunter. Comanchero called him *pal cazador nocturne*. I believe you would say 'night hunter.' "

Earlier in his life, the boy's left arm had been broken, and it had attached back together in almost unmatched places, causing it to angle away from his body like a broken wing. Two heavy scars, shaped like the *f* hole in a violin, marred his right cheek.

"The Comancheros who stole him from the trader's wagon couldn't sell him to the Kiowa 'cause they were suspicious, called him *niño fantasma*," Gray Spot told Frank. "At first, the old fathers at the big white church down on the Mexican border wanted him. Then the priest found him to be opposed to their wishes and apt to scream and struggle against their nighttime fumblin'. So, finally, the Comancheros gave up and brought him to me. We gave them a blanket and a flute made from the bone of an eagle wing."

The boy had appeared at some point during Gray Spot's explanation—not there one minute, there the next. He stood at the Indian's side, a short, stubby bow in his right hand, his poorly healed arm hidden behind the old man.

"Why isn't he wearin' clothes?" Frank asked.

"The dog does not feel at home yet, and he made water on the boy's clothes last night. They're dryin' on a bush."

Frank removed his glasses, blew on the lenses, and wiped them with his shirttail. "You have The Hanrahan's dog. That's what you took, wasn't it? You took the dog?"

The Indian adjusted his robe. "Yes. We told you that. We take something; We leave something."

"I don't understand."

"We have already explained it. We gave the women to protect the old man. We sent the bird and the buffalo to guide you. We took the dog. Wing needed one."

"But it doesn't seem fair that you would take the old man's—"

A frown swept across Gray Spot's face. "You can't answer for the old man. As much as he misses the dog, We think he would agree that it was a trade in his favor."

The two men had sat in the shade of a stunted oak for most of the afternoon. Now the dark veil of night was approaching from the east. The dull gray bones of the rabbit, stripped of meat, lay like an undecipherable puzzle on the sand at their feet.

"We have a pipe if you have tobacco," the Indian told Frank.

Frank left the camp and walked the fifty yards to where he'd tied Red to a mesquite. The reins had become untied, and the mule had wandered a hundred yards past the soddy. Frank fed her a handful of grain, then searched the saddlebags and found an oilskin pouch of loose tobacco.

From a different direction than he'd left, he stumbled back through the darkness until he neared Gray Spot's camp. At first, he thought he'd been bitten by a rattler. Both feet felt as if they had been poked into a campfire, and he danced the way a man will do when he's gotten into a yellow jacket's nest. Ghost-like, the boy rose up out of the darkness. "No one walks behind a Comanche medicine man," the boy whispered. "They have things protecting them that you can't see. You must return to GrPa the same route you left."

Frank retraced his steps to the camp, and gradually the stinging went away.

Near sundown, Wing had killed two early-roosting quail, and they were skewered on the spit, miniature droplets of grease falling from their carcasses and causing small, fiery explosions in the hot coals. The old man sat on a rock outcrop with his legs extended toward the small fire, the boy at his feet. While Frank attended the mule, Gray Spot had dressed in a cavalryman's dark pants and a cotton shirt with flamboyant sleeve buttons.

"You've brought the tobacco?" Gray Spot asked, then, without waiting for an answer, extended the clay-bowled pipe.

Frank loaded the pipe and returned it to the Indian. Gray Spot passed the tobacco under his nose, sniffing it as a man would to capture the fragrance of a warm-night lover. He took a flaming twig from the fire and ignited the tobacco. "We miss this," he said. "Once when We were young and strong, We traded buffalo hides to the Comancheros for tobacco, beads, and foolish things. That is no longer."

"I noticed your fine clothes," Frank said.

"Yes. We wear them for important meetings. The shirt belonged to Our brother. We got the pants from a trooper who fell from his horse and died."

"A trooper fell from his horse and died?"

Gray Spot nodded as if to confirm Frank's comment.

Frank grinned, walked his fingers across the dust, then collapsed them in the manner of a falling man. "Cavalrymen not good horsemen," he said.

The Indian ignored Frank's try at humor.

Frank examined the coin-sized, smooth-edged, blue-ringed holes on the front of Gray Spot's shirt and then the larger red jagged ones in the back.

"It was called a ghost shirt. An untruthful man convinced my brother that the white man could not see him if he wore this shirt. Said my brother could attack without fear. Would be invisible. It was a lie. We buried my brother and others who believed the untruths down by the river that runs dry."

"I'm honored that you chose to wear it tonight."

Gray Spot puffed twice on the pipe and fanned the smoke back over his head. "We know that you have a reason to search for Us. But your mind is not at peace. It is looking for something, but it is also afraid that it might find it. We think it is a dead woman. Your wife? And there are children. Some are dead. Others may be alive."

Frank tilted his head downward so his hat brim hid his eyes from the gaze of the Indian.

That's good, Frank, don't let him see into your eyes. Old Scratch has told you a thousand times that you're easy to read. That's why you never win at poker. Can't hide what you're thinking. He's just guessing. Talking to you about dead women and children. Hell fire and damnation! Half the white men living out here has got dead wives and children.

The old man puffed the pipe again but this time spread his fingers over the smoke and watched as the vapor rose upward in divided, wavering silver streams. "This tobacco was once alive and had a spirit. We can feel its knowledge as it moves between Our fingers."

"I never believed in spirits and such until The Hanrahan got lost. But he saw . . . felt . . . something . . . something he couldn't explain. Pretty much the same for me."

"Yes. People are like this the first time they witness Our miracles. White men mostly feel that way. It frightens them sometimes."

Frank moved away from the fire, out to a place where its redness caused no shadows, and stood looking into the night sky. As a child, he'd been taught of a power that lived beyond the heavens. An all-seeing power that parted seas and raised loved ones from the dead. Who was to say what powers Gray Spot possessed?

The Indian sat, patiently waiting for Frank to emerge from the darkness.

The rancher came back into the light, reached for the Indian's pipe, and refilled it. Gray Spot leaned forward and cupped one hand around his ear because Frank spoke so softly. "I want Ellen back."

"Yes, We know Ellen is your wife."

The rancher nodded.

The Indian rubbed the warm bowl of the pipe against his wrinkled cheek. "It is much easier to prevent someone's death than to bring them back into this world. When We were younger, We brought two people back, but now Our power is not strong. There is a danger. Once We brought a person back—but only half. We had their spirit but not their body. It was a sad thing to witness."

Frank waited for the Indian to continue but when he didn't, asked, "What happened?"

"There was madness. And death. We believed that someone of Us had evil thoughts, and that was why We failed. A relative of the spirit forced my eye from its socket with a sharp stick. To protect myself, We had to kill him. We have not tried to bring a human back since then."

"What happened to the spirit?"

"We could not control it. It wanders in the moonlight, crying like lost puppies. Some of Our young hunters have shot arrows through it, and still it moves. It is a terrible thing."

"Would you try again? My life is not worth living. At times, I have thoughts of taking my—"

"Your life is not yours to give or take. It belongs to something stronger."

"Will you help me? I'll give you everything I own."

The Indian stared into the fire, closed his eyes, and puffed the pipe again. "Tomorrow. We will tell you tomorrow."

Frank nodded and turned to face the dark trail back to his camp.

Gray Spot tapped the pipe against the ground and separated the burnt tobacco from the unburnt. "Frank, I will give you counsel. Don't listen to the voice in your head. It tries to trick your mind with bad thoughts. And do not go to where you heard the pups last night."

Frank rode back down the draw to his camp. He attended to both mules, then unrolled his bed cloth. He removed his boots, rolled up in the tarp, and lay in the darkness, eyes closed, waiting for a sleep that would not come.

This is what Old Scratch thinks, Frank. He thinks the Indian is playing you for a fool. If he had the powers he brags about, he would not be living out here in a thicket, eating jackrabbits and begging for tobacco. He would be somewhere perched on a throne of gold advising generals and kings. And don't you think he would have cured that boy, healed up that scarred face, made that arm so it would work right? You ain't got much, Frank, and now you are offering everything to him. Thought I'd taught you better than that, old son. We need to spend some time talking in a bar over a glass of buzzard juice. Top the night off with a bit of female companionship. I'm thinking of the one with red hair in the saloon down in Longsought. Maybe she can get you in the proper frame of mind.

Frank woke cold and wet from the dew that had arrived silently as the crescent moon slid soundlessly across the sky.

In a metal pot over a small fire, Frank boiled coffee and wondered if there would be anything to eat at Gray Spot's soddy. Probably not. He took bread from his pack, scraped the mold off, and searched until he found a tin of apricot preserves. Wasn't really enough, but it beat nothing. With the provisions in his saddlebags, he climbed on Red and started up the draw to the Indian's camp.

A hundred yards from the soddy, Wing squatted alongside the trail in the shade of a stunted oak, removing a jackrabbit from a wire snare. "Glad you come," he said. "GrPa never slept last night. Stayed up talkin' to the old ones that's done gone."

Frank dismounted and held the hind legs while the boy stripped the rabbit's pelt like pulling the sweater off a dead man. "Old ones that's done gone?"

"Yeah. His father and some others that I never knew."

Frank stared at the boy. "You think Gray Spot is talking to people that are dead?"

Wing gutted the rabbit and wiped his hands on a tuft of dead grass. "Well, 'least one of 'em. He's got his daddy's skull, you know. Keeps it in a piece of white buffalo hide. Says it's sacred. The skull, I'm talkin' about."

"Gray Spot is waiting to talk with me this morning?"

"Yeah. Don't be surprised if he's outta sorts. He gets that way when he don't get no sleep." Wing stooped and pulled small tufts of white hair from the breast of the rabbit's pelt. He spit in the dirt, combined the hair with the mud, and spread the mixture in a series of small circles over the stake that anchored the snares.

"What are you doing?" Frank asked. "Tryin' to kill your scent before you reset the snare?"

Wing turned to Frank, white brow wrinkled as if the cowboy had asked him in what direction the sun set. "It is for the spirit of the rabbit. I want it to know that We appreciate it giving Us its son and will not make waste of any of the body."

"You always do that?"

"Yes. We want the spirit of the rabbit to not be sad. You don't do this?"

Frank cleaned his glasses. "Well . . . mostly. Sometimes I forget."

Wing frowned and shook his head. "White men can sometimes be ungrateful."

The Indian sat at the mouth of the dugout before the fire pit, its ashes cold and falling victim to the morning's swirling wind. He raised his eyebrows in surprise when Frank took the bread and preserves from his saddlebag.

Gray Spot was much as when Frank last saw him, but the old man had braided owl feathers in his thinning, iron-gray hair and, using red ocher, painted oval symbols above and below his eyes. "Last night," he said, "I caught a locust and put it in my mouth so that it would be easier for the old ones to hear Our singing. Our voice is not as strong as it was years ago, and it must travel a great distance."

Frank nodded. "You are talking with old ones?"

The Indian busied himself dividing the bread and smearing preserves over the pieces. He took a bite and looked at Frank as a wise man looks at an ignorant man after explaining something childishly simple.

"Yes. They live out past the stars. In a place a breathing man cannot go. They have seen everythin' that has ever passed under the sun. They know what will happen after a thousand tomorrows. We talked with them about your wife. They know where you buried her under the great rocks. They were not happy that you had not shown the same respect when burying the Indian father and his sons."

Frank stared at the old man. "They killed my wife and daughter. Do you understand? Women! They killed women.

207

They did not ride into my camp like braves. The man lured me up into the rocks. He set a trap. He treated me like I was a fly, and he was a spider. Then when they thought they were safe, his boys rode through the darkness and attacked my family. They were not honorable. They did not deserve an honorable burial."

Gray Spot licked the sweetness from his fingers before removing a cowrie shell, a worn coin, three small, smooth rocks, an owl's foot, and a dried root shaped like a man from his antelope-skin medicine bag. He spread them on the sand with the dried root in the center. "We know these things. Their actions were not respectful. Because of this, We will try to help you. To bring your wife back."

"And my daughter?"

Gray Spot rearranged the items until the coin lay beside the root. "We can try to bring your daughter back. But it is difficult to move a young one, because their spirits are thin and break like mornin' ice on a blade of grass. Let Us try with your wife first."

"When will you do this?"

"The moon must be in the right shape. And the stars must be bright. We think when as many days pass as you have toes on both feet and fingers on one hand. Then the time will be right. But you understand We must have a gift. We give you something; you give Us something."

"I have money." Frank stood and moved toward the red mule's saddlebags.

"Wait," the Indian said. "We have no use for the white man's money."

"Then what do you want?"

The Indian traced the stick image of a horse in the sand. "We want a horse."

"A horse? What kind?" Frank asked.

"A white horse with red spots. One that can carry a colt in her belly and the boy on her back."

"Anything else?"

"No, that is all. You give Us something; We give you something."

Frank traveled northward toward Mobeetie, the Great Plains an expanse of undulating grass ending at the horizon spread before him.

He'd not felt this near Ellen since her death. Might it be that a spotted mare and fifteen days were all that separated him from his wife?

Lieutenant Flipper sat in his cramped office at Fort Elliott, his bearing rigid as when Frank first saw him. "Well, Mr. Rule, were you successful? Did you turn up the one-eyed Indian?"

"Yes, sir. Your directions were good."

"And was the ghost boy with him?"

Frank nodded.

The lieutenant leaned forward and propped his elbows on the desk. "I'm not one to poke into another's personal business, but could he help you in your quest of spirits?"

"I reckon that's still to be settled. It's pretty complicated."

"Yes, I can understand that it would be."

"I've got another favor to ask," Frank said. He'd not been asked to sit, and he stood in the doorway, tracing meaningless patterns on the brim of his hat with an index finger.

"And that would be . . . ?"

"I'm needin' a paint horse. A mare."

Lieutenant Flipper laughed heavily. "Mr. Rule, you'll not find one at this outpost. Or at any other outpost in this man's army, as far as that's concerned. The army found that paints don't have the endurance needed to carry fully equipped troopers

209

over the distances we travel in a day. And they are slow. And easily spotted from great distances. Our Comanche scouts jokingly tell us that the only reason Indians ever rode paints was because they were the only horses they could run down afoot."

Frank grinned. "Yeah, I've heard that, too. It's not for me. It's for a boy."

"Sorry, I can't help you. Anything else?"

Frank stared at the floor. "I'm needing a job. Nothing permanent. Short time. I know where there's a couple of paints, but I don't have money . . ."

Lieutenant Flipper knew other men like Frank: men who fought to get ahead; men who never had enough money; men without families. The army was full of them—especially the cavalry where thousands of struggling men found jobs after the Civil War. "Again, I'm sorry. Our quartermaster sees after things like odd jobs and such. He's gone to Dodge and won't be back for two weeks. If you were an Indian, I might give you something to eat. Not much I can do for a white man." He smiled as if to soften his own words. "Or for a black man, as far as that's concerned. Less'n you want to join the cavalry."

The conversation ended, and the silence was uncomfortable for both men. After shuffling through a stack of papers on his desk, Lieutenant Flipper said, "You might have a look over at Mobeetie. There's a lot of goods and materials that comes through there. Might get a job with a freighter."

As the rancher rode out of Fort Elliott, dark tower-like clouds with bulging cauliflower tops rose from the western horizon and tried to block the sun.

A cold drizzle fell as Frank rode into Mobeetie. At Lou's Livery, the proprietor sat in the barn on an upturned bucket and gawked at Frank as he unsaddled Red. "You the man that come through here couple of days ago, ain't you? Best I recall, lookin' for a one-eyed Injun."

Frank nodded and stripped the gear from his pack mule. He lifted a dry gunnysack from a nail and dried the mules' sides and backs, then forked grass hay into the racks.

"Well, did you have any luck? And if you spotted him, did you shoot him? Reckon you know the sayin' 'bout the only good Injun is a—?"

Frank stood in the open hallway of the barn and watched the downpour gouge miniature rivulets in the sandy street. "Yeah, you let me know last time I was here how you felt about Indians. Any chance I might sleep in here tonight?"

Lou grinned. "Reckon we might do a deal. You see after stuff here, and I might slip down to the saloon and have a snort or two. We'd call things even that way."

Frank nodded. "Done."

Lou pulled on his slicker. "Probably won't be nobody 'round. Mayhaps, McGregor from up in Ochiltree might stop by and get his rig. More than likely be mornin' if he does. He owes me six bits. You'll have a helluva time gettin' it from him. He's a stingy old bastard and would try to barter his soul with the devil." The liveryman stepped out into the rain and turned to look back at Frank. "I done said that I ain't gonna charge you for the night. But if you'd spot me a drink, I might go lower than that. Throw in some grain for them animals."

Frank swept water from his hat with the back of his hand. "Told you I ain't much of a drinkin' man. And not much for buying whiskey for others."

The rain had intensified. Lou buttoned the slicker to his neck and slogged down the muddy street, mumbling.

Frank sat cross legged and leaned back against the tack room door. He fished a foot-long piece of twine from his shirt pocket and tied a thumb knot at the end, then stuffed the cord back into his pocket.

Rain hammered the tin roof all night but by morning had slackened to a drizzle. Frank scattered hay in a vacant stable, spread a horse blanket over his upper body, and had the best sleep in days. The incessant crowing of a bantam rooster woke the rancher, that along with a calico cat sitting six inches from his face purring and peering at him as if he were a huge sacrificial mouse.

Frank fed his mules, then stood watching them eat. His first thoughts of the morning were about the pinto mare Gray Spot wanted. He knew of two: one owned by the mail carrier in Longsought and a second owned by an Oneida dentist. Frank wasn't sure he could even scrape up twenty-five dollars, and he had almost nothing to trade for the horse, even if the dentist or the mail carrier would sell.

Just as well. Save yourself a bunch of trouble. That old Indian can't no more bring Ellen back than I can cook a cherry pie and organize a baptizing at the same time. 'Course, Old Scratch does have other skills. I can line up a few men, two former preachers, and a whole lot of women who will testify to that being a shore-'nough fact. And I'll even throw a few politicians in the mishmash who will vouch for me.

As best he could, Frank ignored the voice while he saddled Red and harnessed the pack mule. If things went as he hoped today, he might be home before dark.

Lou sat in the drizzle outside the barn, one shoulder against the watering trough, legs crossed at the ankles. Rain had softened his hat, and it drooped around his face, hiding everything except his gaped mouth. While his raincoat was still buttoned at the neck, the other buttons had come undone, and his pants and shirt were soggy.

With his back toward Frank, a hefty man wearing a poncho stood over the still-drunk liveryman. "How come th' bugger urr ye sittin' thare?"

Frank had never heard but one man who talked like that: McGregor from up in Ochiltree. "Say there, Mr. McGregor. How 'bout we drag Lou inside 'fore he catches pneumonia. Or drowns."

Water dripping from his beard, the big man turned toward Frank. "Weel, guid day tae ye, Frank. Let's do that."

With Frank grasping Lou's shoulders and McGregor holding his feet, the two men carried the senseless man into the barn and laid him in a stable. The Scot stepped back and stared at the drunk. "Put him face doon in case he pukes and drowns in it."

McGregor pulled the poncho over his head and shook hands with Frank. "Glad a' caught ye. Git something that ye might hae an interest."

Frank grinned and shook his head. "No bulls. Not taking that ol' big bull anywhere."

" 'Tis something else. Last month I visited up into the Territory. Bought a string o' horses from some of the aboriginals. Ponies ur a skinny-malinky lot, and I thought we'd fatten them up a bit, make cow horses oot o' thaim. But fatter they get, th' mair ornery they are."

Frank raised both hands. "I'm not much on breaking rough stock anymore. It's too hard on a man my age."

"No, no," McGregor said. "I've misstated the problem. They're nae that ill. It's just that most of my men are tied up workin' wi' mah freish herd. If it wasn't for that, I'll wager they'd have them whipped into shape. In na mair than—two days, maybe."

Lou struggled to his knees, opened his eyes, and moaned. He pressed the heels of his hands against his temples, retched twice, then sat back on the ground.

"They're in a pasture ower oan th' east side o' toun. Let's ride thare'n' hae a look."

Frank Rule was not an impulsive man. He spent hours mentally debating any horse trade, weighing the pros and cons, and attributes most traders never considered. "Not smooth, juist break thaim tae a point sae ma cowboys can finish thaim off," the Scot had said.

The two rode out to the pasture in McGregor's buggy where eighteen horses, ears pricked forward, watched the men's arrival with suspicion. They were typical Indian horses, a mixture of whatever had escaped the Spanish conquistadors crossed with early High Plains stock. Frank opened the stock gate, and McGregor pulled his rig inside the pasture fence. The horses grew inquisitive and trotted around the buggy, snorting and whinnying, nostrils flaring. Then, as if possessed by something unseen by human eyes, they turned into a whirlwind of color and energy as they circled the men ever faster in an equine frenzy.

"It's because of the rain an' coolness," McGregor said. " 'N they're just excited at seeing mah buggy an' horses. Usually, they're as tame as kittens full o' aff warm milk."

Frank looked at the mass of horses that now resembled a muddy stampede. "Yeah, I can tell that by looking at them. More like tom cats tryin' to get out of a barn on fire, if you ask me."

Well, all right, Frank. I do believe you've got the old bastard by the short hairs. The only reason the Indians sold them to him was because they could never break them. Old Scratch has been looking at wild horses for thousands of years. I'm telling you, the Romans and even ol' Genghis Khan would have killed the whole bunch and just gone somewhere and stole a new herd. Every damn one looks like a bad apple to me. You let that old man off with anything less than ten dollars a head, and he's skinning you alive. I'm tellin' you, that old man is about to pull one over on you.

The two men bargained for an hour, neither willing to give in to the other's price. Frank seemed adamant: five dollars a head to gentle them to the saddle, room and board at Ida Halter's boardinghouse for two weeks, and two horses of his choice. McGregor argued for two dollars a head and room and board at Halter's for one week. Early afternoon, the two men sealed the deal: two dollars and four bits a head, stay at the boarding-house for as long as needed, and Frank was to get his choice of one horse from the rough string.

"Ye take a solid bargain, Frank," the Scot said, secretly relieved the rancher had chosen one of the least likely horses in the herd, a pinto mare with medicine hat markings. "Ane other thing, Frank, I'll no pay ye for breakin yer own horse."

As the sun dropped below the horizon, Frank took the twine from his shirt pocket and tied a second thumb knot next to the first.

Had it not been for the string, Frank would have lost all concept of the passage of time. Every day was the same: out of bed at daylight; climb into his dusty and still damp clothes, breakfast; ten hours at the corral riding horses that seemed more determined each day to kill him; a sparse supper, then collapse onto the bed and enter a jagged sleep accompanied by throbbing muscles and aching bones.

The knots increased by one each day.

It was nearing sundown when Frank hobbled up on the porch at Ida Halter's boardinghouse and slumped onto a wooden rocker. His shirt was sweat-stained, half the buttons missing. One britches leg was ripped, and a hip pocket dangled like a reluctant fall leaf waiting to depart from an oak tree. A narrow strip of dried blood reached from his left nostril and disappeared into his beard.

A thin young man with a scarecrow frame and skin color of a catfish's belly sat on the edge of the porch drinking coffee from a blue enamel mug. He had lived his entire twenty-three years in St. Louis, and until three weeks ago he had never been out of sight of the Mississippi River. He stared at Frank. "Looks as though you've had a difficult day."

Frank glanced at the young man and wondered at the pad and pencil on the floor beside him. "Oh, I don't know, 'bout average I reckon."

"I don't mean to be intrusive," the young man said. "My name is Galamore Franklin. I'm with the *St. Louis Globe-Democrat*. I've come west to write a series of articles about the American Indians. Have you been fighting them today?"

"No. Been fighting their horses, I guess you might say."

Furrowing his brow, Galamore scribbled on his pad, then looked up at the cowboy. "I'm not sure I understand. I thought we fought the Indians. I didn't know we fought against their horses, too."

"No. Breaking them for a man up in Ochiltree, so's his cowboys can ride them."

Galamore looked up from his writing. "His cowboys would have trouble riding horses?"

Frank stuck his hand under his shirt and rubbed a place where ribs might be broken. "Yeah. These, they would."

"Fascinating. Right there is enough for a good story. Mind if I come and watch tomorrow? You ride these wild horses, I mean."

Frank nodded, though he wished Galamore Franklin would take his pad and pencil and irritate somebody else. "Come ahead. I've got 'em in a corral behind Lou's Livery. I'll be there

216

when the sun comes up and stay there 'til I can't take no more."

Ida sashayed onto the front porch and ran the striker around the inside of a triangle dinner bell. "Vittles in five," she shouted in an upper range that would have made the opera singer Belle Cole envious.

Galamore sprang to his feet with the agility of a startled cat. Frank leaned forward, rested his hands on his knees, and brought his weary body into a semi-crouch before standing upright. Inside the boardinghouse, a dozen town residents and four other people passing through Mobeetie sat at a long table, napkins spread in their laps, flatware at the ready. The rancher waited for Galamore to sit, then chose a spot at the opposite end of the table between a widowed schoolteacher and a toothless pensioner.

After supper, and before he climbed into bed, Frank took the twine from his pocket and tied the twelfth knot.

Just after noon the next day, Galamore arrived at the corral in time to see a roan drive Frank headfirst into the churned-up sand. "Good heavens, Mr. Rule, are you all right?"

"No, I'm not all right," Frank mumbled through clenched teeth.

"Why put yourself through such torture?" the newspaper reporter asked.

"This is the last of McGregor's devils. Been working on this rascal for better than a day. Telling you, dark comes and I ain't got him calmed down—I'm gonna shoot the sumbitch 'tween his ears."

The reporter shrank back from the corral fence as if he'd just seen a nest of rattlers. "Oh, my word, you wouldn't shoot a horse, would you?"

Frank reined the horse's head tight against its body and climbed back into the saddle. The roan charged across the corral, head down, hindquarters bouncing high in the air, kicking out violently with his back legs and landing on stiff front legs. The rider clung to the saddle with one hand, the other hand wildly waving as if summoning help from all points of the compass, bouncing forward and backward in counter-concert with the roan's movements.

Galamore moved back to the fence and stood, one hand on the top rail, the other flourishing his hat madly above his head. Never had he seen such violent movements or such a determined man.

Minutes later, the roan tired, stopped bucking, and stood nose near the ground, sides heaving, coat wet with streaks of foamy sweat. Frank slumped in the saddle, as spent as the horse.

Galamore sat in his room until midnight, crumpled pages from his pad littering the floor like white snowballs lined with thin, blue stripes. He could not get the vision of the battle between the man and the horse from his mind. Yet he wasn't able to write it so that St. Louisians might feel the thrill he'd experienced that afternoon.

Frank tossed in his bed. Every muscle ached. He'd torn a bed sheet in half and wrapped it around his torso so tightly that breathing was difficult. His job done, he was one step closer to seeing Ellen.

Mid-morning, Frank, with forty-two dollars and four bits of McGregor's money in his hip pocket, limped down the sandy street to Lou's Livery, where he'd stabled his mules. Lou leaned against the barn gate picking his teeth with a straw and waiting for breakfast to digest. "Well, there, Mr. Rule, looks like I ain't gonna be seeing so much of you. McGregor's boys come down and picked up that herd of horses you been fightin'. Left that paint mare. She's a right purty thang. Don't reckon you'd be interested in gettin' shed of her, would you?"

"No, reckon I better keep her. Got a use for her, but thank you anyway."

"Okay," Lou said. "Then I figure you owe me five dollars for stabling your mules."

Frank stared at the liveryman. "I figure it to come to a dollar. They ain't eat much and you didn't have a need for their stable."

Lou shook his head. "Four dollars."

"No. Tell you what. Two dollars and four bits."

Lou wanted three dollars. But Frank had saddled Red, put the harness on the pack mule, and a halter on the paint mare. If the cowboy decided to ride out without paying . . . "All right, Frank, I'll take what you've offered, but don't look for no favors from me in the future."

Frank paid Lou in coins. The cowboy ran his hand along the mare's flank, an unexpected, gentle caressing movement from a man of his disposition. He pulled a knife from his pocket, cut four hairs from the mare's tail, and with a quick movement of his fingers developed a series of graceful loops. Kneeling on the packed earth of the barn floor and using his knife, the cowboy dug a narrow trench. He poked the hairs into the slit, then raked dirt over the opening.

"What the hell you think you're doin'?" Lou asked.

Frank thought about Wing thanking the spirit for the rabbits. If horses had spirits, he wanted to show his gratitude. Take something; leave something.

Stiff as a man twice his years, he eased up into the saddle and headed south.

Lou watched Frank until the man was no taller than the length of a child's thumb. "Stingy turd," he muttered and, clutching the coins Frank had given him, started toward the saloon.

Frank Rule nudged Red into a trot, the pack mule and the

paint mare following at a matching pace.

Toward the south, the prairie rolled forever, broken occasionally by a dry riverbed and the small branches that fed it during the rainy season. Frank rested the livestock at noon and made coffee. He'd taken three leftover biscuits from Halter's boardinghouse at breakfast and wrapped them in a page of newsprint. A cold dinner was better than no dinner—even if the biscuits were soggy. Frank wondered if the food at Halter's might have turned his taste away from roasted rabbit and quail.

Frank camped a half hour before dark at the same place he had stayed before his meeting with Gray Spot. He fed the livestock and picketed them fifty yards away in a patch of dry grass. After starting the fire and while waiting for it to die down to coals, he put coffee on to boil. Miss Halter had given him a half-dozen eggs, and he'd wrapped them in a bandana and stored them in a small bucket. He unwrapped them and chose the smallest one. Frank placed his small iron skillet over the coals, added a narrow strip of pork, and, when the bottom of the skillet was greasy, he added the egg. When the grease stopped popping and the egg was almost done, he lifted the skillet from the coals and dropped the last biscuit into the grease.

After he finished eating, he wiped out the skillet with his fingers and drank a second cup of coffee. There were no coyotes whining, no wild animals moving in the darkness, only the blue-black sky dotted with pricks of light. Frank sat staring into the dying fire. He took the twine from his pocket and tied the fifteenth knot. Gray Spot had said fifteen days. The paint mare grazed nearby. Take something; leave something.

Gray Spot was dead.

His gaunt body lay atop a funeral pyre, the west wind spider-webbing silver hair across his pale forehead. A folded buffalo robe lay under his head. His feet, clad in ornately beaded moccasins, extended from the edge of a worn blanket draped over his lower torso. An ancient sun-bleached, buffalo-bone breastplate decorated with porcupine quills covered his chest.

Wing, body covered with ashes and red paint and slashes of yellow smeared across his face, leaned over Gray Spot's corpse arranging trinkets, a worn knife, and a ceremonial bow and quiver of arrows along the edge of the pyre. The boy did not raise his head nor did he acknowledge the approaching horseman.

Frank dismounted and stood with his hand covering his mouth. He'd seen death. Had killed men. But other than the bodies of his dead family, nothing had driven the blade of anguish into his soul like seeing Gray Spot's corpse.

Words would not form on his tongue or in his mind, and if they had, he would not have been able to express them.

Wing moved back from the pyre and stared at the lifeless Indian.

Frank stepped forward and touched the boy's shoulder. "What . . . why . . . ?" His voice was just above a whisper.

The boy turned. His forehead was wet with sweat and tears streaked the ashes on his cheeks. "GrPa wanted it this way. He did not want to come back. He said that if a body was burned, there would be nothing for the spirit to come back to."

"When . . . how . . . ?"

"Yesterday morning. Just like I'd been doing all along, I'd heated stones and dipped a bucket of water. GrPa'd spent the night with the others praying inside the sweat lodge. I stopped outside the wolf-hide door and whispered his name. Told him I'd leave the stones and water where I always did. He didn't answer. I called his name again except louder this time. He still didn't answer. I didn't hear any noise, no chanting, no whispering. I feared that he might be gone—him and the others just disappeared into the night wind. I moved the hide just a crack and looked inside. His face was against the floor. Hands over his ears." The boy stopped and swallowed. "I asked if he was sick. He didn't answer. I crawled inside and touched him. There was no warmth to his body."

"You said there had been others inside with him, praying?"

"Yes. Remember he talked to you about We? It was him and spirits of long dead shamans.

"After we got the sweat lodge built . . ." Wing closed his eyes and nodded his head as if counting. "That was about ten days ago. GrPa went inside. He'd only come out just 'fore daylight. Said I wadn't to look at him, made me put a blanket over my head."

"But the others . . . ?"

"Most times, they'd be with him, I believe. I'd hear them walking around. Little light footsteps. Sound like small children. Sometimes they'd talk, but it was never more than a whisper. Couldn't understand what they were sayin'."

"How many, do you think?"

"Dunno. They never made no markings. GrPa and them would go back in the sweat lodge. I'd come out from under the blanket, wouldn't be no signs 'cept what GrPa made."

"Damn!" Frank circled the small, dome-shaped hut, looking for man tracks. "But you would hear their voices inside?"

"Yeah. Purty clear. Hearing 'em prayin' and chantin'. Sometimes, they'd sing."

"Always the same?"

"No. The night 'fore I found GrPa dead, there was a woman's voice. She was screamin' and cryin'."

It was hard for Frank to breathe, and the hair rose on the back of his neck like it will do sometimes before a lightning strike. "Could you understand her?"

Wing went to the pyre and rearranged the trinkets. "Yeah. She called your name. Twice."

"You're sure, about my name, I mean. She called, *Frank?*"

Wing nodded. "Wadn't no doubt."

The cowboy walked a hundred yards down the draw and sat on a rock outcrop, face resting in his palms. He shook like a man with high fever, then his body spasmed, and vomit gushed uncontrollably. After his stomach was empty, he lay in the sand and howled with sounds probably used by the first man after wolves took his mate.

When he awoke, the night birds were flitting across a darkening sky. He smelled the smoke before the throbbing glow of the fire came into focus. He lay back in the sand, exhausted as if he'd fought a yearlong battle.

White hair slanting across his face, Wing sat before the cold ashes. He sifted their grayness between his fingers, occasionally capturing a bone fragment or a burned bead and dropping them into a leather pouch. "This is all that's left of GrPa. For one year, I will carry bits of him with me. His body, I mean. His spirit and wisdom will be with me forever in my heart and mind. When I see a cloud, feel the wind, or touch water, I will know he knew it before I did. He taught me things I don't understand now, but I will in time. I will."

"I can't understand him just up and dying," Frank said.

"I think he died of sorrow. He wanted to bring your wife back. But he couldn't, and they couldn't help him. I believe they almost succeeded, but when they didn't . . . GrPa's spirit left. And the others went with him."

"But you never saw them. Just heard them."

"No. Never saw them. But I know they were there. GrPa believed they would come to help him. It may be good that he is not with us anymore. He talked about how most of the buffalo were gone. How the white man had killed many of his people or

223

were fencing them in like a farmer's milk cow. Wadn't any freedom no more. I think his time was gone, and he would never be happy in this world again."

Frank moved to the boy and stood uncomfortably. Finally, he said, "I brought the horse. The paint mare."

Wing nodded. "GrPa said you would. He thought you were an honorable man."

Frank handed the horse's reins to the boy. "And I believe he was an honorable man, too."

Wing said, "This morning, up near where his hands would have been, I found something. I don't know how it got there. It wadn't GrPa's; it's not mine; I never saw it before today."

"What is it?" Frank asked.

"It's a gold ring. By the size, a woman's, I think. Here, take it," Wing said and handed the ring to Frank.

The rancher recoiled as if the boy had dropped a firey coal into his hand.

Around noon, the bespectacled cowboy and the teenaged albino set out toward the southwest, the boy's three-legged dog hobbling along behind. The wind had lazed early, and clouds, their rounded masses like dirty sheep's wool, partly shielded the riders from the sun.

Earlier in the day, Frank had loaded the boy's meager belongings—a couple of tattered shirts, a pair of pants, two pairs of worn-out moccasins, and a rawhide bag containing his bow and arrows—on the pack mule. Wing secured the leather pouch containing GrPa's beads and bone fragments with a long rawhide string and looped it around his neck.

Frank warned Wing about the wildness of the mare and cautioned him to watch himself around her. On the way down from Mobeetie, the paint mare had struggled against the rope halter that tied her to the pack mule. She'd hung back and was skittish at anything unusual, a blowing tumbleweed, a bird that came too close, a bolting rabbit. But, by the morning, the horse had taken to the boy and followed him around the camp as they were preparing to leave.

"Maybe the mare thinks that we've been together before," Wing said. "What if when we were in an earlier life, we hunted buffalo together? Or rode with other Indian peoples on raids against our enemies?"

"Maybe," Frank said. "But Gray Spot said your folks were English."

"Yes. But who knows who I was before that. I may have been an antelope. Or a cloud. Or a lizard. GrPa said we should respect people and animals. We never know when we come back who may be the horse and who may be the rider. I want to think that when I come back, my arm will be healed, that I will be equal to other men."

Before they left Gray Spot's camp, they had discussed the ring again.

"I think it belonged to your wife," Wing said. "I believe they almost brought her back. I never saw nothing, but I heard a woman's voice, and she was calling out. Maybe it was another woman. Maybe it was another Frank, but I don't think so. GrPa had been a powerful man when he was young. Had great medicine. A great healer. Even when ancient, you saw his power when you were hunting for the old man and his dog. You were not the first man to come and ask his help. Twice I saw some things that GrPa warned me to never tell anyone about. A sacred secret, he called it."

Frank again examined the ring. "I don't know," he said. "I want to believe it is hers, but I just don't know."

Wing petted the three-legged dog's head, then turned toward the cowboy. "If you aren't sure, you can't keep it. The ring, I mean."

Frank, voice rough and tone belligerent, looked into the danc-ing bluish-pink eyes of the albino. "What do you mean, I can't keep it? What if it's Ellen's?"

"But you don't know."

Frank rubbed the pitted surface of the ring. "But it might be."

"That's right. But it might not be. If you keep the ring and it belongs to another woman . . . it would be as if you had kidnapped her. Taken another man's wife. You are not a stealing man. GrPa trusted you."

Frank clenched the ring until cords rose up in his forearm. "Then, what—?"

"Here. You bury it here. In a place that not even I know. Someday, a spirit may tell someone about the ring. Who it belongs to. If it belongs to you, you come back and get it. If the spirit does not talk with you, you leave it. Maybe long after we are gone and everyone who knows us or ever saw our ashes is gone, the children of the blood owner will be led to the ring."

"But what if . . . ?"

"I will go into GrPa's house once more. I need to spend time where he lived. It will be the last. Here. Maybe in the future . . ."

Less than a hundred yards from the soddy, an immature scrub oak, already leaning under the influence of an insistent west wind, grew at the edge of a rock outcrop. Frank dug a hole to the depth of a man's knee. He'd taken his enameled coffee cup from the pack and with the point of his knife scratched his initials and the date on the bottom. The rancher kissed the ring and then held it against his heart. After placing the ring in the cup, he cut a strip from a horse blanket and made a firm bundle no larger than his hat. As if burying a baby, he placed the bundle in the hole and covered it with dirt. When he finished, he dragged a large rock over the fresh earth.

The rancher stood and covered his face with his hands, body

slumping forward, knees bent. To the east, a mourning dove's sad call was answered by its mate.

Frank dropped to his knees beside the freshly covered grave, took an empty cartridge case from his jacket, packed it with dirt, and dropped it into his pocket. When he walked away, he did not look back.

Gray Spot had said, "Take something; leave something."

★ ★ ★ ★ ★

María de los Ángeles

★ ★ ★ ★ ★

"Howdy. Name's Frank Rule, ain't it?"

Frank turned toward the source of the question, a lanky young man with protruding ears and a significant underbite. "Yep. Last time I heard, nobody else was using that name."

"Yeah, well, okay. Pap's got somethin' for you."

Frank and Wing tied their horses at the rail in front of the Longsought Mercantile. The building not only had Longsought's best general stock but also served as the town's post office, funeral home, and gossip center. The owner's son, Bulldog White, sat in a straight chair on the wooden sidewalk at the front of the store. This was his favorite post—gettin' somethin' past old Bulldog is like tryin' to sneak daylight past a Dominicker rooster, the townspeople said—and he'd been there since the sun was an hour high.

Bulldog unfolded his lanky frame and stood. "Ain't seen you for a while."

"Not needed nothing," Frank said.

" 'Nother reason I didn't know who you was, I thought you always rode a red mule, if I rightly recall."

Frank beat the Texas Panhandle dust from his pants. "You recall right. Still got her. Traded for this horse last week. Might do most of my travelin' on him. Easier on my ass."

Bulldog looked at the horse. "Right good lookin' animal. Got a name?

Frank was tiring of the questioning. "Yeah. Call him Socks,

231

'cause of the coloring on his front legs."

Bulldog turned his attention to Wing. "Did you trade for this feller, too? And his clothes. My God, why you could put two of him in them britches and wrap his shirt around him twice. And he's just about barefooted. Pretty dang pitiful, if you ask me."

Frank frowned. "No, wadn't no trade. His name is Wingford. Wingford Street. He goes by Wing. Don't you be concernin' about his clothes."

Bulldog moved to Frank's side and whispered behind his hand, "Don't recall ever seein' a man that was kinda' . . . you might say . . . kinda' pink. Ain't got no more color than one of them fishing worms that I dig up behind Pap's toilet."

Frank frowned again. "Well, Bulldog, I don't expect Wing's ever seen anybody that looks like you. Reckon that makes the two of you about even."

Wing was not a part of the conversation. While the men were talking, he had stepped up onto the porch and, with the timidity of a Baptist preacher looking into a whorehouse on a Saturday night, poked his head into the dark interior of the store. It had been years since he had seen so many clothes, ropes, glass cases, tins of food, and sacks of flour and meal. The alien smells of wagon grease, peppermint, and leather dressing added to his bewilderment.

Bulldog's father, Charlie, sat slumped on a tall stool behind a long wooden counter, sleeves gartered, a green celluloid visor perched barely above his eyebrows, elbows resting on the glass top. Wing's body interfered with the light flow, and the merchant looked up from the column of numbers he was tallying. "Come on in, son," Charlie said. "You're blockin' my light."

Wing retreated to the porch where Frank had dismissed Bulldog. Wing looked at Frank, raised his eyebrows, and blew a gust of air through his tightly circled lips.

The rancher grinned, stepped through the doorway, and

motioned for Wing to follow.

"Morning, Frank."

"Mornin' yourself, Charlie."

"Looks like you've got a new partner."

"Yeah. Name's Wing. He comes from up north 'round Fort Elliott. Seen some hard times, you might say. Gonna need to get him some clothes. Pair of pants, couple of shirts, shoes, pair of drawers, some socks. And a hat with a broad brim. His skin don't favor the sun too much."

With an experienced eye, Charlie surveyed the young man. "Believe I can take care of that. And I got in some used shoes and pants yesterday. Save you some money. That be okay?"

Frank nodded. "Just do us right."

From the doorway, Bulldog listened to the conversation. "Ain't never skinned nobody in a deal yet, have we, Pap?"

Charlie ignored Bulldog; he'd had a lot of practice at that over the years. "Looks like the boy's gonna need about size twenty-eight pants, a medium shirt, and I'd say 'bout size seven brogans. Reckon a medium in a hat ought to work. That'll be a startin' point anyway."

The clothes fit—shirt might have been a little big, but he'd grow into it, Charlie figured.

The shoes were a problem; Wing had never worn anything except antelope-skin moccasins. He clomped across the floor, lifting his feet high as if he were wading through tall grass.

"Take getting used to," Frank said. "He'll be all right after a while."

Charlie settled the hat on Wing, then held up a looking glass so the boy could see his new image. He had seen himself in small bits of a broken mirror, but seeing his entire face and the hat perched on his head was startling. He ran his face through a series of expressions—scared, happy, frowning, menacing, and, finally, flicking his tongue out like a frog capturing a mosquito.

He laughed at the last action and covered his eyes with his hands.

The merchant wrapped the other dry goods in brown paper and tied the bundle with white string.

Wing, followed by Bulldog, walked out onto the sidewalk and stood with his thumbs hooked behind his galluses, admiring his big-hatted shadow.

"Charlie, Bulldog said you had some mail for me," Frank said.

Charlie laid the clothing parcel on the counter. "Yeah," he said and turned to a series of cubbyholes in the wall behind him. "Here it is. Two messages. One's a letter. Came last month. The other one's a newspaper clipping a woman dropped off few days ago and said to give to you when I saw you. Or if I saw you."

"What woman?"

The merchant leaned across the counter and whispered as if he were divulging a secret that would have a permanent effect on the High Plains or maybe the entire state of Texas. "She's from Oneida. Widow woman, somebody said. Must have a lot of money 'cause she was ridin' in a fancy rig with a darkie in a shiny yeller suit drivin'. He was sittin' up there on the front seat actin' proud as a dog with two . . . uh . . . two tails."

Frank held the letter up toward the dim light seeping through the window. "Pretty fat," he said. "But I don't see no money inside. Kinda disappointin'."

"Cowhand was in here buying horseshoes saw her. Said her last name was Harrington, and her family had enough money to burn a wet mule with hundert dollar bills. Bulldog followed her down the street. Says she's staying at the hotel. Took the black feller three trips to carry her trunks and grips up to her room."

"Must change clothes right often," Frank said as he folded the letter and the newspaper clipping and tucked them in his jacket pocket.

Curious as to the content, Charlie was disappointed Frank hadn't opened the envelope. The merchant had tried to open it with teakettle steam before Frank's arrival, but the wax seal on the back held fast. "Let me know if there's anything in the letter that I might help you with," Charlie said.

Frank picked up the bundle of clothes and walked to the door.

The merchant's last chance was slipping away. "I'm guessing that she'll be taking her meals at the hotel." He pulled a heavy-chained, silver watch from his pocket. "Comin' up on noon. Mayhaps catch her in the dining room."

Frank and Wing tied their horses behind the hotel in a copse of cottonwood spread alongside the creek. A black man decked out in a yellow suit sat on the back steps of the hotel, a plate balanced on his knees, eating beans and drinking water from a glass jar.

"Take you to be the Harrington woman's driver," Frank said.

"Yes, suh. Conro, that would be me," the black man said as he sopped bean juice from his plate with a fist-size chunk of bread. "She don't trust nobody else with the job. Not since Mr. Harrington . . . uh . . . was took from us, anyways."

"Reckon I need to see her. She inside?"

"Yes, suh, that she would be. She be eatin' just 'bout now."

Frank tucked his shirttail in and raked the dust from his boots with his fingers. "Wing, you want to go inside with me?"

The albino shook his head. He had never seen a structure the size of the three-story hotel and was not sure he would be safe inside such a huge building. And he had never looked at a black man up close and wasn't through looking at him.

Frank nodded. "Suit yourself."

He took a step toward the hotel, then turned toward Conro.

"Oh, how will I know her? What does she look like?"

Conro had tilted the plate and corralled the last of the bean juice with the bread. His hand paused in transit, suspended halfway between the plate and his mouth. "You won't have no trouble pickin' out Mrs. Harrington. No, suh, no trouble, no trouble a'tall."

Conro was right. Frank could have picked her out in any Long-sought crowd. And probably any crowd in Oneida, or Dodge, or Dallas. Once in a fancy Tucumcari hotel, he had seen a portrait of two Spanish women, a mother and daughter with red dresses frilly with white lace and pearl combs in their glistening black hair. The rancher had thought he would never see a woman as pretty as the two—and he had not, until now. He did not know the term handsome and, if he had, he would never have thought about applying it to a female. But Mrs. Harrington was a handsome woman.

Her late husband, Houston Harrington, was an adventurer. He thought no more about crossing the border into Juárez or over the Sandia Mountains into Albuquerque than he did about pursuing stolen cattle up into the Oklahoma Territory. But his most successful adventure was a few years after the Civil War when he brought the beautiful María de los Ángeles from Tubac to the sprawling family ranch in the Texas Panhandle near Oneida.

After their arrival from the desert southwest and the subsequent wedding, townsfolk agreed: he got a beautiful woman, and she got a very wealthy man. And they noted she was years younger than he—young enough to be his daughter. Generally, the women frowned on this while the men passed it off with a wink and a grin.

María de los Ángeles

★ ★ ★ ★ ★

Frank removed his hat and stood before María de los Ángeles. "I'm Frank Rule."

The woman, heavy Bible at her elbow, lowered her coffee cup, touched her lips lightly with the white napkin, and smiled. Because of his reputation, she had a mental picture of Frank Rule: big, strapping, tough looking. But the man before her needed a haircut and shave and, other than the glasses, looked no different than a couple of cowboys who worked on her husband's ranch. "Yes, Mr. Rule. I've anticipated seeing you. My friends call me Ree."

"You sent me a letter, and left me a piece of newspaper at Charlie's store. I was surprised. Believe it is the second letter I ever got, but I ain't read it yet."

María de los Ángeles smiled, her teeth dazzling white against her olive skin. "Won't you be seated, Mr. Rule? Perhaps have coffee and a sweet with me?"

"I thank you, ma'am, but, no. A few things to pick up here in town. Then gotta get back up to the north. Got a sick cow to tend to."

"Please sit, Mr. Rule. I'm sure your cow won't begrudge you spending a few minutes talking with me."

"No, ma'am, I—" It occurred to Frank that he was speaking with a lady and had not removed his hat, a serious breach of Texas etiquette he immediately corrected. "I'm all right standing up . . . been setting most of the morning. In a saddle."

"Very well, but if you change your mind, the invitation remains. I'll try to keep our conversation brief."

"Yes, ma'am."

María de los Ángeles crossed her fork and knife on the far edge of her plate and corner-eyed the couple at the table to her left. She lowered her voice. "I want you to kill a man. And I want him to know why you are killing him." She paused and

237

daintily touched the corners of her mouth with the napkin. "And who hired you to do it."

Abraxas Escovedo sat on the veranda of the Tumblebug watching the cone-shaped shadow of the Capulin volcano move toward the bar's hitching rail. A few miles northeast, the Oklahoma and New Mexico Territories cornered into the Colorado state line.

Other than his muscular build and the scar traversing from the center of his close-cropped cranium to his ear, he was as unkempt as any of the cowboys lounging on the porch, drinking cheap whiskey and smoking dark cheroots.

Escovedo walked to the edge of the shadows, unbuttoned his pants, and peed an arching stream out into the dusty road. He rebuttoned, then locked his fingers behind his head, and stretched his shoulder muscles. "Freedom. Ain't nothing like freedom, boys. And I owe it mostly to you."

"Houston Harrington was a kind man," María de los Ángeles said. "He was an adventurer at heart. Had he lived a few hundred years ago, he would have been on the *Mayflower* and the first man off the ship. He was always looking for something different to do."

Frank nodded. "Known a couple of fellers like that. Seems mostly they don't come to a good end."

María de los Ángeles shook her head. "You don't understand Houston. He was not that kind of man. He weighed risks. Not overly careful, you understand. He would laugh and say that I was the biggest risk taker he ever met. Marry a man who was old enough . . . you know what I'm saying without going into all the details. Houston said a man should marry a woman half his age plus seven years."

This kind of talk made Frank uncomfortable. "You said

Houston . . . Mr. Harrington was a risk taker."

Mrs. Harrington noted Frank's reactions. "I insist, Mr. Rule, that you be seated. You are making me tired by just standing there, and I am straining my neck looking up at you."

Frank sat and placed his hat, crown down, on a corner of the table.

María de los Ángeles pushed a cup toward Frank and nodded at a waiter standing inside the dining room door. "Houston had mined for gold in California, hunted grizzly bear up near the Canadian border, and sailed around Cape Horn. Mind you, most of this had taken place before we married. I would like to say that I would not have permitted such folly, but that would not be truthful. He was very much his own man."

The waiter refilled María de los Ángeles's cup, then filled Frank's.

Abraxas Escovedo was born in Las Animas County, years before Colorado became a state. His Mexican father left his Italian mother with three children, Abraxas the oldest. At seventeen, tired of supporting the family by working in a primitive open-pit coal mine, he stole a horse and traveled southward into New Mexico Territory.

"A bad choice," he told anyone who would listen. "The sheriff at Willow Springs made a living putting horse thieves in the pokey. He read the brand on the mare I was riding. Throwed me in the hoosegow for eight months and sold the mare to a buffalo hunter.

"I'd still be behind bars if he hadn't got tired of feeding me. But I evened things up. Waylaid him one night when he was headin' to the barn. Busted his head in with a wagon spoke. Took his horse and gun and headed out again. Wound up here in Black Cherry. Never lived nowhere else permanent, 'cept when I was locked up or on my way to jail."

The hotel dining room emptied. Trying to hide their curiosity, many of the departing diners stole glances at the two who remained—the stunning, obviously wealthy woman sitting with the bald, bespectacled cowboy—and, dismayed, wondered what they could possibly have in common.

"Ma'am, I'm sure your husband was a fine fellow. 'Preciate you telling me about him. And 'preciate the coffee. But this country is different than it was a few years back. You can't go and shoot a man just 'cause somebody else don't like him."

María de los Ángeles placed her dainty fingers atop the rancher's hand. "It is not dislike, Mr. Rule. It is loathing."

"Maybe he needs killin', but I'm not your man."

"No, I believe you are the man I need."

"Where did you ever get the idea that I went around killin' men. 'Specially for money?"

"I . . . my late husband and I have . . . had a business acquaintance. A banker. His son was killed in Tascosa. You went over there and—"

Frank nodded and raised his hand. "If you know all that, then you know I never got his son back."

María de los Ángeles smiled. "I know all about that, Mr. Rule. I realize that the men who were responsible for the young man's death . . . died. I know of your agreement with the banker. The terms. The money he paid you. You see, his wife was a cousin of my late husband."

Frank drained his coffee and swirled the grounds in the bottom of the cup. "Hope the woman was a better person than her husband. I never cared for him."

María de los Ángeles chuckled, an amazingly deep and husky sound from such a petite woman. "She was sweet. Kind. Gentle.

It took a while for the sadness over the loss of her son to go away. When she found out that the men responsible for her son's death had been . . . were no longer among the living, it made . . . made things easier."

"Guess you know that I almost had to take it outta the banker's hide to get what he owed me."

María de los Ángeles smoothed a wrinkle in the tablecloth and rearranged the alignment of her plate and saucer. "Yes, that's what I understand. His wife told me he was a changed man—for a few weeks. Collecting your fee will not become a problem with me. I am prepared to pay you before the sun sets today."

Frank cleared his throat and looked over the vacant dining room. "What's this feller's name?"

A cathedral of clouds rested against the northern horizon, anchored there for days, unmoving, hoarding its rain.

Escovedo spread the dominoes face down on the front table in the Tumblebug. There was an unmistakable clicking as he mixed the tiles on the scarred surface. Three empty chairs at the table were quickly occupied. One by Joe Sherman Lee, a thick-chested freighter ferrying a load of goods to Walsenburg. The other two chairs were taken by cowboys Mute Williams and Herb Pierce, both cronies and partners in crime with Escovedo. "All right, fellers," Escovedo said, "it's Muggins and a penny a point. And since I'm the only hombre that can count past ten without taking his shoes off, I'll run the tally sheet."

Herb reached across the table, gave the dominoes one final mixing, and drew five. The freighter stared at the back of the tiles as if he could see their spots, then carefully chose five. Mute Williams closed both eyes, danced his fingers through the dominoes, and pulled five. Escovedo dragged five from the edge, then shoved the remaining dominoes aside and spread his fingers over the jumble. "It's a rich boneyard; I can tell by the heat rising up from it."

"I ain't got all day," the freighter said. "I ought to be on the road right now. If you got the double six, put her out there." No one moved, and he slapped the double five on the tabletop. "See it and weep. Looks like you gents are a dime in the hole, and the game ain't hardly started."

Two hours later, Herb stood and said, "I'd love to stay here and play 'til dark, but I've got a couple of Roman-nose mules to shoe 'fore sundown. What's my tally over there, Abraxas?"

"Well, let's see here, you mostly broke even with everybody 'cept you owe me four bits. Pretty cheap entertainment if you ask me. Play two hours and lose a half dollar."

Mute smiled, tapped his index finger against his chest, and raised his eyebrows in a silent question.

Escovedo scanned the tally marks, made a few diagonal lines, and said, "Not bad. Not bad at all. You in the hole to Herb for a dime, the freighter fifteen cents. And eighty cents to me."

Mute whistled, a flat toneless note, but his eyes twinkled at the excitement of the game.

The freighter rubbed his hands together. Their roughness gave off a raspy sound. "What about me? Looks like I'm a winner here today."

Escovedo consulted the tally sheet and frowned. "Yeah, you done pretty good." He frowned again, smudged a few marks, and added a half-dozen more. "Hell fire, if I didn't see it with my own eyes, I wouldn't believe it. You pretty much broke even. 'Cept against me. Best I can tell, you owe me five dollars and six bits."

The freighter leaned across the table and snatched the tally paper from Escovedo. "Why hell, this ain't no tally. It's just a bunch of marks, looks like chicken scratching to me."

Escovedo looked shocked. "You accusin' me of cheating?"

"Well, I damn sure am, and, furthermore, I'll not put up with it. Not a damn minute."

"Sorry you feel that way about it," Escovedo said. "Hurts my feelings."

"I gonna hurt more than your damn feelings," the freighter shouted. Without rising from his chair, he leaned to the side and reached for his pistol.

Hidden by the table, a sawed-off double-barrel shotgun lay across Escovedo's lap. He fired both barrels. The buckshot pattern did not spread more than a foot, and from his belt line to his knees, the freighter's body jellied.

Escovedo walked to the saloon window and looked at the freighter's loaded wagon. "Fellers, I'd say that there's about enough goods on that wagon to pay me what the freighter owed me."

María de los Ángeles smiled and said, "His name, Mr. Rule . . . does his name really matter?"

"Well, yes," Frank said. "I'm not gonna go and take on a Texas Ranger or the governor of Texas. I'm kinda thick between the ears, but I ain't that thick."

"Mr. Rule, I would not do anything like that. The man's name is Abraxas Escovedo."

"Can't say as I've ever heard of him. Whereabouts is he?"

"Black Cherry," she said, her lips compressed as if she had tasted something sour. "Up near that old volcano called Capulin, halfway between Raton and Clayton in the New Mexico Territory."

Travel from Old Moses to Loma Parda was not easy. Tom Mc-Masters's wife, Felicia, had told him this at least a hundred times—maybe a thousand. But Tom's brother operated a combination saloon-mercantile store in Loma Parda, a blow-off town for Fort Union troopers guarding the Santa Fe Trail. "Brother says I can come down there and in a couple of years make enough money to add some sure-enough acreage to our ranch up here," Tom told Felicia. "He's got a good business, selling feed and groceries and such."

Tom did not see any need to tell Felicia about the prostitutes operating out of caves north of Loma Parda, especially since Cavalry Captain Skools had already caught most of them, shaved their heads, and named their former camp Cañón de Las Pleones. Also, it would not have interested Felicia to know that Loma Parda sat on the bank of the Mora River, but she would have been interested to know the town was also known as Sodom on the Mora.

"I'll take David with me," Tom told Felicia. "With two of us working, we'll probably be back in less than a year. Maybe nine months."

"Well, least you ain't taking the oldest. Stafford oughta be old enough to handle things 'til you get back."

Tom laughed. "He's twenty-one. If he can't run the place and look after the cattle, he damn sure ain't gonna learn no younger."

On a fine day in mid-September, a day when the blowing grit was sandblasting the bushes and dying grass, Tom and David set out on a southwest course for Loma Parda.

On that same day, Escovedo and his two compañeros, Mute Williams and Herb Pierce, left Loma Parda traveling northeast toward Black Cherry. It had taken almost a month to sell the murdered teamster's wagonload of rifles and pistols. They sold the last of the firearms at a sheepherder's camp outside of Las Vegas. Nothing remained except the long trip back to Black Cherry.

The men took a side trip over to Loma Parda, where Escovedo had achieved a brief splash of fame. On horseback, he had taken a late-night woman in the street, pulled her belly-down across the saddle in front of him, and rode right into a saloon, where he demanded the bartender serve drinks to everybody. But, when his horse would not drink, he shot the animal through the head. Seemingly satisfied, Escovedo threw the woman over his shoulder, walked out the door, and left his dead horse on the saloon floor. After a night's stay in the jail, the local sheriff escorted Escovedo and his buddies to the edge of the town and threatened them with castration if they ever set foot in his county again.

The distance from Old Moses to Loma Parda was just over a hundred miles as the crow flies and something over a hundred and fifty miles as a horse travels. Other than the Turkey Mountains, scattered barren hills, and the Canadian River, most of the journey was through monotonous, rolling rangeland.

On a cool night, Tom and David McMasters chose to camp at Taylor Springs near the confluence of the Cimarron and the Canadian Rivers. It was almost sundown when the two got camp set up. David had killed an antelope late that afternoon. Both men, tired of dried beef, looked forward to a meal not related to a cow. David rode down the river looking for suitable grazing for the horses while his father prepared to roast a hindquarter of the antelope.

Three men crossed the river and stopped fifty yards from the McMasters camp. "Hello, mister," one of the men shouted. "Mind if we ride in? We're needing directions to get up to Raton Pass."

Tom McMasters moved back from the fire. Other than David, he had not seen another living soul in almost two days. Now these men appeared out of the desolation. He wished he had his saddle gun in hand, but there was no need to stir up unnecessary trouble or show his fear. "Yeah. Come ahead."

The three men rode into the camp and dismounted.

The largest man removed his hat and hung it on his saddle horn. The thick scar extending from the center of his head to an ear was an angry red in the firelight. "I'm Abraxas. These other two fellers are Mute and Herb. We took a few cows down to Santa Rosa. Comin' back, we musta took the wrong fork this morning. We kinda know where we are. Just need to know for sure."

Herb grinned. "Kinda embarrassing. Makes us seem like greenhorns."

McMasters nodded. "Go back across the river, head toward that low range of hills. You'll pick up the trail as it goes through the notch."

" 'Preciate that. We . . . uh . . . might bed down with you tonight. Seeing that you've already got a fire goin' and all. If that's okay?"

McMasters stared at the three newcomers. He had seen men like them before. Drifters. Ne'er-do-wells. Two-bit horse thieves. "Mayhaps you might want to give us a bit of room. There's four of us. And nobody wants to be crowded."

Mute walked about the camp, eyes straining to pick up hoof-prints in the fading light.

"Four of you?" Escovedo said. "Didn't have no idea there was that many in your party."

"The rest of the men have gone down the river. Looking for a place to pasture the horses tonight."

Standing behind McMasters, Mute looked toward Escovedo, grinned, and raised one finger.

". . . he'd been shot once in the back of the head," María de los Ángeles shuddered and said. "David heard the men talking with his daddy. Then there was some shouting. The boy is just a kid,

246

maybe fifteen or so, and he was horrified. He tied his horse and sneaked to the edge of the camp. Got there in time to see Escovedo shoot his father in the head again. Of course, he was terrified. He ran back and got his horse. Rode down the river as fast as the animal could run."

Frank Rule nodded, picturing in his mind the scared boy. "The men—the killers—didn't come after him?"

"Yes, but he outdistanced them. The saints must have been with him because around noon the next day he encountered troopers from the Ninth Cavalry. David took them back to camp, and that's where they found his dead father.

"And the killers?"

"As luck would have it, the troopers found them in a box canyon up near Tinajay. One of their horses had thrown a shoe, and one was killed by a rattler. Three men and two horses. They were not making very good time. Foolishly, the heavily armed outlaws chose to enter into a gunfight with the cavalrymen."

Slight smile lines gathered at the corners of Frank's eyes. "Three men against the Ninth Cavalry. Don't sound very smart to me."

"Wasn't." María de los Ángeles toyed with the pie crumbs on her plate. "Only Escovedo survived."

"So the Ninth captured him. I don't understand why you're trying to get me tangled up in this."

The cavalrymen buried Herb and Mute in shallow graves and piled rocks on the fresh dirt.

With Escovedo handcuffed and sitting dejected in his own saddle, the cavalry rode west toward Fort Union. Two days later, and in considerably worse shape than he was when first placed on his horse, he was delivered by the soldiers to the county jail. The following month, the Mora County Territorial District Court tried him and, based on David McMasters's testimony, sentenced him to be hanged.

A boisterous crowd of five hundred or more from every corner of the territory gathered to witness the hanging. Sheriff Raúl Hernández chose a large cottonwood by the river and hauled the handcuffed and fettered Escovedo to the site in a wagon. Velton Smith, the territory's semi-professional hangman, climbed up into the wagon and dropped the noose over the outlaw's head, being careful that the knot rested under the angle of the left jaw. Velton uncuffed Escovedo's hands, then pulled them behind his back. But, before he could properly tie them together, a fight between five inebriated spectators broke out accompanied by at least two blasts from a shotgun. The encouraging screams of a dozen dancehall girls, who had not witnessed a fistfight in the last two hours, panicked the horse. He lunged forward, snatching the wagon from beneath the sheriff, the outlaw, and the hangman. Instead of having his neck broken, Escovedo was being choked. He grabbed hold of the rope and frantically tried to pull himself upward toward the strangling noose. Sheriff Hernández scrambled to his feet and grasped Escovedo around the waist, trying to pull him downward. Eyes protruding and face redder than a beet, Escovedo desperately clung to the rope with both hands.

But the spectacle of the sheriff swinging from the waist of the dangling outlaw was too much for the startled crowd; they rushed forward and cut Escovedo loose. Sheriff Hernández protested, hollering that justice had not been done, but the crowd, who contended that the outlaw had been hanged, shouted him down. While it was unsuccessful, the sentence had been carried out.

Two regulators took Escovedo and his rope-burned neck to the county line and issued the standard Mora County warning:

"We catch you 'round here again, we'll cut 'em off even with your belly."

The late-afternoon sun poured through the hotel dining-room windows, thatching the floor with golden shafts.

"Sounds as if he got out of there by the skin of his teeth," Frank said.

María de los Ángeles stroked the tablecloth, chasing away the wrinkles. "If Sheriff Raúl Hernández had been allowed to finish the hanging, do his job properly, we would not be having this conversation."

Escovedo set out afoot for Black Cherry. For a man who had barely evaded the hangman's noose, the outlaw could not put Mora County behind him quickly enough. The sun made the rope burn on his neck sting as if it were a noose of nettles and they were on fire.

Near dark, he came across a tired little ranch sitting forlornly against a low hill. The corral fence lay in a jumble of rotting posts, and the buildings, including the house, were little better. A white-bonneted, stooped woman carrying a small tin milk pail stood in the path between the barn and house watching his approach.

"Evenin', ma'am. Don't reckon you'd give a weary traveler a bite of something to eat?" Escovedo said.

The woman's mind wrestled with the man's question and especially with the "weary traveler" part. He wasn't just a weary traveler. His name was Joe, and he was her oldest son. He might have been traveling, but it was just back from the war. She'd received a letter from him last week, or maybe it was twenty years ago, telling her he was recovering in a hospital and should be home by the time the grass started greening.

"Joe, my sweet, sweet boy. Of course, you can have something

249

to eat. Why don't you look after the milk? There's a straining rag out by the well. I'll go in the house, warm up the beans, make some cornbread. Extra crisp just like you've always liked it."

Escovedo waited until the woman went inside. He drank the warm milk straight from the pail, and, when he had his fill, he flung what remained in a wide arc in the grassless backyard. At the barn, he eyed the emaciated milk cow, opened the gate, and turned her loose in the unfenced pasture, then moved to the horse. The animal was a faded roan and, judging by the grooves in her teeth, was at least thirty years old. "Got 'bout seventy-five miles in you 'til you keel over," he muttered as he threw the battered saddle across the horse's swayed back.

"Well, that worked out just right," the woman said as she set beans and cornbread on the kitchen table as the man entered the house. "Joe, you barely got home in time. I'm just about starved out. Mr. Rancy is coming tomorrow to buy the horse and the cow. Ought to barely be enough money to see us through to spring. Joe, I was always convinced that you'd be coming home. Let me ask you somethin': ain't we living on the grace of God?"

"Ma, you go along, and I'll clean up in here," Escovedo said.

The old woman fell asleep in the rickety rocker. The chill of the morning woke her, and she was not sure that she had really seen her son. She did not notice that her long-dead husband's shotgun that had rested for years in an antelope-hoof rack over the mantle was gone. Late afternoon, she walked to the barn with the milk pail hanging from the crook of her arm, the wire bail squeaking rhythmically. The cow had disappeared, and the horse was missing. Maybe Mr. Rancy had already been here and picked them up. But perhaps they had never been there at all.

She sat peacefully on a three-legged milk stool as the dull

clouds crept stealthily up from the south and choked off the light.

"Sheriff Raúl Hernández was a stubborn man," María de los Ángeles said. "Later, after the tragic incident on the train, the sheriff and I became good friends. He told me about the unsuccessful hanging and the murders. He believed that, even after Escovedo had left Mora County, he should not be able to escape punishment. So, the lawman followed him for a week, claimed if he could have gotten within a quarter of a mile he would have shot him with a buffalo gun. But Escovedo traveled too quickly, and the sheriff never got in sight of the outlaw."

María de los Ángeles watched as Frank walked to the back door and seemed to check on something or someone. When he returned to the table, he no longer sat but stood as he had in the early part of their conversation.

Frank fidgeted, and she knew he was losing interest. "Bear with me just a few more minutes," the woman said.

"Sheriff Hernández gave up after six days. But he did find the poor demented soul wandering through her house calling her son—telling him that his supper was ready. Later he found two ranchers had been murdered and their horses stolen. He knew Abraxas was the killer, but he could never catch up with him."

"Don't seem like you need me," Frank said as he retrieved his hat from the table.

"That's not true," María de los Ángeles said. "You see, the outlaw hated the sheriff as much as the sheriff hated him."

It took Escovedo several months to recover from his desperate flight back to Black Cherry. His reputation also suffered. He left with two cronies, Herb and Mute, and a wagonload of dry goods in addition to the firearms; he returned on a gimpy horse, his neck with a coarse rope burn, and with no money.

"Comancheros," he alibied. "Took us by surprise, robbed us, and killed Herb and Mute like they was dogs . . . took our horses." He gave no explanation for the scar on his neck.

But Black Cherry collected drifters like hairy dogs collect fleas, and it wasn't long before three ne'er-do-wells—Pigmeat Phillips, Whitey Decatur, and Camden Lake—joined Escovedo. Moonless nights were ideal in this desolate country for stealing a couple of cows or a wandering horse. Livestock buyers at Folsom paid no attention to brands, especially since they were only paying a thief's price.

But this kind of thievery was hard work, the returns niggardly. On a night at the Tumblebug when the four men were reduced to playing poker for kernels of corn, Escovedo pushed himself away from the table and said, "Enough of this being pore as prairie dogs; by gawd, it's time we made ourselves some real money."

"Doin' what?" Camden asked.

"Yeah, I ain't much into sweatin'," Pigmeat joined in.

Escovedo stood, dropped into a gunfighter's crouch, and pulled two imaginary pistols. "Robbin' trains. That's where the money is, robbin' trains."

"They were not very good train robbers." María de los Ángeles chuckled, the timbre husky. "The first train they held up didn't even have a mail car. The second train had one, and the scared clerk was glad to open the safe. It was empty.

"Escovedo and his men climbed into the passenger cars. Three spinsters, two children, and a cattle buyer were terrified as the bandana-masked men walked down the aisle, guns drawn and cocked. No one but the cattle buyer had any money, and he was returning with a mostly flat wallet after buying cattle in La Junta."

Frank grinned. "Sounds like they oughtta go back to stealing milk cows and such."

María de los Ángeles said, "I wished they had done just that. Houston might still be alive, if they had."

"But they kept robbing trains?"

"Yes. The third train had a locked safe in the mail car. But the clerk was a seasoned postal employee and had gone through a half-dozen earlier robberies. He refused to open the safe and Escovedo shot him in the foot. The man still refused. This time Escovedo shot him in the head and killed him.

"The fourth time, they thought they had hit pay dirt. Three passenger cars, two boxcars, and a mail car. They broke into the mail car. It was empty."

"Empty! They were slow learners."

María de los Ángeles smiled and held up two fingers. "The boxcars contained five Pinkerton detectives and the retired Mora County sheriff, Raúl Hernández. And the territorial governor had allowed some of the local citizens to form militias to hunt down the culprits. One Pinkerton had been a cavalryman, and he said he'd not heard that much gunfire since the Battle of Glorieta Pass in '62."

"All right. I know what happened. One of the outlaws got away."

"You are right. Escovedo got away."

Escovedo might not have been the most talented robber in this part of the country, but he was hell at hide-and-go-seek. If the law was not too hot after him, he hid out south of Old Moses at Seneca right near Rabbit Ears Mountain. The railroad footed the bill for the Pinkertons, and Sheriff Raúl Hernández was in the hunt mostly because he was still pissed at the outlaw. Most of the militias were still in the hunt because they were enjoying themselves. They almost hemmed Escovedo up twice, but, both times, he got away and hid out in the No Man's Land, a fifty-mile-wide strip of land that years later would become the Oklahoma Panhandle. That was rough country. The Osage and the Pawnee lived there and were more than a little tired of white men hiding out in their country, because it brought lawmen and those damn Pinkertons in their round, black hats. Perhaps tired is an understatement—extremely hostile is more fitting. And, to make matters worse, occasionally, if the U.S. Cavalry was bored, they might make a swing through to show the Indians that they could.

But Sheriff Raúl Hernández followed Escovedo like a bad smell. On a summer day, when the outlaw was hunkered down in a mesquite thicket seeking refuge from a dust storm, the sheriff poked a scattergun in his ribs and said, "Got you, you sumbitch."

The lawman tied Escovedo's hands behind his back, then slip-knotted a rope around his neck and tied it to the back-rigging ring on the saddle. "Shore hope your horse don't run off with you," Hernández said. "And, if he does, really hope you don't fall off, 'cause you'll damn sure swing from your neck 'til you're way past dead. The way you was supposed to in the first place."

Five days and a hundred miles later, the sheriff and the outlaw rode into the Texas town of Lone Tree. The little town was accustomed to having rustlers as guests and had constructed a holding cell comprised of a heavy chain bolted to a large rock. "A circuit magistrate will be by here in a week or so," the blacksmith said as he manacled the outlaw's ankles and chained him to the rock.

"We got more time than anything else," the sheriff said.

Folks passed by occasionally and helped Escovedo pass the time of day, gossiping, playing dominoes or just watching the rock's shadow as it moved across the sand. They did not linger due to the absence of shade.

One of the visitors was a dry goods salesman traveling up to Raton. After leaving Lone Tree, he stopped to have a beer at the Tumblebug saloon in Black Cherry. That night, five heavily armed men left the saloon riding southeast.

"Don't make a good-God-damn," the magistrate said. "I'm the closest thing to a judge in a hundred miles. Gimme one witness and five citizens in good standing, and we'll have a trial right out there under that tree."

Thirty-eight minutes later, Escovedo had been found guilty and sentenced to life in prison at the Texas State Penitentiary at Huntsville. The magistrate's final words were, "You'll have to take his sorry ass down there 'cause I ain't sending nobody up to get 'im."

"Be a train through here in three days," the blacksmith said.

The magistrate turned to Sheriff Raúl Hernández. "You be on that train. I'll give you an order so that the folks down at Huntsville will take the prisoner and pay you sixty-five cents a day for your travel."

The train was eight hours late, but its tardiness did not bother anybody except Escovedo, who was getting tired of the rock and sitting in the hot sun.

"Okay, so if Escovedo is in jail in Huntsville, why are you still bothered with him?"

María de los Ángeles frowned. "But that's not where he is, and that's why I need you."

Sheriff Raúl Hernández left the manacles attached to the outlaw's ankles after unchaining him from the rock. On board the train, he looped a lariat through the shackles and tied it to

255

the seat behind Escovedo. "Old son," the sheriff said, "that ought to hold you. If it don't, I'll tie the rope around the train's axle. See how you like that."

Other than the outlaw and the lawman, there were only three other people in the rail car: two women who, to use a local saying, looked like they'd *been rid' hard and put up wet*, and a dark-suited man with shiny, custom-made boots and a broad-brimmed, white, felt hat. The women, Faustine and Earnestine Müller, were sisters. The man was Houston Harrington.

Sheriff Raúl Hernández took a seat across the aisle from the outlaw and facing the Müller sisters. At the opposite end of the car, Houston Harrington sat reading a newspaper and smoking a Vicente Martinez-Ybor Havana cigar.

There was a delay leaving Lone Tree; the pump supplying water to the train was having problems and required extra cursing and kicking. Sheriff Raúl Hernández took the opportunity to impress the Müller sisters with vivid tales of being a lawman; the sisters took the opportunity to idly loosen the top two buttons of their dresses and accidently impress the lawman with their cleavage. The sheriff allowed the German women to examine his pistol; they unintentionally allowed him to see their legs almost up to their knees as they shifted into a better position to look at his firearm. The three had emptied a bottle of schnapps before the engineer blew two long blasts, and the train, hooded by steam and smoke, snaked away from the makeshift depot.

Escovedo, hat tilted forward until it almost hid his eyes, leaned back into the corner formed by his wooden seat and the side of the car. His jaw loosened, mouth sagged open, and he breathed with the regularity of a sleeping man. Unwary rabbits have fatally observed the same actions in coyotes.

Ten miles south of Lone Tree, the engineer yanked the train's whistle in a succession of short blasts. In this part of the High

Plains, it usually meant livestock on the tracks. The train slowed, then stopped with a teeth-rattling slam. Houston Harrington poked his head out the open window and saw a cowboy trying to move a small herd of scrawny cows away from the tracks. Harrington stepped out of the train car and stood on the rail bed, watching. The engine noise prevented him from hearing the approaching horsemen.

María de los Ángeles's face slipped into something resembling a sickened smile. "Most of what happened next is secondhand and came from the terrified engineer and his brakeman."

A cowboy's horse slammed into Houston Harrington, knocking him head first into the side of the railcar. He careened away and fell onto the rail bed, unconscious.

"He was on the ground when I first saw him," the engineer said. "Your husband, Mr. Harrington, I'm talking about. I started back to check out what was going on. Them two women come outta the car dragging the sheriff like he was a rag doll. He wadn't puttin' up much of a fight. He was plumb limber-legged."

"Yeah, we wadn't fifty feet from 'em," the brakeman said. "I hollered 'what the hell?' Bout that time three fellers come out from behind the train and pulled down on us—their gun barrels looked to be the size of cannons. Said to not move a damn peg.

"Quicker than a hiccup, one of 'em wuz in the passenger car and come out with Escovedo. Still had them manacles 'round his ankles, rope draggin' behind him like some kinda long snake. One of the cowboys had a sledgehammer and a cold chisel in his saddlebags. Took him 'bout a minute to get the manacles cut off."

The engineer said, "It was hard to look at, but Escovedo like to have stomped Sheriff Hernández to death. The two women

257

started screaming and pulled him off, or I believe he woulda done it. Finally he stripped the sheriff naked and tied him to a telegraph pole. Mr. Harrington kinda come to and sat up, had blood runnin' down the side of his face. Escovedo walked back to where he was and kicked him in the head. Your husband rolled down the railroad bank. The outlaw leaned down and picked Mr. Harrington's hat up off the ground, put it on, and come swaggering back down the tracks like he was some kinda big shot or other."

"Scary, I tell you. Scariest damn thing I was ever mixed up in," the brakeman said. "And I was on two trains that was robbed. But, this time, I thought for damn sure I was a goner."

"We didn't have no idea of what was fixin' to happen," the engineer said. "But Escovedo told us to get back on the train. Ever'body except one cowboy got on. That cowboy got in the engine cab with us. We run about ten miles, and the cowboy said for us to stop. There was two more cowboys and a whole bunch of horses waitin' at a road crossin'. Escovedo and his bunch got off. The cowboy that had been ridin' in the cab with us told me to get the hell outta there. I was damn glad to do it. And that was the last we ever saw any of 'em."

María de los Ángeles moistened her lips and drew in a breath. "I was at the station to meet Houston when the train arrived. The engineer and the brakeman were still terrified. The depot agent found the Oneida sheriff and a couple of deputies. Sheriff finally convinced the train crew that they had to go back. I got on the train—the Seventh Cavalry could not have kept me off. We stopped when we saw Sheriff Hernández hanging on the telegraph pole. He was gone—probably died while he was unconscious. Houston was a little farther up the tracks. He was dead. Just . . . dead. We did not even have a chance to say goodbye."

Expressionless, Frank Rule said, "Where you reckon Escovedo is?"

"The railroad didn't have any more interest in the outlaw," María de los Ángeles said. "Sheriff was dead, and there hadn't been any more robberies. Besides, the Pinkertons were too expensive. But I hired one on my own to keep hunting my husband's killer. Told him not to try to bring him in. That I needed to know where he was. He came back in a couple of months and said he had found him."

"Where was it?"

"Right where most of this mess started. Black Cherry, over in the New Mexico Territory."

"You know what he looks like?"

María de los Ángeles nodded. "I sent a photograph in the letter I mailed to you. The one you picked up this morning. I even had some *Wanted* flyers made. Left one of them for you at the store."

Frank sat at the table, took the folded paper from his pocket, and flattened it on the white tablecloth. He studied the poster for a minute, then nodded. "Tough looking feller."

"I'll pay you whatever you ask. But I do ask that we be discreet. I . . . we don't want to do anything illegal. That would not look good in the light of the legal day."

"I'll see what I can do."

María de los Ángeles gasped and tears welled in her eyes. With her right hand, she made the sign of the cross. "I'll pay you in advance. Give you anything you want."

"Like to have a piece of that pie. Got a young feller waitin' out in back. Don't believe he's ever eat pie, and I'd like to take him some."

". . . but that's the best place I've got to leave you," Frank Rule said. "Can't leave you here at the hotel. Wouldn't feel right leaving you out at the ranch. Charlie would have something for you to do around the store. Might learn something."

Wing looked away from Frank and shook his head. "No. Can't do that. You don't let me go with you, I'll go back up to where we left GrPa. I'm used to living there."

"But there's nobody there," Frank argued.

Wing still would not look at Frank but instead looked northward across the plains toward Mobeetie and Fort Elliott. "You don't take me with you, that's where I'll go. Not be here when you get back, 'cause I can make it on my own."

Rail service at Longsought was not much more than a one-room depot, a freight platform, and a pen that wouldn't have held fifty head of livestock.

María de los Ángeles sat on one of the two wooden benches in the Longsought depot, the chattering of the telegraph key filling the room with staccato dots and dashes. Frank stood by the window, looking down the tracks and watching Wing press his ear against the steel rails.

"It will be faster and easier," the woman told Frank. "Take the train up to Des Moines. I'll rent a cattle car. You can ride in it with your horse. Houston did when he was going hunting up in Colorado. He seemed to enjoy it. The Pinkerton man said there's a switching station there. Be less than a half-day's ride from Black Cherry."

Frank nodded. He knew what it was like traveling across the prairie in a cattle car with horses; the hot wind whistling through the slatted sides, blowing sand, and the horses spooked with the floor seeming to move without reason beneath them.

"I've instructed Mr. Jones, the engineer, to leave the car at the siding. Maybe you can come back in it after you kill . . ." her words trailed away. "After you've completed your business with Escovedo."

"Maybe." Frank paused as if weighing possibilities against realities. "Most likely not. Things might get kinda . . . hurried 'long toward the end of this thing."

"Just trying to help, make things easier."

Frank almost grinned. "My leaving schedule might not fit in with a train schedule."

". . . and I'll have this yellow bandana," Frank told the engineer. "You come back and see me waving it, stop and let me on. Hope I'm waving it at the siding, and we can load my horses. Might not be that way. Might have to leave my horse. Might have a man with me. Might not."

"That feller be with you?" The engineer nodded toward Wing, who was standing beside the train passing his hand through vapor drifting from the engine.

"Yeah," Frank said. "He'll probably be at the siding. If he is, pick him up even if I ain't there. Understand?"

"Yeah, I understand. Who is the man you might have with you?"

The hiss of escaping steam from the locomotive drowned out Frank's response.

The train followed the steel rails in a generally northwestward direction, traveling across the monotony of the High Plains, through endless miles of a grass sea marred occasionally by a small assembly of buffalo or a solitary bull too old to stay with the herd. Mesmerized by the train's speed and the sight of the plains as they floated by, Wing stood slit eyed, staring through the cracks of the wooden sided car. Frank sat cross legged on the floor cleaning his weapons. He'd not used either the L.C. Smith double-barreled or the Sharps .50 buffalo gun in weeks, and dust had accumulated in their actions. At the opposite end of the car, four horses tied to a series of metal rings stood awkwardly swaying with the movement of the train.

A mile south of Des Moines the train slowed, then stopped. The brakeman slid the door open and poked his head inside. "It'll take us a few minutes to get situated on the spur. You'd probably be better off if you got out—'less you enjoy being bumped around."

Frank and Wing waited in the shade of a small mesquite as the locomotive maneuvered the cattle car onto the siding. One hundred yards to the south, the buildings that once made up the town of Des Moines squatted in various stages of dilapidation. Never more than a dozen half-soddys and a wood-frame store, the village died a quick death after the buffalo hunters decimated the huge herds and moved on. Some cowboy with a sense of humor and a bucket of black paint had lettered two words on a plank leaning against the store: *Town Closed*.

A brakeman reconnected the train, and the engineer leaned from the cab of the locomotive, waved, and gave two blasts of the whistle. " 'Bout the same time tomorrow, 'cept going the other way," he shouted as the drive wheels clawed at the rails and the couplings tightened.

Thirty minutes later the train was no more than a speck against the horizon.

"Here's enough food and water for a couple of days," Frank said as he saddled his horse. "Pick you out one of 'em buildings over there. Hide if you have to. 'Less I run into bad luck, I'll be back by then. Mayhaps even tomorrow. But don't wait past day after tomorrow. If I ain't back by then, I ain't comin' back. You understand?"

Wing nodded. "What you want me to do if you don't come back?"

Frank jammed the Sharps into the scratched leather scabbard and climbed up on his horse. "Go back to the hotel. Tell the woman—woman they call María de los Ángeles—that I never turned up. She'll pretty much know what took place. Believe she'll look after you 'til you get on your feet." Frank grinned, leaned down from the saddle, and tousled Wing's hair. "I figure that oughtta take 'bout a week."

Wing would not look at Frank. "You'll be back," he said.

"I'm leaving the shotgun with you. You did pretty good the other day shootin' at them prairie dogs. Same way as shootin' at a man, 'cept it'll be closer. But don't let him get too close. You'll know what to do."

Wing wrapped the horses' reins around his hand, shouldered the gun, and started toward the dilapidated store. He stopped, half turned toward Frank, and shouted, "You'll be back."

Three men stood on the dirt road in front of the Tumblebug watching the rider approaching from the east.

"Don't believe I know that feller," the one with the blond beard said.

"No. He'd be damn hard to forget—that round hat and them spectacles. Dang shore ain't from 'round here." This from the second man, the one with a missing ear.

"Wonder if he's got any money on him," the man with the rope burn scars around his neck said.

As Frank got closer, the men quit talking. Simply stood and stared.

Frank nodded to the three men, dismounted and stretched his back the way a man will do after a hard day's ride, and tied his horse to the rail in front of the Tumblebug.

"Good lookin' hoss you're riding," Blond Beard said. "Reckon I could talk you into sellin' it?"

"No," Frank said. "I'm more in the buying notion than the selling."

"Know what you mean," the man with the scarred neck said.

"I'm a horse trader. Not much good at it. But I never saw a horse I wouldn't buy; never owned a horse I wouldn't sell."

Frank laughed. "Yeah, I've heard that before. Man said that before he sold me a blind mule."

The interior of the saloon was dark but no cooler than the outside. A wizened man wearing a shirt that had not seen the inside of a wash pot in six months stood behind the bar poking a wooden match into his ear. He extracted the match and examined the captured yellow residue.

"Ye needin' somethin'?" he asked.

"I'd take a glass of beer, if you had any," Frank answered.

The man turned, took a flyspecked glass from a shelf, then leaned down out of sight behind the bar. A faint gurgling sound wafted up. He stood and handed Frank the glass, partly filled with a pale-yellow liquid.

The three men came inside the saloon and sat at a rickety table. Escovedo stared at Frank as if looking at a critter alien to the New Mexico Territory. "Don't believe I've ever seen you before," he said.

Frank took a drink of beer, turned, and spit it on the floor. "Damn, that's bad. You ought to have to pay a man to drink stuff like that."

The men laughed. One Ear said, "That's the drainings from a couple of weeks. Ain't had no fresh beer here in a month."

Frank swiped his shirtsleeve across his mouth. "Yeah, well, I'll not be paying for it. Mayhaps take my pocketknife and scrape that stuff off my teeth."

It was apparently no surprise to the bartender that he would not be paid for the ruined beer. He leaned on the bar, gouging in the other ear with the matchstick.

Escovedo said, "What kinda horses you lookin' for, Mister . . . ah . . . what did you say your name was?"

"Frank. Frank Rule. I'd buy about anything that still had

some road left in 'em. A dozen or so. Nothin' less than three years old, nothing older than ten. You asking me, but you ain't told me your name."

"Yeah. Sorry 'bout that. Name's Escovedo. Might have somethin' that would interest you. Got four head that sounds like they might work."

"Close?" Frank asked.

"They ain't behind the bar," Escovedo said and looked at his companions to gauge if they appreciated his witticism. They did.

Frank glared at Escovedo. "Didn't come over here for no jollification or to drink bad beer."

Damn, Frank. Old Scratch thinks you might be walking on mighty thin ice here. Come in this ratty old saloon. Poking this bad man in the butt with your finger. Better start watching how you talk or go back over to Des Moines and get your shotgun. Old Scratch don't want to see us get hurt.

Escovedo gauged Frank. The stranger didn't look like he had two coins to rub together, but he was talking about a number of horses. Man could never tell these days who had money and who didn't.

"Where 'bouts are your horses?" Frank asked.

"Over there." Escovedo pointed to the west, toward Capulin Mountain. "Old mountain got a hollow place in the top of it. Folks say it was one time a volcano. A fair spot to graze a few head of livestock and a damn good place to hide 'em."

"And that's all you got? Four head?"

"Well," Escovedo said, "might be able to scrape up 'bout ten more. These two fellers here can go out to a pasture we got south of town and bring the rest of 'em to a lot over there by that dry wash."

"How long that take them? To get back here with the horses?"

"Couple of hours. We'll be back 'fore they are."

"All right," Frank said. "We're wasting daylight. Looks like I might need to go somewhere else to find what I need. But let's go look at what you got."

Escovedo turned to the one-eared fellow and the bearded man and said, "Okay, boys, skedaddle."

". . . what the hell?" Escovedo muttered. He lay in an uncomfortable position on the ground, head throbbing, a sticky warmth covering the left side of his face. He tried to wipe his eyes, but his hands were tied and the rope secured around his ankles.

His last memory: he and Frank Rule starting the ascent on the road leading to the top of Capulin, and Frank saying, "Well, look here." He'd turned in time to receive a rifle butt to the head. He'd felt himself falling and everything went black.

"Your head stopped buzzing so we can talk?" Frank asked.

"What the hell is wrong with you?" Escovedo said, wriggling as he tried to rub the blood from his left eye against his shirtsleeve.

"You and me are gonna take a little trip together," Frank said. "We can take it with you sitting up in the saddle like a man with your hands tied together. Or, if you don't like that, I'll tie you belly down across the saddle like a sack of horse feed and you can spend the next few days looking at the ground."

"Mister, I don't know who you are and where you think you are takin' me. But I can damn guarantee you that you are a dead man."

Frank adjusted his glasses. "Tougher and better lookin' men than you have threatened me with lots worse stuff."

Escovedo tried to stand, wavered, and fell face first into the dirt. "You ain't never dealt with nobody like me. I've killed better men than you for spittin' in the road."

Frank led the outlaw's horse from the brush and stopped

beside Escovedo. "What's it gonna be? You gonna sit on the horse like a man or ride across the saddle like a sack of feed? We gotta be going, and I ain't got time to hear your threats."

"My men come back to the Tumblebug with the horses and I ain't there, your ass is—"

Frank hoisted the outlaw over the saddle and tied his feet to his hands beneath the horse's belly. "Most folks puke after an hour of riding like that. We'll see what you're made of."

Escovedo turned his head to the side and eyed Frank upside down. "We'll see what *you're* made of, you sumbitch, when the boys catch you and roast your ass over some hot coals."

"Guess I'll cross that bridge when I get to it. I've tied your horse to a D-ring on my saddle. Wouldn't want you wandering off nowhere by yourself." With Escovedo's gun tucked into his saddlebag, Frank put the spurs to his horse.

"Where're you tryin' to take me?" The outlaw's speech rose and fell with the movement of the trotting horse.

Frank looked over his shoulder. "Mayhaps Des Moines, or Lone Tree, or Longsought, or perchance Dallas. We'll travel 'til we get where we're goin'."

"I ain't never done nothin' to you. What in the hell do you think you're doing?"

"Got a woman that wants to have words with you."

"A woman! I don't even know a woman in any of them towns."

Frank checked the trail behind him. "Well, you're 'bout to."

"What's her name?"

"María de los Ángeles. Her husband was named Houston Harrington."

"I never knowed folks with that kind of name."

"I done told you that you was 'bout to."

The one-eared man was named Goochie, and the blond-bearded man was called Merle. They gathered the horses from the south pasture, then waited an hour for their boss and Frank to return from Capulin Mountain.

"Reckon they got lost?" Goochie asked.

"Or run into some kind of trouble." Merle ran his fingers through his beard, searching for lice or something else foreign. "I didn't like the looks of that little fat feller. Why a horse trader would be carrying a Sharps .50 is beyond me, 'less he's a part-time buffalo hunter or a man lookin' for trouble?"

Goochie laughed. "Don't think that feller looked like a buffalo hunter. I hear tell that Billy Dixon killed a damned Indian over near Adobe Walls with one of them Sharps. Claimed it was 'bout three quarters of a mile away.

"And 'nother thing. Heard it'll knock a buffalo bull down at five hundred yards."

Merle looked up at the sun, then down at the lengthening shadows. "It's gettin' on over in the evenin'. Won't hurt for us to ride out there to the mountain, have a look."

An hour later, at the base of Capulin Mountain, they found Escovedo's hat and three flies crawling on a fried-egg–sized puddle of dried blood.

While the moon had diminished as it rose from the eastern horizon, it had cast enough light across the prairie for Frank and his prisoner to travel until almost midnight. They camped for the night in a shallow draw, their horses tied to a dead mesquite.

Shortly before sundown, Escovedo's stomach had emptied for the third time. Frank stopped and untied the rope that secured the outlaw's hands and feet beneath the horse. "I'm gonna let you get in the saddle. You behave yourself, and that's the way you'll travel. You try anything, you'll ride like a sack of oats the rest of the trip."

"Oh, you'll not have any trouble outta me. It's them two fellers followin' us that'll give you trouble."

"I reckon I'll be able to handle 'em."

"What are we gonna eat tonight," the outlaw asked. "I'm empty."

"Ain't. That's what happens after all that puking. We're not having a fire. Makes it too easy for anybody that might be followin' us. I believe you'll be all right for a day or two."

Frank had pulled Escovedo from his horse and tied his hands and feet together behind him. The outlaw lay in the dirt on his side and glared at the cowboy, thought about his own pistol in the saddlebags, and the Sharps in the scabbard. Wondered how well he could handle the pistol with his hands tied. Probably not very well. If they were not eating tonight, they probably would not in the morning either. That meant they might be close to where they were going. Goochie and Merle would catch up with them tomorrow. Then he'd see how much the bald-headed cowboy enjoyed riding strapped under the belly of a horse.

"Know you ain't accustomed to sleeping on the hard ground," Frank said. "Can't give you a straw mattress, but I can loan you a horse blanket. And you'll be happier if you don't try to cause me trouble tonight."

Escovedo squirmed around until he got the blanket across his shoulders. *Oh, you got trouble coming,* the outlaw thought. *You figure Goochie and Merle are laying up for the night. Goochie was raised by Indians, and Merle was a scout for the cavalry. They can track a fish swimming down the river. They ain't sleeping, I'm bettin'. It ain't easy, but they are after us right now.*

After Frank left, Wing allowed their horses to graze and watered them from a last month's rain that had collected in a playa. Before dark, he stabled the horses in the dilapidated store. He looked at the sign that read *Town Closed* and wondered if GrPa had ever been here.

He ate some of the food and drank some water that Frank left, then crawled into a soddy. He wasn't scared, but it was not easy to go to sleep knowing that somewhere to the west Frank was hunting a man. Or a man was hunting him. Three night-hawks soared through the dark sky, sharp-tipped wings beating frantically as they flew higher. Then, folding their wings, the birds dropped toward the ground. Yards above the earth, they extended their wings and rose up again with a faint *barrouppp* sound.

Wing crawled from the soddy and stood watching their flight. He raised his hands over his head and made a fluttering motion. The nighthawks circled the boy once and flew westward.

Merle leaned down from the saddle and studied the hoofmarks in the dirt. "Hey, Goochie, over here. They came through this little low place. If they're heading straight, and I'll bet they are, that means that ought to be—" The former cavalry scout pulled a military compass from his pocket, settled the needle, then pointed ten degrees south of east and said, "Right out there. If they've laid up for the night, I'm betting right now we ain't five miles behind them."

Frank jerked awake at the *barrouppp* sound. He had spent the darkness fighting off the urge to sleep. Escovedo had a long history of treachery, and Frank was determined not to become the next victim. Once, he'd drifted off into a fitful nap when, as clear as a bell, Ellen called his name. Confused, he had answered aloud and felt foolish when the outlaw wanted to know who he was talking with.

The *barrouppp* sounds continued. He crawled out of the wash, hunkered down, and scanned the horizon. Three nighthawks appeared from the lightening sky and repeatedly dove toward his fireless camp, pulling out of their dive before launching skyward again.

"What the hell is wrong with 'em birds?" Escovedo asked.

Frank took his horse to the top of the wash and came back for Escovedo's. "Mayhaps you slept in their nest last night," Frank said as he untied the outlaw's feet and helped him up in the saddle. "Start you off up here," he said. "Act up and you'll spend the rest of the trip on your belly tied across the saddle."

Escovedo glared down at the cowboy. "Ain't no need in tellin' you this, but this trip is gonna be a whole lot shorter than you think it is. You'll be a lucky man if you witness the noonday sun."

Frank wrapped the rope attached to the animal's bit ring around his hand and led Escovedo's horse out of the wash, the outlaw sitting uncomfortably in the saddle. He stood for a minute, surveying the horizon for any sign of pursuit. Nothing in sight except the lazily waving prairie grasses and a few scattered clumps of mesquite bushes.

Goochie and Merle had traveled all night. As daylight approached, they lost the trail and had ridden in an arc searching for hoofmarks, broken bushes, or bent grass—anything to show that horsemen had passed. They decided that, somehow in the darkness, they must have passed Rule and Escovedo.

"We'll lay up here," Goochie said. "Tie our horses in that mesquite thicket over there. We'll let them come to us. They get close enough; we'll shoot that sumbitch right through his glasses."

Almost as one, three things happened: rifle fire cracked, a half-inch deep gash opened across the top of Escovedo's horse's rump, and the wounded horse reared, jerking the rope from

Frank's hand.

The outlaw's horse wheeled, plunged off into the wash, and emerged on the other side, bucking wildly. Escovedo, hands tied through the gullet of his saddle, hung on.

Frank grabbed his own horse's reins and pulled it toward the wash. Two shots echoed in rapid succession. The horse grunted, and his front legs crumpled. The animal fell, thrashed briefly, and lay still.

"Damn, Goochie, why did you do that?"

"Hell, I had a clear shot. Figured he'd be harder to hit once he was in the saddle and moving. Why you cussing me, when you shot, too?"

Merle frowned. "Well, yeah. What did you expect me to do? We was gonna wait 'til he got closer, then you opened up. I didn't have no choice."

Goochie grinned. "At least we got Abraxas outta there. Now, only thing we gotta do is catch his fool horse."

"What about that Rule feller? What we gonna do about him?"

"What about him? I figure I got him with my second shot. You don't see him up runnin' around, do you?"

Merle smoothed his beard away from his mouth and shook his head. "You ain't got no idea if you hit him. Ain't got no idea if he's dead or if he's crawlin' through the grass comin' toward us. Only thing we know is, his horse went down."

Goochie rolled a cigarette and lit it. "No. I'm okay with it. I had a fine bead on him. He's dead; I'll bet my boots on it."

Two hours after the shooting, Merle said, "You sure enough about your shot that we can go down there and have a look?"

"Yeah, I think so. We'll take it kinda easy. He pops his head up, I'll lay a slug 'tween his eyes."

Separated by fifty feet and with saddle guns resting in the

crook of their arms, Goochie and Merle moved through the waist-high grass toward the spot they had last seen Frank.

As his horse went into the final throes of death, Frank jerked the Sharps from the scabbard and rolled off into the wash. He sat with his back against the shallow bank trying to catch his breath and waiting for the hammering in his chest to subside. His hat was gone, his glasses askew, and drops of blood from a shoulder wound plopped on the ground. Frank ran his hand under his shirt and felt the damage. An entry hole and a larger exit hole; he was comforted that no bullet remained in his body.

Gritting his teeth against pain from his wound, Frank crawled up and peered over the bank. Nothing—just the movement of the grass in the dry wind. Five yards away, his slain horse lay on its side. The cowboy crawled to the horse and pulled .50-caliber cartridges from the saddlebag, then scooted on his belly back into the wash.

He knew the direction of the shooter; he did not know how many. There had been three shots. Certainly, the last two were so close together; it could not have been only one shooter. So, there had to be at least two people—maybe three.

Running stooped and with bent knees, Frank moved back up the ravine. He stopped a hundred yards from where his horse had been shot and crawled to the edge of the wash. He raised the rear sight on the Sharps and waited.

"Look there," Goochie said, "there's his horse. Deader'n four o'clock." He built a cigarette, inspected his work, then struck a match on the butt of his rifle. "Bettin' we'll find that old cowboy right beside his—"

Merle glanced to see why his friend didn't finish the sentence. One side of Goochie's face was gone, and the other side had

273

sagged into a deformity. Then he heard the boom of Frank's rifle.

Frank jacked the lever, extracted the casing, seated another cartridge, cocked the hammer, and waited.

Facing Goochie, Merle lay on the ground, his face screwed up into a tight grimace. He'd seen a dead man before, but not a friend and not at arm's length. The impact of the bullet had lifted Goochie and driven him backward ten feet. Merle tried to convince himself that as long as he lay still, the shooter could not see him, and he would be safe.

He was breathing almost regular when a blowfly appeared and began to examine the gaping hole in Goochie's head. Rolling onto his stomach, dragging his rifle like an extra appendage, Merle started crawling back to where the horses were tied. It had taken the two men five minutes to walk to where Goochie's body now lay, but it seemed he had crawled for hours. His eyes filled with dirt and grass seed, and his mouth suffered from dryness as if stuffed with cotton cloth. Heart pounding and breath coming in short, shallow jerks, he was afraid that Frank could simply follow the sound of his movements. But, at least now, he could hear the horses moving uneasily as they smelled the blood and heard the uneven noise of him moving through the grass. If he could reach his horse, he would get the hell out of this ugly mess. Go to the Tumblebug, get some of the boys, come back, and kill that damn Rule feller.

As he reached the horses, Merle rose from his belly to his knees. Goochie's horse shied away, pulling the reins through the dead branches of the mesquite bush. Once free, the horse turned and raced across the prairie as if being pursued by wolves.

For five minutes, Merle sat in the grass, trying to control his breathing. His horse tilted its ears forward and studied him.

Slowly he reached for the reins and talked to the animal in a calm and soothing voice. "Whoa, boy. It's all right. It's me. We'll get out of this. Just be easy. Be easy."

The mid-morning sun warming its back, a hawk wheeled overhead, riding the updrafts rising from the plains. Its cry was piercing, designed to frighten rabbits or field mice from their burrows. The man below was oblivious to the circling raptor.

Merle stood, unfolding in sections like a carpenter's rule. He looked toward the place where he was sure the shooter waited. No movement, nothing but the hypnotic billowing of the waving grass. He pulled himself into the saddle, and his left knee seared with pain as bone and cartilage shattered. The horse grunted and lurched to the side. Its hind legs collapsed, and Merle slid backward over the horse's rump and sprawled on the ground, thrashing in the dirt like a tormented bug. The horse scrambled to its feet, squealing in pain and terror. Merle tried to step up into the saddle again, but his left leg was useless, and his boot was filling with blood. The horse stood, front legs spavined, blood frothing in its nostrils. Merle grasped the horn, trying to pull himself up. He did not hear the second shot, nor did he feel the bullet that tore through his chest. He and the horse collapsed to the ground and lay together centaur-like in the warm sun.

Frank shouldered his buffalo gun and moved down the wash to where his horse and Goochie lay dead. Out past that, he saw the trail of broken grass Merle made as he crawled to the east. He took the saddle from his dead horse and stood, studying the dead gunman. With the toe of his boot, he rolled Goochie over onto his stomach.

The best he could, he hid his saddle and Goochie's weapons

under a narrow rock outcrop. With the Sharps cradled in his uninjured arm, he followed Merle's path. Both the horse and Merle had suffered serious damage from the buffalo gun before they died. Frank was sorry about the pain he'd caused the horse, but the man got what he deserved.

Frank rummaged through Merle's saddlebags, found a partial bag of coffee and a battered pot. But there was no water, so he tucked a double pinch of coffee grounds behind his lower lip. Then he set out to the north. Escovedo was somewhere out there. He shouldn't be too hard to find. Not being under the control of a bridle, and with a man floundering awkwardly in the saddle, Escovedo's horse had probably shed its rider or had wrecked in one of the shallow ravines leading over toward the river.

In less than an hour, Frank picked up the horse's trail. A mile later, he found where the animal had fallen to the ground, and two trails diverged after that point. Thirty minutes later, he came upon Escovedo staggering through the brush. The outlaw carried his saddle against his stomach, gripping it with his tied hands.

Frank moved up behind the struggling Escovedo and kicked his feet from under him. The outlaw sat up and stared at the cowboy. "You'll pay for this," he said. "My friends will string you up by the thumbs when they catch up with us."

Frank grabbed Escovedo by the back of his shirt collar and pulled him upright. "You gonna have to get some new friends. Looks like your last ones have laid down on you."

Escovedo glared at Frank. "Yeah, you talk pretty big. I see you're afoot. See you've been shot. Bet the boys killed your horse and are coming after you right now."

"You're 'bout half right. One of them did kill my horse, but they ain't comin' after me or anybody else. Wouldn't be surprised if the coyotes were dragging both of them through the brush. Or flies were laying eggs in their carcasses."

The outlaw's shoulders sagged. "You ain't killed them?"

Frank nudged Escovedo in the belly with his buffalo rifle. "No, I didn't, but this old Sharps did."

Escovedo trudged eastward, the evening sun hot on his shoulders. Frank walked a couple of strides behind, occasionally delivering the same commands he would have given a plow mule: gee ho, haw, whoa, and git-up.

The outlaw was still tied to the saddle, and he hugged it against his stomach as if he were lugging a fifty-pound pumpkin. With no free hands to swat them away, the sandflies had easy access to his eyes and nose. This, along with wrists rubbed raw by the ropes, did little to improve Escovedo's already foul disposition.

They were traveling a line ten degrees south of due east. Frank checked his battered compass again. When he raised his head after looking along the sighting wire, he saw dust rising from the plains ahead. Five minutes later, he could see three horses traveling on a bearing that would intersect his path.

Escovedo saw the horses at the same time. "Told you. They're coming after me. I've been in a whole lot more of these scrapes than you have. My men'll not let me down. We're fixin' to see how you like carryin' a saddle. Might let you dig your own grave. Buzzard bait!"

"We'll stop right here," Frank said. "We are gonna get flat on our bellies. You holler or make any kinda fuss, I'm gonna put a slug through your head. After that I'll deal with whatever comes from your friends."

Escovedo sank to his knees and rolled over onto his side, the saddle attached to his hands like some gross appendage. He grinned at Frank and said, "They'll get you. You are same as dead."

Frank laid a half-dozen .50-caliber shells in his hat, sank to one knee, and pulled the Sharps against his good shoulder. "You may be right, but you'll not live to know it."

Two men sat cross-legged in the shade of a small mesquite. Nearby, shiny iron rails rayed away in opposite directions like a sunburst. A third man, both hands tied to a saddle, sat dejected in the sun twenty feet from them.

"Durn glad to see you," Frank said. "Escovedo was probably gladder. He was complaining something terrible 'bout how heavy the saddle was and how his wrists were burning."

Wing looked out from under his big floppy hat at the outlaw and grinned. "Still don't look too happy."

"You showing up with the horses made our trip a lot easier. And quicker. We'd have still been walking."

To the north, a train whistle blew, a low quavering sound that snuck across the desolate prairie like the cry of a lost soul yearning for home.

Frank looked at the sun, then toward the hair-thin stream of smoke trailing from a dark speck that was rapidly increasing in size. " 'Bout on time I'd say." He took the yellow bandana from his pocket and gave it to the albino. "Go out there and wave the engineer down. I'll get Ole Happy over there up on his feet, and he can load when the horses do."

The train rumbled southward toward Longsought. In the cattle car, the horses swayed with the unevenness of the rail bed. Escovedo sat at the other end, untethered from the saddle but tied to the slatted side of the car. His disposition had not improved.

". . . and I'd never seen anything like it," Frank continued. He and Wing leaned against the back of the car, talking. "I woke up and those night hawks were diving and making that *whooping* noise. Came up out of that dry wash and those two fellows opened up on me."

Wing grinned. "I saw them before you did. The birds had come to look about you. See if you needed help. Or that's what GrPa would have said."

Frank nodded, amused. "Yeah. The hawk circlin' 'round over that last man. Whistling like he was showing me where he was hidin'. Guess GrPa would have said the bird was helping me out with that, too."

"Maybe. What would you say?"

The train blew two long blasts, a short one, and another long one for a road crossing. It was a waste of steam. In its five years of service, there had never been anything at the crossing.

Frank studied the question before answering. "Well, if I hadn't known your grandfather, I'd say it was an accident. Now, I don't know.

"And another thing. How in the world did you find us out there in all that open country? We could have been anywhere. If you'd have been an hour earlier or an hour later, you'd have missed us. You could still have been lookin', and we could still a'been walkin'."

The train's momentum lessened, and the engineer blew two long blasts and a short one. The horses shifted uneasily at the noise and change of pace.

"You gonna laugh when I tell you," Wing said. "I woke up this morning, and things just . . . just . . . just didn't feel right. Felt it in my stomach. Felt it in my head. Got on my horse and rode around. Not much better. Took the other two horses down to the creek and let them drink. Felt some better."

"You wasn't sick or nothing? Dizzy? Light headed?"

"No. Just wasn't right. I came past the rail siding and kept going—didn't have no reason—kept goin' west. The feeling went away. 'Bout an hour, and I saw you."

"You don't know what made you do it?"

"No. I could guess, but you wouldn't believe me."

"GrPa?" Frank said.

"Maybe."

The train stopped at Longsought, and Wing unloaded the horses. Conro, still wearing his yellow suit, sat in a buggy and called out when he saw the boy, "Y'all git him?"

Wing nodded.

Conro tapped the horse with the buggy whip, and they moved down the dusty street at a smart pace.

María de los Ángeles, elegantly dressed as always, was drinking coffee on the hotel veranda with the wives of two cattle buyers when Conro stopped the buggy at the street's edge. He stepped down from the rig and stood patiently, hat in hand.

"Would you ladies excuse me? I am expecting a message, and it may have arrived." She stepped to the edge of the veranda, and Conro crossed the board sidewalk. She leaned forward as Conro whispered a few words.

María de los Ángeles returned to the table and lifted her large, leather-bound Bible. "I'm afraid I must cut our visit short. Perhaps you might visit with me another day in Oneida. I have so enjoyed talking with the two of you." And with that, she crossed the sidewalk, and the driver helped her into the buggy.

Along with a half-dozen professional loafers, Sheriff G.W. Satterlee stood in the shadow of the depot. "Well, I'm mightily impressed," he said. "What was you gone, one day, two? Come back here pretty as you please with one of the worstest men in a thousand miles. Hardly a scratch on you."

Frank grimaced. " 'Less you count a .30-30 through the side of my shoulder. You don't count that, then I'm as good as I was last week."

"Oh, I never meant to make light of it," the sheriff said. "I've had a couple of them myself. They do sting for a while."

Vulgarity erupted from the cattle car. "Done near forgot about him," the sheriff said. "Now that you've got 'im, what are you goin' to do with him? Guess you'll be takin' him down to Oneida. Understand they've got a warrant for his arrest. Think there might still be a reward."

"Yeah. That's where he needs to go," Frank said. He rubbed dried blood from his shirt with a thumbnail and flinched when he got too close to the wound.

"Train not scheduled to leave for another thirty minutes. Why don't you run down, let Doctor Munro check you out? Let him patch up 'em holes in your shoulder. I'll look after Escovedo 'til you get back."

"Right lucky man, I'd say." Frank, stripped to his waist, sat on a wooden chair in Doctor Munro's office, the smell of alcohol and iodine strong and off-putting. "Bullet been an inch more inside, it would have got a bone or artery," the doctor said, leaning back to survey his work. "Couple of weeks and you'll be 'bout good as new."

"That's good, Doc. I didn't figure it was anything to worry about, but the sheriff thought it might be a good idea if you looked at it."

Fascinated, Wing stood by the doctor's cabinet looking at the shiny surgical tools and mysterious bottles with indecipherable labels.

Doctor Munro helped Frank back into his shirt. "Be careful. Don't be rasslin' no steers or breakin' no wild horses."

"No danger in that," Frank said. "How much I owe you?"

The doctor ran his hands through his gray hair. "Didn't have to dig out no bullet; I'd say give me 'bout . . . 'bout six bits, and we'll call it even."

At the depot, the crowd grew as the word spread through town that the infamous Abraxas Escovedo had been captured and was tied up in a cattle car. Deputy Frank McCormick was occupied shooing away small boys who were entertaining themselves by shooting peas through hollow canes at the outlaw.

Sheriff Satterlee stood on the load platform, uneasily watching the growing crowd. María de los Ángeles's rig sat in the road across from the depot.

The sheriff stepped down off the loading platform and said, "Frank, do you believe all these folks have come down here to look at Escovedo? Last time we had this much excitement here in Longsought was when you brought McGregor's big Highlander bull through town."

Frank smiled. "Tell you one thing, we might put this town on the map after all."

The sheriff grinned, and his face wrinkled like an apple left too long in the summer sun. "Well on our way; might have to change the name to something fancier. Guess you've heard Houston Harrington's widow has been in town for a few days. When Harrington was livin', he was a pretty important man up here in the Panhandle. Richer than ten feet up a black bull's ass, I hear."

"I've heard about him," Frank said.

"Yeah, you know she was up here when Escovedo killed her husband. Rode out on the train with us. Found her husband graveyard dead. I hated that she saw it."

The crowd increased when several cowboys from the Emerald Isle Saloon showed up.

"Mrs. Harrington is a real looker," the sheriff said as if he were appraising the fine points of a horse. "That's her rig out there in the street. You ain't gonna believe what I'm about to tell you. Her and that Conro nigger come up to me while ago.

She was carryin' a Bible. Said she wanted to look at the man that killed her husband. Wanted to pray for his soul."

"You didn't let her in the car, did you?"

"Yeah, I did. Finally. Told her how dangerous he was. She said she'd keep her distance. And that Conro feller was with her. I went up and checked the ropes that was tyin' Escovedo. Tell you what, Frank, you're a good hand with a rope. He couldn't get loose if he had a week and a chopping ax."

"She's in there now?"

"Yeah, been in there 'bout five minutes. Oughta be comin' out any minute now."

Frank elbowed his way through the crowd and was climbing into the loading chute leading into the open cattle-car door when he heard the two shots.

"Well, who'd have thought it?" the sheriff said. The train had left, the cowboys gone back to the saloon, the loafers drifted away, and Doctor Munro returned to his office. Sheriff Satterlee, Deputy McCormick, Wing, and Frank stood looking at the body of Abraxas Escovedo. "Don't look so dangerous with them two holes in his forehead, does he?" the sheriff said. "She was either a real good shot or Escovedo was awful unlucky."

Deputy McCormick squatted and stuck his index finger in one of the bullet holes. "Tell you what, fellers, a .41 that close does a hell of a lot of damage. Bet old Escovedo never had no idea of what was about to happen to him."

Satterlee shook his head. "Had that Remington double-barrel derringer in her Bible. Place cut out that fit the pistol just as pretty as you please."

McCormick wiped Escovedo's blood on his pants leg and grinned. "Turned out, it was a dang good thing she was in there. It wouldn't have been the first time he escaped the law."

Smiling sheepishly, the sheriff turned to Frank. "You had him tied good. I seen them knots my very own self. Ain't got no idea how he got loose."

Frank looked at Satterlee and slowly shook his head. "Yeah, he was one bad man. Got what was comin' to him. Reckon it come in a different way than he figured."

"Didn't take Judge Snodgrass long to make up his mind, did it?" McCormick said.

"No; reckon the judge has seen lots of that self-defense stuff. Made it easier on everybody the way he handled it," Frank said.

Wing and Frank walked down the dusty street leading their horses. A tumbleweed ambled along the board sidewalk, pausing occasionally to wait for more propulsion. A spotted dog lying beside the saloon stood, inspected its dirt bed, and lay back down in it.

"Frank, there's things I don't understand," the boy said.

"What are they?"

"Them ropes never come loose from Escovedo. He was still laced up tight against them sideboards. He wadn't about to get away."

"You're right."

"Then why did the woman kill him?"

" 'Cause he needed it. He was a bad man."

They stopped in front of the mercantile store and tied their horses to the hitching rail. Bulldog White sat on the porch in his accustomed place, spitting tobacco juice on ants convened around a dead grasshopper.

"Okay. But why didn't the sheriff take her to jail?"

" 'Cause she was a woman. Escovedo had killed her husband. Sheriff figured it was her right. Now, just let all this go."

"But if it was wrong for Escovedo to kill her husband, then why wadn't it wrong for her to kill—?"

"I told you, she was a woman. Now, I'm not answering any

more questions. Need to get some stomach drench for the cow and get on home."

Darkness swept in from the east and congregated over the men, leaving them faintly silhouetted against the sickly yellow western horizon.

The albino, concerned about his three-legged dog at the isolated ranch, rode twenty feet ahead and occasionally looked back over his shoulder as if his furtive glances at Frank might hasten their journey.

Frank rode slouched on his horse, the way horsemen had done for centuries here on the High Plains. He was hungry. Tired. His shoulder throbbed. He wondered if it would have ached had Doctor Munro not probed around in it. And he was not happy with the happenings of the last few days.

Say there, Frank, good buddy. Old Scratch has a new name for you. Judas Goat! Yes, sir, Judas Goat. Guess it goes without saying that Abraxas Escovedo was one of my favorites. Old boy was quite a hell raiser. Hadn't done a damn thing to bother you. Now he is dead, thanks to you. You led him to that woman, that María de los Ángeles, Mrs. Harrington, whatever she calls herself. She used you. Maybe going down to the prison at Huntsville would have been bad, but being tied up in a cattle car and shot by a madwoman was a whole lot worse. Sometimes, Frank, I just think you don't give a tinker's damn.

The two men unsaddled their horses and fed them grain. "Go on to the house," Frank told Wing. "See about your dog. I'll brush your horse down. Be on up there in a few minutes."

Frank watched Wing disappear, his albino-pinkish skin ghostly in the light of a fading moon. He finished with the horses, turned them out into the pasture, and stood looking across the dark plains. The loneliness came back to him as it did so frequently this time of night. There was no solace. And he was tired. He took the cartridge case—the one he had packed with dirt when he buried the ring—from his vest pocket and deeply breathed the earthen scent.

Leaves on a mesquite that survived on the leakage around the horse trough moved, a delicate quiver. The windmill blades shifted gently, and the shaft squeaked in its housing. A feathered wind breathed across his face.

Heat lightning flickered in the west and then encircled the entire horizon in three dim pulses.

And they came.

His youngest son, Joseph, trailed by the brindle dog, walked in front singing about a man named Old Joe Clark who had a yellow cat that could not pray.

His daughter, Shirl, was a young woman now and, in her outstretched hands, an apple pie, steam rising from the vents in the crust.

Ellen's hair was gold, and he could smell her freshness. She reached out, trailed her fingertips across his cheeks, and smiled. Her eyes were dewy, skin soft and lustrous. "Oh, Frank, Frank, we've waited so long. Won't you come?"

286

ABOUT THE AUTHOR

John Neely Davis was raised in the sandy hills of West Tennessee, an area east of the edge of the Mississippi Delta. Most of his working years were spent in government land acquisition stretching from the Appalachians to the river valleys of New Mexico.

Previously published novels include: *Bear Shadow* (winner of the Janice Keck Literary Award for Fiction); *Stephen Dennison; The Sixth William;* and *The Chapman Legacy* (Western Fictioneers Peacemaker Finalist for Best First Western Novel of 2018). He has also contributed to numerous anthologies: *Hobnail and Other Frontier Stories; Filtered Through Time; By Blood or by Marriage; Comanchero Trail;* Western Trail Blazer Series; *Contention and Other Frontier Stories; Sundown;* and *Words on Water.*

He lives with his wife, Jayne, in historic Franklin, Tennessee.

The employees of Five Star Publishing hope you have enjoyed this book.

Our Five Star novels explore little-known chapters from America's history, stories told from unique perspectives that will entertain a broad range of readers.

Other Five Star books are available at your local library, bookstore, all major book distributors, and directly from Five Star/Gale.

Connect with Five Star Publishing

Visit us on Facebook:
https://www.facebook.com/FiveStarCengage

Email:
FiveStar@cengage.com

For information about titles and placing orders:
(800) 223-1244
gale.orders@cengage.com

To share your comments, write to us:
Five Star Publishing
Attn: Publisher
10 Water St., Suite 310
Waterville, ME 04901